Naked In A Coat of Armor

By

Eugene A. Aichroth

© 2003, 2004 by Charlene Knadle.
All rights reserved.

No part of this book may be reproduced, stored in a retrieval system, or transmitted by any means, electronic, mechanical, photocopying, recording, or otherwise, without written permission from the author.

First published by AuthorHouse 04/07/04

ISBN: 1-4140-2088-0 (e-book)
ISBN: 1-4184-0901-4 (Paperback)

Library of Congress Control Number: 2003098997

This book is printed on acid free paper.

Printed in the United States of America
Bloomington, IN

This book is dedicated to Charlene Knadle, who believed in my father's writing from the start. Her untiring efforts, patience and advice helped to make the book a reality. Thank you, Charlene. My father gave you his manuscript knowing it would be in good hands.

Special acknowledgements also go to Enid Graf, the late Sue Kain, the late Shari Gladstone, and the late Richard Elman, whose suggestions were carefully considered along the way.

Dad's number-one critic, proofreader and original encourager was my mother, Lillian Aichroth, who I believe was the actual "Lora" throughout the book.

I am sure that there are others I have missed, and I thank them for also having a part in my dad's "autobiographical bit of fiction."

Gail Suzanne Aichroth Maas

Contents

Part 1 1

   Chapter 1 5

      Germany-England-Germany, 1888-1915 8

      Earlsfield, 1915-1925 16

   Chapter 2 22

   Chapter 3 34

   Chapter 4 42

   Chapter 5 55

   Chapter 6 64

      Animal 68

   Chapter 7 73

   Chapter 8 80

   Chapter 9 86

      Books 97

   Chapter 10 101

Part 2 107

   Chapter 11 109

      1935-1945 109

      Out of the Mud, Into the Blue 114

   Chapter 12 121

- Chapter 13 137
- Chapter 14 149
- Chapter 15 161
- Chapter 16 177

Part 3 193

- Chapter 17 195
- Chapter 18 202
- Chapter 19 209
- Chapter 20 217
  - Observation 224
- Chapter 21 228
  - The Kid Next Door 231
- Chapter 22 239
  - Shower 241
  - Nightmare 243
  - Poetry 244
  - Id 246
  - Aud 247
  - Lottery 248
  - Halloween 250
- Chapter 23 253
  - Adventure 258

    What's His Name 263

    Beggar Man 265

    Morning 268

Chapter 24 273

    It Hurts Only When I Laugh 273

    A Wee Dram 281

    Hitch Hike 283

    Terminal 286

    Magnus (Tribute) 287

    Surprise 292

    Last Exit 295

[Photographs](#) 3

.... 106

.... 190

.... 298

Part 1

"A child's life is like a piece of paper on which every person leaves a mark."

Chinese Proverb

"We could never learn to be brave and patient if there were only joy in the world."

Helen Keller

Eugene A. Aichroth

Naked In A Coat of Armor

Eugene A. Aichroth at 9 (in sailor suit) with his mother, Daisy Wenham Aichroth (later Lundstrom), his Aunt Frida, and younger brothers Dick (L) and Bob (R)

Eugene A. Aichroth

Gene at almost 14, on his way to America. (Passport photo)

Chapter 1

I opened my eyes wearily, felt a cold breath drift across the room and noticed the curtains ripple ever so slightly. I turned my head and there, in the corner, stood Rigor Mortis.

"Do you always barge into people's rooms unannounced?" I asked. Mortis didn't answer; he just coughed and his skeleton rattled like a clay wind chime. Stomping his feet and brushing the weather off his shoulders, he pulled his black cloak tighter around his frame and pinned it in place with three knuckles of a bony finger. What ever for? I thought; he has nothing left to keep warm. Looking out the window along the garden path just past the woodshed, I saw Lora struggling with a bundle of firewood. She stopped to catch her breath, and looked up at the bare stems of the climber rose, clinging desperately to its trellis; she was probably remembering how beautiful it was just a few weeks ago.

My wife looked pretty, bundled up in her down jacket, with a wool cap pulled over her ears. Little silver ringlets framed her face, and her cheeks were burnished like red apples by the spiteful wind. She puckered her lips and I knew she was whistling. We kidded her about it, but I hoped she'd never quit.

Lora picked up her bundle again irritated at having to stop to rest, and bent into the storm with determination. We old timers are like that, determined to defy Mortis and his deadline. We fly off in all directions, like sparks off the blacksmith's anvil–not long-lasting but positive in direction. We volunteer for more committees than we have time for, take more courses than we can cope with, attend too many lectures and reviews, baby-sit, travel, and entertain. We're resolved to somehow hold back time, because there are some things we forgot to do and don't want to admit that we can no longer do them.

Often when retiring from one rat race we create another. I remember that when I retired I wanted to slow down and sit on the sidelines and contemplate the stampeding herd going by. I planned to cut the telephone wires and throw all the clocks away. Of course I never mustered the courage to do so. Are we running scared and whistling in the dark?

I sank back into the white cloud of pillows and wiped the beads of sweat from my forehead. "You know, Mort," I said, When life's express slows down at its destination, the blurred landscape of memory comes into focus."

"So, all is terminal, and some lives are diseased," Mortis said, shifting from one foot to the other.

"Look, I've made no profound mark on my biography, no earth-jarring accomplishments, but I've had a good life. I did what society brainwashed me into thinking was right. And even with all its complications, there's little I'd care to change."

Rigor answered me as though he heard my thoughts. "Let me tell you something, Burt," he said, waving a bony finger at me. "You think you're so important, saturated with wisdom, constipated with brag, boast and bologna. You think you're justified to purge yourself to the world, when in fact you're nothing more than a pebble in the driveway."

Naked In A Coat of Armor

Mortis, gliding across the room, moved closer to my bed. "When you're dead and on the compost," he went on, looking down into my face, "there'll be no more playing 'Can you top this?' Friends and relatives will gather around the pit and your loved ones will say, 'We loved him so.' And your wife will mourn the loss of you as her best friend. One will say, 'He was my best friend; he was a good man.' The clergy will announce in exaggerated eulogy and pray that the Almighty will carry you to your blessed reward. Some will think, 'Too bad they didn't bury the son of a bitch sooner.' After a while, a concave spot will appear on the perpetual care lawn to remind all that you, too, are biodegradable. People will say, "Burt. Burt who?' The world will have felt no weight loss, nor will there be the slightest skip in its rotation."

I could see that Mortis was getting impatient, as time was running out.

"What I'm telling you, Burt, is that you won't be missed for long. You had your 'three score and ten,' and you're lucky. You beat the odds. You've been on overtime."

"Thanks a lot. You're so kind, you old crepe hanger. You made my day," I gasped. "That is, my last day. You win, but you must admit I stayed in there and competed with the rats. After all, a race this far is a pretty long haul."

"So what are you trying to tell me?" Mortis asked gloomily.

"Look, Mort, I'm ready to pack up and pack it in. Give me a little time to say my good-byes, and I'll tell you a story when I get back.

Eugene A. Aichroth

Germany-England-Germany
1888-1915

It was 1888 and conscription was the law in Germany. Even small hamlets like Bell in southern Germany were expected to meet their quota. Grandfather Johan Eichwald was devil-may-care in his younger days while his brother, Walter, was more serious. Both were ripe for the draft at seventeen and eighteen years of age and were soon shipped out for basic training. The story that follows is true, according to my mother and other gossips. It's as true as I heard tell and as honest as my tired memory will allow. It's as reliable as the characters that I quote. (So much for truth.)

Grandfather Johan took to military life with enthusiasm. He was thrilled to join the elite Lancers, a cavalry outfit of the times. Johan was tall, lean and handsome. He posed a striking figure in uniform, mounted on a fine horse and sporting the famous Kaiser mustache. But Johan's brother Walter, a gentle easy-going sort, wanted no part of this military regime. He had a baby face with fat, rosy cheeks and a roly-poly belly. It was while passing in review on the parade grounds one day that Walter's bowels began to protest and rumble and it was obvious to him that a movement was certain. When the troops were ordered to halt and stand at ease, Walter, now desperate in his predicament, stepped out of ranks and asked the drill sergeant for permission to go and relieve himself.

"As you were, soldier," bellowed the officer, glaring at his subordinate. "You've just earned three

Naked In A Coat of Armor

demerits for breaking ranks and three more for talking. Get back into formation."

Walter's bowels churned, growled and groaned. A dull pain stretched across his stomach like an uncomfortable cummerbund. No longer able to control nature's demand, Walter shit himself–there on the drill field, in the heat of the day, standing at parade rest. The ruthless discipline so humiliated him that the next day he went over the hill and the Kaiser's army never saw him again. He spent the night with a friend, Carl. "You know what they do to deserters don't you?" Carl said with concern.

"Yeah, I know, but I'm not going back."

"Where will you go?"

"I don't know. Maybe England. I hear there's a shortage of bakers there. And butchers, too. Why don't you come with me? We can find work there."

"Not a bad idea. I hate not having a job; I'll pack some gear and get ready to move out."

In the morning the boys started out on foot across country into Luxembourg to Belgium. After several days' hiking, they crossed the border into France and to Calais, on the English Channel. They had traveled at night to dodge the gendarmes, hostile dogs and bounty hunters. They slept in haystacks, manure heaps and cattle barns. One night the boys stopped at a prosperous-looking farm and Carl remarked, "Wow, look at that manure heap!"

"What about it?" said Walter, irritated.

"Don't you know that the bigger the manure pile the wealthier the farmer, and the wealthier the farmer the better the menu? Hope they invite us to supper. Another thing to remember, if you're courting the girls: it's the farmer with the biggest manure heap whose daughter will bring the most generous dowry."

"How come you're so smart?"

"Oh, I've been around."

"Well I'm not chasing girls just now. All I want is to get to England as soon as possible."

The two young men found the people of Belgium to be friendly and helpful. The French were another matter, and the boys had to be very careful not to be apprehended. There was a rivalry between the French and Germans in those days, what with Kaiser William II aching for a war.

At Calais Walter and Carl managed to stow away on the ferry to Dover, England. As the ferry pulled into the slip, they jumped overboard and swam ashore. It took three days for the fugitives to dry out. They learned that British weather was rain, fog, showers, and more rain. In England, few ventured outside without an umbrella. In summer one wore a sweater at the beach.

Walter and Carl found employment soon after they landed and served an apprenticeship in the baking business for several years. Eventually they formed a partnership, went into business for themselves, and prospered. In 1902 they parted and Walter established a flourishing bakery in London on Lambeth Street, where it remained in the family.

In Germany, Walter's brother, Johan, had finished his enlistment in the Lancers and moved to a small picturesque village north of Stuttgart on the Neckar River called Neckarweihinyen. There he established a business as a wagoner and wheelwright. He earned a reputation as a fine craftsman, and business was good.

Naked In A Coat of Armor

Johan was a happy-go-lucky fellow, always thirsty and always in pursuit of the girls. Erica was his true love, but the thought of marriage, and confinement to dull domestics, frightened him. It was much more fun to frolic and flit from blossom to blossom. Erica gave birth to their firstborn on September 30, 1893. It took two years of much deliberation before he was finally persuaded to marry her. In the meantime, Johan's sister, Johanna, an Evangelical nun and the matriarch of the family, a stern disciplinarian, a bible puncher, was determined to keep the neighbors from knowing that all was not quite on the straight and narrow. She thought it prudent to take the boy, Walter, to her brother in England, the boy's uncle of the same name. And so the little hamlet was deprived of a scandal.

Walt lived with his uncle until he was fourteen. It now occurred to Johan that his son was old enough to earn some money to contribute to the household, and he demanded that young Walter be returned to Germany. Walt was unhappy in Germany. His mother and father were strangers to him and now it seemed he had a brother, Paul, eleven, and a sister, Johanna, eight.

Walt was put to work delivering bread and rolls for the local bakery. But he longed to be back in England, and one day, after being in Germany for month or two, he took the bread money and the bakery bicycle and rode off. Walt worked his way through Belgium to France and eventually back to London, just as his Uncle Walter had done many years before. Happy to be back with his cousins and school chums, he settled down to learn the baking business. He became part of the family and considered his cousins as brothers and sisters—more so than his own kin in Germany.

Eugene A. Aichroth

Walt eventually left his Uncle's establishment and struck out independently. He found work at the Palace Hotel in Southend-on-Sea, a posh summer resort at the mouth of the Thames. Occasionally he would ride the tram out to the dance hall at the end of the pier. One evening he saw a lovely blond girl in the lobby and asked her to dance, and she agreed. "Are you from Southend?" he asked.

"No I'm from London. My name is Dorothea, and I'm on holiday."

"A pretty name, and what do you do in the big city, Dorothea?

"I'm a bar maid at the Bow Bells, my dad's pub. And you–are you from around here?"

"No, in fact it seems we have something in common. I used to work as a baker for my uncle in London." They laughed at the coincidence. Later in the evening he asked, "Shall we get some fish and chips?"

"I'd like that." They rode the tram back and stopped at one of the fish stalls along the waterfront. It was a lovely evening, so they strolled along the beach munching on their food and happily chatting.

"May I call you when you get back to London?" Walt asked.

"Yes do; I shall look forward to hearing from you," Dorothea said.

It was August 14 when the German armies marched into Belgium and the Great War began. Convinced, along with many others, that the conflict wouldn't last beyond Christmas, Walt and Dorothea were married on October 28, 1914 and moved to the north part of London.

Naked In A Coat of Armor

In November, the British government interned all so-called enemy aliens, including Walt. London experienced the first of a new kind of warfare—aerial bombing. These frightening raids came as a shock and the citizens went on rampage and smashed the shop windows and dragged the foreign merchants out into the streets and beat them. Uncle Walter thought it prudent to change his foreign name on the storefront to something more British. A Scotsman working for him suggested using his name. Thus the Eichwald establishment became known as Kerr's Bakery. Walter also thought it would be a good idea to have a pretty blond, blue-eyed girl behind the counter, rather than a fat man who spoke with a foreign accent. But when he asked his nephew's wife to come and work for him, Dorothea refused, thinking it was beneath her status.

The door of the pub swung open and the light spilled out across the pavement like a carpet rolled out for some celebrity. A horse and carriage stood waiting at the curb. In the illuminated fog, they appeared as stage props. A man stepped into the flood of light and, when the door closed behind him, the sudden darkness was like a curtain drop at the end of a performance. He whispered something to his horse, unstrapped its nosebag and hung it under the carriage, between the high wheels.

"Hey Cabby!" Peg's voice was muffled in the mist. "Cabby, look smart, get us to the Lying-in Hospital at Earlsfield."

"Earlsfield? That might as well be on the other side of London."

"I don't care if it's on the other side of the bloody moon, now get cracking!" she demanded.

"Half a mo lady, half a mo, it'll cost you ten shillin' and I'll take it now, if you please."

"Ten shillin'! Mind you, I was only joking about goin to th' moon."

"Ten bob, or you can walk."

Peg dipped into her bag. The fog, thick enough to drip off the brim of her hat, didn't help as she frantically rummaged in the dark for the coins. She came up with a handful of something and said, "Eight shillin' tuppence apenny is all I've got."

"Walk," said the man, dripping with compassion.

"Bugger!"

Dorothea clung to the carriage for support, handing her bag to her friend. Peg finally came up with enough silver. "Here," she said with contempt. "Here's yer bleedin' pound of flesh."

Peg and Dorothea had known each other since school days. Peg helped her friend up and they tumbled into the Hansom. "Now get a move on, Peg shouted. The driver said something only his horse could understand. The old mare shifted her weight from one hind leg to the other, reluctant to risk the effort to move out. The Cabby flicked her gently with the tiny tassel at the end of his whip, letting her know that it would be all right to try. She leaned into her collar and, when she felt the load, she dug her hoofs into the ground and the carriage began to move ever so slowly. Almost immediately, they were swallowed by the fog.

"Ain't it eerie?" Peg mumbled to herself. "Here we are, the three of us and a bony old nag in a low cloud and God only knows where." She put her arm around her friend, to comfort her, and listened to her moans mingle with the clippity-clop of the horse's hoofs. "Sounds like bloomin' Big Ben, tick-tock...click-clock," she said, trying to get Dorothea's mind on something else. Then, to the driver, "Can't you get this damn plow horse to move a bit faster?"

"Look here, lady, don't you get your knickers twisted. This old girl does the best she can, and if you don't want her to collapse right here in the middle of Lambert Street you'd best leave the driving to me...right?"

"Coo," breathed Peg, "Uncanny how he can pin-point our location and he cawn't even see 'is horse's arse. Dorothea's moans grew louder as the pains became more frequent. The cab rattled across a stretch of cobblestone and, for a dreadful moment, she thought her time had come. If only Walt were here, she thought. I'd be so much braver. Oh why did they have to take him away?"

"Hurry driver, hurry," called Peg.

"Right, Mum, mind you I'm hurrying."

They pulled up to the hospital a year later, or so it seemed. "Here, Governor, give a lift," ordered Peg, as she nudged Dorothea out of the carriage. The old man climbed down off his high perch in time to catch her. He slung her arm around his neck and over his shoulder and all but carried Dorothea into the somber building. Bloomin' good of the bloke, thought Peg.

A crisp nurse marched up and greeted them with, "Hallo, whot 'ave we 'ere?"

"Ain't it damn well obvious? Get me friend in bed. Call the doctor! Do something! Now!" Peg screamed.

They got Dorothea into a room and Peg tagged along, mumbling something about wot 'ave we here? Blimey, how daft can she be?

"Cheerio," called the Cabby, as he pulled away. "Good luck to our chum."

"Ta very much," Peg answered as she turned to her friend. "He's a good bloke; he is, you know."

Dorothea had a nasty time giving birth to her first born. She was young, frightened, and felt terribly alone. The doctor was a bugger. "If you had married a good Englishman," he said, "instead of a barbarian Hun, you would not be hurting so."

When the child arrived he smacked him extra hard, venting his hatred on another foreigner. The baby let out a yelp, already protesting its new environment.

Dorothea looked down at the bundle cradled in her arms and thought, My God what have I done to you, my son? Giving you a German father. Could it be that the doctor is right? No, no, Walt isn't like that. He is a good man. Kind and compassionate. She loved him very much...and yet...The wartime propaganda posters that she'd seen around the city flashed before her: pictures of women, raped by the enemy, and babies skewered on German bayonets. No, no, it's my English doctor who is the barbarian!

**Earlsfield
1915-1925**

It happened on the twenty-seventh day of the ninth month in the year of our Lord, one thousand nine hundred and fifteen. That was the day Burt was born, right smack in the middle of a monumental celebration

Naked In A Coat of Armor

on September 27, 1915. Fire and brimstone rained from above. Artillery cannons boomed, machine guns saluted, and the new aerial bombs added excitement for the people of the city. The place was Earlsfield, London, England. He learned later that the jubilee was not to celebrate his arrival. Instead it was called the Great War, whatever that meant. Of course he couldn't remember the particulars, but there was a paper that verified that indeed he was born. He seemed to remember being snatched up periodically (always at a most inconvenient moments) when his mother dashed off to what was known as an air raid shelter. His father, in the meantime, was locked up in an interment camp, classified as an illegal alien.

Dorothea felt so very homesick. But her father, fanatic in his hate and prejudice, all but disowned her for marrying a foreigner, especially a German. So intense was his feeling against his son-in-law that he would not call his first grandchild by his given name, Ernst. Grandpa Whendam declared that while the boy was in his house he would be called Burt.

Dorothea took her son to the Whitehall internment camp to introduce him to his father. "Walt, it's a boy," she said.

Tears welled up as Walt kissed Dorothea. "And he's a fine one, he is, thanks to you. Here let me hold the little nipper. I know that everything is going to be all right," Walt said. "The news is good. Rumor has it that an armistice is to be signed soon. Then they'll let me out of this blasted place and we'll be together again." No one thought it was possible that it would be three more long, terrifying years before the war would cease. Nor did Walt expect to be moved to the

Isle of Man, a lonely, wind-swept speck in the Irish Sea, off the coast of Scotland. There he would stay interned for the remainder of the war. After the armistice, the British government deported all aliens without notifying their next of kin.

Dorothea had pleaded with Uncle Walter, "Won't you please vouch for your nephew to keep him from being sent back to Germany?"

"You forget, my dear Dorothea," Walter had said, "when you refused me a favor at the outbreak of the war, a time when I needed you to work for me in the bakery. Now it is my turn to refuse. You can go with my nephew to Germany for all I care."

Walter's nephew was sent back to his place of birth, a foreign country to him now. Dorothea did not learn of her husband's whereabouts until she received a card from him instructing her to meet him in Stuttgart.

She said goodbye to her dear friend Peg and wondered if they would ever see each other again. She clung to her son, now three years old, as they sloshed through the drizzle to the ferry that would take them across the channel. It was crowded with women, who, like Dorothea, were going to meet their deported spouses. The soldiers escorting the women treated them with contempt, as though they were traitors to the British Crown. When they arrived at Calais they discovered that their baggage had been searched and precious items like soap had been stolen along with other valuables. Walt took his wife and son to Osswiel, a pretty little hamlet, in Wurtenburg where an aunt and uncle owned a small farm. They made a temporary home with the Shulthises, good people who tried to make them welcome. But Dorothea, a city girl, was bewildered and frightened to suddenly find herself in a tiny foreign village where people spoke with a strange guttural language, so different from England.

Mrs. Shulthise invited her nephew Walt, his wife, and their son Burt for their evening meal. The strange supper consisted of black bread, sausage and ersatz coffee, made from chicory and ground acorns. Little Burt was wide-eyed as he watched Mrs. Shulthise, a buxom woman, slicing the crust off a huge cartwheel of homemade bread. She held the loaf wedged between her large breasts as she sawed back and forth toward her with a long, sharp carving knife. The boy held his breath, waiting to see if she would stop in time.

"Come," Uncle Erwin said, breaking the spell. "Eat up. We have a long day ahead of us tomorrow."

"Yes", Ursula, his wife, chimed in. "We are threshing the wheat, starting early in the morning."

Walt and Dorothea were happy to finally be alone as they retired to the little room above the cow barn. It had been a long, trying day for both of them, but she couldn't help feeling homesick. She wondered what the morning would bring. Was there a sunrise in this strange land? She felt reassured when she woke to a bright day. Already there was much activity in the yard. Chatter and good-natured banter came drifting from the threshing barn, which aroused her curiosity. She dressed hurriedly and shook her husband—she needed an interpreter—and they both went to see what the excitement was about.

"What's going on?" Dorothea asked Mrs. Shulthise. "What's all the commotion?"

"My, but you're up very early," Aunt Ursula said. "Come, have some breakfast, then we will go and see. Did you sleep well?" She commenced to cut great strips of smoked pork and dropped them into a hot pan on the wood stove. She brought steaming coffee and slices of black bread to the table. The sound of the sizzling meat and the warmth of the kitchen with the smell of the cooking relaxed Dorothea. She felt that she could trust this woman and that they would be friends.

"Thank you, Mrs. Shulthise. That was very good," Dorothea said, and Walt translated for her as she began to clear the table. "I'll do the dishes," she offered.

"We'll do them together, and please call me Tante."

After they were finished tidying the kitchen, Aunt Ursula said, "Come, let's see what those noisy men are doing." A large canvas had been spread on the floor of the barn and grain dumped on it. Several men and boys were positioned around and had started to thresh the grain with crude flails. An old man sat in the corner and played a smart tune on his violin. All began to sing in unison as the workers flung their flails in rhythm. It was a pleasant scene, albeit foreign to Dorothea. These are happy people, she mused.

"Now watch." Tante's voice startled Dorothea.

The workers had stopped the threshing. A door on each end of the barn was thrown open and the men lifted the canvas and snapped the grain into the air several times as the fiddler slowed the tempo.

"See, they let the breeze do the work of separating the chaff from the seed. After, it will be put into bags and hauled to the miller. But now it is time for some refreshments. See—they draw their kerchiefs to wipe their brows; that is our cue to bring the beer and apple schnapps. That keeps them in good humor and they work faster. Soon it will be time to feed them—and of course they drink more beer."

Dorothea noticed that the pace slowed in the afternoon. There seemed to be more song and laughter than work.

After the evening meal, the old man struck up a fast polka and all began to dance—and the harvest was celebrated. Walt put his arm around Dorothea and twirled her to the music. She smiled up at him and for a moment thought it was all right to be happy.

Chapter 2

He dragged her across the field, she, struggling against his grip.

"Let go of me," Dorothea shrieked. "What are you doing?"

"Come, schatz, you und I are going to have a little romp in der hay stack together."

She screamed for help.

Walt heard her from across the other side of the field where he was pitching hay onto a wagon. He raced toward them, clutching the pitchfork like a javelin and knocked the man to the ground, bringing the weapon so close to his jugular that the old man could smell the dried dung on the long sharp tines.

Dorothea screamed as she flung herself across the prone man.

"No, Walter, no!" she shouted. "You can't kill your own father."

Walt raised the weapon to arm's length, and the sudden motion sucked in all the frightful human emotions he had wrestled with during the last four long years. A flood of terrible rage and bitterness, hate and frustration crammed the block of time he spent as prisoner of his beloved England. Men, who spoke with the accents of England, Ireland and Scotland had been rounded up and corralled in a barbed-wire compound. 'Aliens' they were called and then, with the war, they were "enemy aliens." The only wrong they had committed was to be born in the wrong place and had neglected to pledge allegiance to England.

Then when his uncle refused to vouch for him after the armistice to keep him from being deported, the shock and fear were devastating. What despair and hopelessness he felt when Dorothea's parents rejected him and all but disowned their daughter for marrying a foreigner. The violent rage for revenge when he heard that the English doctor told his wife, had she married an Englishman instead of a Hun she would not have suffered so when giving birth to their firstborn. He would never forgive Britain for shipping him off to the Isle-of-Man, separating him from his wife and newborn son. And now to find himself in his homeland...homeland? He felt as though he was a man without a country, devoid of friends, not knowing relatives, hated by strangers for having married a woman from England. He didn't even recognize his parents, whom he hadn't seen in many years. All this pressure welled up inside of him like a dangerous head of steam that threatened to tear him apart. Then, as if to pin these terrible thoughts to the earth forever, he brought the fork down with all the force his emotions propelled and drove it deep into the hard soil. Walter shook as though possessed by some violent convulsion.

Dorothea took his hand and whispered, "It's all right, Dear. It's all over." The old man got up and brushed himself off. Bewildered and confused, he could not understand what would motivate a son to turn on his father and attack him with such determination. And for what? What did he do to deserve such a violent reaction from his own flesh and blood? Those English dogs have distorted his mind, he thought. They certainly haven't taught him to respect his elders. He even speaks with their peculiar accent. The swine have stolen a father's son. "You had better take your golden princess und leave," Johan told his son. "Go back to your Englund. Here they will break her in two. Der Fatherland needs strong women, women who can work in der fields and in der kitchens. And women who are good in der bedroom."

"Why you thirsty sot, what do you know about a day's work? I'm told all you ever cared about was your schnapps and a different woman to take to bed. You, who sent my little sisters to deliver bread from door to door before school, and in all kinds of weather. You who couldn't afford to buy shoes for them because you collected their pennies to spend on your booze. Do you know what the penalty for rape is where I come from? You swine! Get out of my sight before I finish you off now." He made a move for the fork but stopped.

"Rape? What...rape? Women are not raped. They are pursued und subdued. They are caressed, und fondled, und pinched, hugged und kissed. Women are put upon a pedestal und worshipped, then knocked down und kicked und fed. But raped? No." The old man walked off, shaking his head, still befuddled, still unable to understand this stranger from Britain.

Walt knew that some men treated women as secondary citizens, that they believed females existed simply to propagate the species. But it was never demonstrated so bluntly as now. Walt turned to his wife. "Yes, I think we had better move away from this miserable place. In the meantime, be very careful of these wolves. If one ever comes near you, I'll kill him, and maybe you, too, if I catch you wiggling your pretty ass for them. "Go on home."

"Walt, now you're being very nasty." She blushed and gave him a peck on the cheek and left, but she didn't turn in the direction of home.

There was something else worrying Dorothea. Her little Roland was suffering from rickets–malnutrition, people said, a post-war curse in that God-forsaken land. She decided to canvass the local farmers for an extra drop of milk for her sick child. She tramped from door to door and was about to drag herself home, weary and miserable, when she saw him. He was standing in a barnyard, tall and handsome, his powerful arms bulging under rolled up sleeves. She walked up to him and explained her need for extra milk, confident those soft brown eyes would not turn her down.

He studied this superb Anglo Saxon blond and wondered if he was dreaming. Could a foreigner be that beautiful? "You are the lady from England, ja?"

"Yes, I am," she said with British pride, and tossed her head like a thoroughbred mare. The man slipped his arm around her and pressed his hand to her breast and bent to kiss her. She wriggled away from his rude advance and demanded, "How dare you?"

"Oh come now, mine fine princess, come down from your royal horse. She was frightened, and turned to leave, hoping she would not panic.

"Wait, please, here wait eine moment bitte."

She noticed his awkward limp as he moved toward the barn.

The war, she thought. Presently he returned with a chipped enamel mug full of milk still warm with animal heat. He raised the mug ceremoniously and said. "This, for English ladies...ist eine prosit."

Was there something ulterior in this kind gesture? Would she be a fool to accept it? Then as she reached for the cup he poured the milk onto the ground at her feet.

Rage welled up inside of her. "You bastard," she screamed and curled her fingers like a cat unsheathing its talons. She snarled like a cur at bay and, with clenched teeth, lunged for his cruel sneer.

He sidestepped and dragged his lame leg to trip her, the fall knocked the breath out of her. She pressed her face into the earth so that he would not see her burning tears. He left her where she fell. She felt the damp spot where the milk had seeped, and clawed a handful of the wet soil as though to salvage a drop of the precious liquid.

It was dusk when she finally turned into the dusty road toward home. She trembled with a terror, not only for her own safety but in fear of such brutal times, such brutal people.

Life was miserable in Germany. Walt was treated with contempt by friends and relatives alike because he didn't fight for Germany in the Great War. Dorothea was despised by some for being an alien. The nation was bitter in their defeat and vented their hatred on all foreigners. Walt moved his family to Neckarweyingeny, his birthplace, a pleasant town on the Neckar River.

A busybody across the street leaned out of the window to appraise the newcomers. "Mataaleee!" She called to her six-year old daughter as an excuse, lest she appear too nosey. Besides, it was time for little

Martha to shepherd the geese down to the river for their morning swim.

This unhappy existence gnawed at Dorothea and she slumped into a melancholy state. On two occasions she took little Burt to the river's edge, contemplating an end to both their lives.

Walt found work with the railroad and they moved to Ludwigsburg. Dorothea improved in this pleasant city and soon found the will to cope. They rented small quarters above a gardener's house in Stuttguta Strass. Mr. Schaffer was a horticulturist who specialized in hybrid rose trees. He also raised rabbits and chickens to supplement the food ration. Pleasant surroundings and a steady income, albeit meager, helped to repair Dorothea's depression. An occasional parcel from England and letters from her mother were also comforting. They brought Frieda, Walt's youngest sister, to live with them and be a companion for Dorothea. Then the birth of their third son, Rolph, kept her happily occupied.

It was payday and Walter brought his wages home in a paper sack and dumped them on the kitchen table: about three million, five hundred and forty thousand reichsmarks. Inflation was out of control. It was no use trying to count it; better to get down to a store and buy something before the value dropped for the third time that day. If he hurried, there might be a couple of loaves of bread left, and an egg. If he was lucky, even some sausage. He returned with one loaf of bread and a half of pound of horsemeat.

Horse meat? thought Dorothea, I wish he hadn't told me till after we ate it.

"What are we doing in this country of madmen?" said Walt, as if reading his wife's thoughts. "I met Carl standing on line. He's wallpapering a room with hundred-thousand-mark bills. On the way home I cut through the park and stopped to watch a couple kids fly their kite and, would you believe, it was made out of paper reichsmarks. Dorth, the barber will cut my hair for four eggs and give me a shave for two, rather than accept the worthless money!"

"What's to become of us?" Dorothea wondered out loud. "What can we do?"

Walt put his elbows on the table and propped his head on his hands. "I've always felt I could cope with the lunatic fringe," he said, "but sometimes I feel as though I'm smack in the middle of the asylum. We've got to escape from this bedlam. I'm not sure how, but get away we will."

These were the worst of times for Germany. The Allies took the spoils and left the country to bleed. This policy created fertile soil for the seeds of rebellion to germinate in the beer hall at Munich, eventually reaping an oppressive harvest of weeds that would become known as Hitler, and Hess, Gobles, and Goering. Farmers and those in rural areas able to cultivate their own food fared just a little better than the urban population. The production and distribution of food crops was closely monitored. A percentage of each crop harvested would be allotted to the urban areas, and it was necessary to obtain a permit to slaughter animals for food.

The railroad company gave their employees permission to cultivate small gardens along the rights-of-way. Walt worked a small plot about two miles away that yielded a fine crop, thanks to the regular application of sewerage from Mr. Schafer's cesspool. A large old wine barrel served as a container for this smelly product. An old bucket attached to a long pole was used as a dipper to transfer the precious liquid from the cesspool to the barrel. Walt, with young Burt's help, hauled it on a wooden coaster wagon made by Burt's Grandpa Eichwald, the wagoner. It was on these trips that Burt learned the difference between "rechts und links" (right and left) after nearly loosing the barrel a couple of times.

Mr. Schaefer thought it would be funny to offer the city girl from England a chicken, a live one, against regulations. Dorothea accepted the gift graciously and thanked the man in her broken German, but could not bring herself to take the bird in her hands.

He set it on the kitchen floor. "Have fun." He laughed as he left.

Dorothea had visions of a crispy brown change from the ordinary fare of boiled potatoes and sour milk. But she felt completely helpless, watching the awkward, squawking feathery thing strut around her kitchen floor. She stood puzzling over the hen, wondering where one began to prepare a live chicken for the pot, and to do it very discreetly?

Little Fredericka, a neighborhood child, in spite of her six years knew all about such things and pointed out that first it had to be caught. Then the bird was to be dispatched, plucked and eviscerated. Ugh. Dorothea's three sons and Fredericka had fun chasing it around the room. Soon the place looked as though a down pillow had burst during a fight. The poor hen all but collapsed from this marathon.

Dorothea finally summoned enough courage and took a carving knife to commence the grisly operation. She was horrified to discover that such a scrawny neck could be so tough. But at last, having severed the head, she let the chicken fly. The woman, in a state of shock, watched in disbelief as the sightless bird flew around the kitchen, ricocheting off the walls and ceiling before it collapsed spread-eagle on the floor. At this point the children were shaken, too. Dorothea was still in a daze when Walt came home.

Homicide, he thought, when he stepped into the blood-spattered room.

Whether that chicken finally appeared on the menu or everyone by then had lost their appetites Burt did not know.

Though life was difficult, the children didn't care about adult concerns; they had their own problems. When a child is hungry he wants to eat; menus mean nothing to him. A crust of bread smeared with lard and sprinkled with salt tasted as delicious as a slice of bread and butter sprinkled with sugar. Either one would fill the void. On sunny days there were meadows and forests to explore and, when the snow came, there was the excitement of skates and sleighs and snowballs. Grandfather Eichwald built a beautiful hardwood sleigh for the kids. He was a master craftsman, though Dorothea, his English daughter-in-law, ever spiteful, said it was more like a rocking horse.

Naked In A Coat of Armor

Starting school, on the other hand, and discovering that he spoke the wrong language complicated matters for Burt even before he stepped into the classroom. When the boys saw him coming across the yard, they gathered together and chanted a sing-song thing like, "Darin kommen die Englander, die drecklokere auslander" ("There comes the Englishman, the dirty foreigner"). Their parents had not yet gotten over the bitterness of defeat, and the children learned that cruelty was funny.

The first lesson Burt learned in first grade was self-defense. Once while fighting with a classmate, he was pushed into the street and knocked down by a hit-and-run cyclist. The result was a broken ankle. A big man in a green overcoat piggybacked him all the way home. The doctor, a portly gentleman, wore a gold watch chain strung across his paunch like an equator around a globe.

He stepped into the room and doffed his hat and coat. Pince-nez, leashed with black ribbon, straddled a big bulbous nose.

He rolled up his sleeves and bellowed, "Veil, what is the trouble here?" Plunking Burt on the kitchen table like a sack of barley, he hurt him even before touching the swollen leg. Burt sensed he wasn't going to get along with this character.

"Ouch, you're hurting me," he hollered.

"Ja, I know, und I want you should be a good soldier."

Burt's mother, on the opposite side of the table, was instructed to hold onto the child while Frau Schaefer pulled his leg out straight so the doctor could wrap it with a bandage. Burt felt as though they were trying to pull him apart. He had visions of his separated leg lying on the floor and twitching like the daddy-long-legs he plucked the day before. He howled and hollered until he wriggled free.

"Ladies, please! If you do not hold der slippery eel I cannot do my vork." They renewed their hold and the doctor began to wind the bandage to the knee. Between each layer he smeared great gobs of white stuff. "Pull, ladies, pull."

Burt struggled and tried to kick the doctor with his good leg.

The doctor was out of breath now. His rosy cheeks were flushed and glistening with perspiration. One lazy eye caused the other to bulge and glare over the top of his glasses, reminding Burt of a cyclops. The doctor thrust his face so close that Burt could count the tiny purple veins that traced a paisley pattern on the knob of his nose. Through gnashing teeth he hissed, "If you dare to kick me, you young snot nose, then maybe we break der other leg. Ja?"

"You're a naughty boy," Dorothea said. "Wait till your father gets home."

The ogre rolled his sleeves down, buttoned his cuffs deliberately, and Frau Schaefer helped him on with his coat. He stepped to the door and, as he turned to bid the ladies good day, caught Burt sticking his tongue out. "Remember, smarty-pants, we are not yet through mit you," he said, shaking a fat finger at the boy.

Some weeks later the cyclops returned, carrying a very large pair of shears. "Veil now, how is der smart-alec today?"

Naked In A Coat of Armor

Burt knew at once that he was in big trouble again. He soon found that the shears did not fit smoothly between the cast and his leg. As a result, Burt lost a couple of chunks of hide as the doctor struggled to cut away the cast. Burt suspected the man was getting even with him, and he yelled very loudly again. The doctor clamped Burt's free leg against the table with his body. He wasn't going to take any chances and had a mean grin on his face as the pieces of plaster fell to the floor.

Burt felt greatly relieved to get rid of that awful weight and, now, after all those weeks of irritating itch, he could scratch his leg.

"Now you are as good as new; come, walk to me here," the doctor demanded.

But Burt wouldn't budge.

"If you do not walk on that foot now, then maybe you don't ever walk again, Ja? Now come."

Burt wasn't going to go near him, he was so scared of him. Anyway, it hurt to put weight on his weak leg.

"All right, shoot yourself," the doctor suggested and, with his shears tucked under his arm, he stomped out of the room and slammed the door behind him.

Chapter 3

Hans, the village idiot, was in GUT class. His face looked as though his mother stepped on it when he was a baby. His hair was cropped close and it was staggered as though a sheep shearer had done the clipping. His black eyebrows grew in a straight line across his brow. A dark shadow hovered across his face and made him seem old too soon. The eyes, close together and pried wide open by constant fear, were vacant like glass pressed into a clay bust.

Hans Schnyder's body looked like a sack of potatoes and was always in the way. It was tied in the middle with a dirty ribbon of rag. His jacket was too long and his feet had no shoes. He shuffled his posture across the yard like an old man, stooped and haggard. His fellow students were cruel to Hans, like boys can be. They never passed him without punching him or poking him. They made fun of him and laughed when he cried. On a rare occasion when one of them showed a spark of kindness or compassion for some reason, or for no reason (they'd offer him a chip of candy or a biscuit, perhaps an apple core they couldn't finish), the boy's face seemed to dissolve. At first he was cautious, for fear that the gesture might be another unkind prank. But then a grin would stretch his mouth, flowing across both sides of his face at once. The wrinkles at the corners of his eyes indicated they were focused and registered an overwhelming gratitude for such a tiny benevolence.

Hans Schnyder's place in the class was in the back of the room. He wasn't promoted to the class; he was

Naked In A Coat of Armor

just there like a desk or waste paper basket. He hardly ever left his corner. Mr. Stern lost all hope of ever teaching Hans anything, and adopted him as a whipping boy. And whip him he did. There was the time Mr. Stern was writing something on the black board and broke the last piece of chalk. Some wise apple laughed, and the teacher marched to the back of the room and commenced to flay poor Hans with his cane. Oh yes! Let Stern be in a bad mood and the boy would get it two and three times a day. He was whipped the first thing in the morning just to warm up the others and to remind them to be very careful. This was very confusing to the docile boy, but he accepted his punishment.

Mr. Stern was a portly gentleman who wore pince-nez. Nearly all professionals wore these special clip-ons. It was the badge of authority. To glare over the top of them was to convey ruthless discipline. High ranking military officers wore monocles, which made them look high ranking and sinister. Youngsters were reminded that all professionals knew all things, that they could do no wrong, and that doctors, clergymen and professors sat on the right side of God Almighty Himself and lawyers and officers sat on the left side. Students were inspected for hygiene when entering the classroom. Heads were scrutinized for "livestock." Fingernails were examined. And ears. God only knows *what* was so important about ears. The inspector would all but wring them off the children's heads to make sure they had been scrubbed. Burt's mother warned her sons that if they didn't keep their ears clean potatoes would grow in them. Ears made convenient handles for bringing incorrigibles up to toe the mark.

The boys carried their schoolbooks and slates in knapsacks. The wooden frames of the slates had to be scrubbed till they were bleached white. A sponge hung by a string laced through a hole in the corner of the frame had to be clean and dry. Pencils, made of slate, were inspected for sharp points. Students carried these brittle tools in a wooden box with grooves to keep them from breaking.

The first lesson of the day was always dictation. The teacher would read a paragraph to the youngsters from the textbook and they would write it down. Those who passed were rewarded with an extra recess, while those who failed took the lesson over again. Poor Hans never passed inspection or dictation. And recess only gave the kids another chance to torment him.

Frieda was Burt's father's youngest sister and lived with them. She was eight and Burt was two years younger. They were like brother and sister. They spent a great deal of time together playing, fighting and getting into mischief. Sometimes they played doctor and nurse. That's when they discovered that anatomies were different. They were given an assortment of chores to keep them out of trouble.

In 1921 a plague of mice infested the countryside, causing serious damage to the crops. At night it was possible to hear the pitter-patter of their feet as they scurried within the walls of the house. If you were real quiet and listened, you could hear them squeal when they got mad at each other. It was an especially trying

Naked In A Coat of Armor

time for the women. One night the excitement reached a crescendo when a mouse got caught in Dorothea's long hair. She passed out three times between screams. It was during one of her moments of unconsciousness that one of the others was able to untangle the little critter.

Then a plague of may beetles followed. They ate what was left of the crops. School children were given small bags of poison to scatter across the fields and were paid thirty pfennig an hour. They earned six pfennig for every litre of beetles they collected. They searched the woods for firewood, since fuel was terribly scarce, and collected beechnuts, valued for their rich cooking oil.

One day Frieda and Burt trudged along the railroad right-of-way dragging a burlap bag searching for bits and pieces of coal that spilled from the speeding trains. It was a hot day, which made the chore tedious and boring. Their efforts were not very rewarding. The firemen were very careful not to lose too much of the precious fuel. Burt and Frieda stopped to rest in the shade of a favorite old chestnut tree. Burt's sleepy eyes followed the two silver rails to where they converged, and he wondered what that place was like. Not far from where they were sitting, a siding veered off to the south and disappeared into a freight yard. Frieda, dreamily, was looking in the same direction.

Suddenly, she sat bolt upright. "I know where we can find coal–lots of coal."

"Where?"

"Down there, where they unload the trains."

"You're crazy."

Eugene A. Aichroth

"No, listen!" Frieda said, the excitement building as she planned. "Tonight after supper we'll take our wagon and go right into the railroad yard and get a real big load." Freda was always scheming up some wild excursion. Burt usually went along with the plan because it was always an adventure, always a challenge. Sometimes it was great fun and sometimes they ended up going to bed without supper. They decided–that is, Frieda decided–to pull this current stunt off the very next night.

Right after supper they took their wagon and set off straight for the freight yard. The sun had settled to the twilight position where it causes shadows that distort the landscape. They slipped through the gate unnoticed and wormed their way along the fence for awhile. Then they veered off and cut straight across the yard to where an empty gondola car was sitting. It seemed so enormous, like a black iron dinosaur that swallowed them up as they crept under it and dragged their wagon along. There was coal, lots of coal. They lost no time in loading their wagon, giggling and proud that they were so smart.

"Shhh." Frieda put her finger to her lips. Burt heard heavy footsteps crunching the dolomite along the roadbed. Two big black boots moved slowly along the siding towards the children. They tried not to breathe as they crouched behind their wagon. The boots stopped opposite the children and they heard keys rattle and a lock snap open. The black boots pulled a lever and the chute of the gondola flew open as if to devour them. Instead, it vomited coal down on the children and pinned them to the ground. Another bushel full and they would have been buried alive.

Naked In A Coat of Armor

They held their heads and screamed as the boots bent to look under the gondola.

"You all right?" a voice asked in mock surprise.

"Squeak, sniff." Frieda snuffed.

"You...boy. You all right?"

"Cough, snuff," Burt answered, too frightened to say words.

"Vell, now you have coal. Get out of here and don't come back. Der next time they vill never find you, yet."

Burt and Frieda burst out of the black pile, Frieda pushing with all her might and Burt pulling frantically to get the wagon out from under the railroad car. They were determined not to give up their hard-earned contraband. Their get-away was hampered as pieces of coal chocked their wheels every few steps.

At last, at a safe distance beyond the gate they dared to stop for a rest. Frieda's head was bleeding and the blood mixed with coal dust made a gruesome shampoo. Their tears made squiggly white streaks down their black faces. They laughed at each other, seeing that they looked as though they might be coming from a minstrel show.

"That bastard could have killed us." Burt said.

"Dad would kill you if he heard you say that word."

"I don't care, it's true." When they got home with their illegal freight, Dorothea, of course went into shock. "Where in God's name have you two been?"

When they had told their story she said, "That bastard could have killed you."

Walt looked like he didn't know whether to laugh or take another bite of sausage. He dipped into the sauerkraut. "Why, that son of a bitch."

That was another word Burt thought they weren't supposed to say. But now he was too tired to care any more.

Walt was a good natured, gentle man and a good father, but he wanted no one to mess with his kids. After finishing his supper, he sat with a faraway look. Burt and Frieda knew he was planning something because his mustache kept twitching. Suddenly he got up, put his coat on, snatched his hat off the peg in the hall, and stomped out of the house. An hour or so later he was back and announced with a big smile, "Well, that bugger won't dump coal on my kids again."

"What do you think Dad did to him?" Burt whispered to Freda later that night.

"He beat the shit out of him, that's what."

"Yeah, like he will you if he hears you talking like that."

"Go to sleep." She giggled.

The next day the newspaper announced that the security guard on the night shift at the freightyard was reported missing in the morning. Later in the day, bloodhounds found him at the bottom of a gondola car with a large lump on his head. "Someone must have tapped him on the head with a blunt instrument," the yard foreman said. But when questioning the guard he couldn't remember anything.

"Peculiar," said the foreman."

"Peculiar," Frieda said with a silly grin as she read the headlines to Burt.

Naked In A Coat of Armor

Walt was determined as ever to leave Germany. He heard from friends who were successful and were prospering in Australia and North America. Otto sat down beside Walt one day during lunchtime and announced, "Kerbach is going to America."

"How do you know?" Walt said.

"He has a knitting machine he wants to sell."

"Wonder what he's asking for it?"

"What do you want with a knitting machine?"

"I'll get it for Dorth. She can knit socks for some extra money so I can emigrate to America, too."

"You in America?"

"Why not? I have a good trade; I speak the language. Kerbach will be established and could vouch for me."

Dorothea wasn't sure she liked that plan, but Walt purchased the machine. She soon learned how to operate it and, with the vast demand for woolen socks, it wasn't long before there was enough money, and Walt booked passage for America.

A year later, in 1926, Dorothea took the family, including Frieda, to England.

Dorothea packed the children up and left Germany to visit her parents. She wanted to see them once more before going to yet another foreign country to join her husband. There wasn't money enough for the children to go with her to America, so arrangements had to be made for temporary lodgings for them.

Chapter 4

Burt and his brothers lived in a place for boys for awhile. The parents who could afford to pay called it a boarding school, but it was an orphanage to those whose parents forgot where they left them. After they said their goodbyes, Burt wondered if he would ever see their mother again. He found out that he was going to be separated from his young brothers, Rolland and Rolph. He was frightened and lonely.

"Burt, it will be just a little while before we will all be together again," Dorothea reassured him. "Be a good boy and watch over your little brothers." There was six and seven years' difference between Burt and his siblings. Ever since Rolph and Rolland were crawling around in dirty diapers, it was always, "Burt take care of your brothers. Burt, mind the little ones. Burt, when you go out to play, take you brothers with you." His chums would tease him and he grew to hate his brothers. But now it was different. With Dorothea and Walt gone, Rolland and Rolph were the only family ties left to him. He wanted to be near them, to take care of them.

Holy Innocence School was an oasis in the center of the city of Chatham in Southern England. It was surrounded by an eight-foot wall with broken glass embedded in the mortar along the top. Perhaps that's why it seemed like an oasis. There was a gatehouse at the beginning of a long driveway, lined with holly trimmed like privet hedge. This roadway escorted the visitor to a large, somber complex of red brick buildings. There a roly-poly Mother Superior officiated over an order of nuns. Besides the convent, there were quarters for elderly ladies and facilities for some three hundred boys, with a corner for little children. Burt's brothers were to be billeted there. A large meadow with a few dairy cattle stretched to an orchard and, beyond that, a vegetable garden. On the other side were a storehouse, a laundry and all the necessaries to provide for the motley group of inhabitants.

At Holy Innocence the proverb, "Spare the rod and spoil the child," was taken literally. There Burt learned the meaning of discipline. He and his agemates were warned that the devil would be beaten out of them and the fear of God will be beaten into them. Should they dare to stray from the narrow path, they were to be thrashed to within an inch of their lives.

The school semester invariably commenced with the cane-peddler displaying his wares with morbid pleasure. He was a one-eyed gentleman with a sinister sneer and a cruel cackle. The type of cane preferred was porous and flexible, ideal for routine flogging. The rods were cut into three-foot lengths. Three diameters were selected by the schoolmaster: quarter-inch to be used on the little ones, three-eighths for those who broke the rules occasionally, and half-inch for the incorrigibles.

When the cane was applied skillfully, the hapless one would wish someone else was in his place. The culprit was ordered to stretch his hands straight out to the sides with palms up so as to present a good target. The boys discovered that if they held their hands extra high the good Sister would lose a lot of leverage. It didn't take long, though, for the nuns to catch on to their game. From then on, they were made to kneel to take their penance and with much more effective results. If Sister was experienced in wielding the cane, she would aim for the fingertips. There the sting was best felt. Most of the boys were callous to a whack across the palm. But let a near miss strike them across the wrist, then the feeling was as though the hand had been severed, causing much dancing and complaining.

Nuns at Holy Innocence wore long rosaries, with beads nearly the size of golf balls from their leather belts. Once when it was Burt's turn for some correction, and Sister Joseph began exercising with much enthusiasm, somehow the cane became entangled in her rosary, causing him to receive a smart clout alongside of the head with a flying "self-ball." This left him dazed for a moment and wondering which he preferred, the cane or the rosary.

The early morning muster was rather rude. The nun on duty would flash the lights on and frighten the boys out of dreamland with a singsong chant of half prayer and half threats. "Hail Mary, full of grace...Up, up you sleepy heads! The Lord be with you, blessed art thou...Up, up you lazy louts! Holy Mary Mother of God...You've wet the bed again! Pray for us sinners now...You're going to get it!...and at our death."

Dressed and washed, beds made and morning prayers completed, the boys would file into the refectory for a hearty breakfast of porridge without milk or sugar and black cocoa without sugar or milk. An unlucky bed-wetter honored that morning was made to stand in the corner with his sodden sheet draped over his head and given no breakfast.

Naked In A Coat of Armor

One good sister, especially innovative, was determined to put an end to the lazy habit once and for all. She thought that to add a chamber pot to be worn as a crown and with a red ribbon tied to the handle would be a sure cure.

After breakfast, the dishes were paraded to the scullery to be washed, acres of red tile floor had to be mopped, sinks cleaned, garbage taken out–all before classes.

Mr. MacMahon, the only male teacher, taught sixth, seventh and eighth grades. He was not tall but well built, and he carried himself in a military posture. Some said he was a graduate of Sandhurst. When lecturing, he would pace the floor with his cane tucked under his arm like a swagger stick. To emphasize a point, he would draw it like a saber or bow it like a fencing foil. Sometimes he would suddenly whip it through the air taking great pleasure in its sound and resilience, scaring the hell out of anyone caught dozing. His preferred method for commanding attention differed to that of the nuns. He would drape the dunce over a desk, stretch the boy's pants tight over his gluteus maximus so the delivery would produce the best results, and then the boy had to eat supper standing up.

Mr. MacMahon also took charge of the Glee Club. He would stand the short singers up front, the taller ones behind, and the third row behind them on a bench. There was enough space between ranks to enable him to walk in between and listen to his songbirds individually. Those blessed with ears allergic to tone and unable to reach a note would get a sharp whack across the back of their bare legs. This quickly brought them up a notch or two on the scale, much to the maestro's satisfaction.

There were four swings on the playground, two low ones for the low ones and two high ones for the high ones. If the boys swung as high as they could, without doing a summersault at the top, they were treated to an intermittent peek over the wall and saw things like motor cars and shops and people and girls. One smart-alec came up with the theory that if you swung high and let go just as the pendulum paralleled the horizon, you could fly through the air like a bird and sail right over the wall. Well, we talked Archie into giving it a go and, just as he came up to the summersault position, he let go, flew through the air like a bird, and sailed smack into the wall...splat! falling to the ground in a heap. Just then Sister Ludavena, steeped in her vespers, passed by and was startled to see this mass delivered from heaven in front of her. Poor Archie lay moaning in pain, his shoulder blade protruding grotesquely and his arm hanging limp. The good Sister quickly surveyed the situation. She placed her foot on the flyer's chest, took hold of his arm, and deftly pulled and twisted it simultaneously. The dislocated shoulder snapped back into place with a grating sound, and the boy got up and took off. The rest of the boys gaped in amazement and stood dumbfounded, vowing never to do anything reckless again–at least not for the next hour or so–while they reflected on the other miracle worker, the one in the Bible.

It was a happy day for Burt when his young brother Rolph was transferred to be with the older boys. He was assigned to Burt's charge, and Burt would be

Naked In A Coat of Armor

responsible for his care. The washroom was lined with pigeonholes where the boys kept their Sunday shoes. Several wooden tubs, supported by wooden sawhorses, stood in the middle of the room. The boys would wash up each evening before bedtime. Boys stripped to the waist would ring the tubs, and the boys in charge would see to it that the young'uns washed behind their ears. Invariably, a happy splashing party would take place. On one occasion when the hilarity reached a crescendo, one of the tubs slid off its support, causing a tidal wave to slosh across the tile floor. The room was in an uproar, with half-naked bodies skating and sliding into each other. But the laughter was suddenly clipped, as there, in the doorway, stood Sister Ludavena.

She was in shock as she surveyed the flood. "What in God's name happened here?" she roared.

"It was an accident," Burt said.

"An accident? I'll give you an accident." With that she began to beat him over the head and shoulders with her cane, the half-inch one. He snatched the weapon out of her hand and threw it at her. The shock of such insolence turned her harsh face to crimson. With clenched teeth and fists, she flew at him anew and beat him into a corner, where she snatched a shoe out of a nearby pigeon hole and brought it crashing down on the bridge of his nose. As the blood gushed down in front of him, she screamed, "How dare you raise a hand to me! Now go and wash your dirty German Jew nose!" Burt reflected that, not much earlier in Germany, they had called him a dirty English foreigner. This was all very confusing; with all that scrubbing, you'd think a body would be cleaned up by now. It's funny how prejudice works.

Once during a stickball game, the champion belted a ball through the dormitory window. The penalty for that was three dunkings in a cold-water bath. The bathroom had two tubs up on a platform much like a stage. Overhead were drying racks on which hung the loincloths the boys wrapped themselves in to cover their nakedness when bathing. The burly lad assigned to do the dunking stood poised in his glory, waiting for the fun. The first shock of the penal bath, of course, drew a breathtaking gasp, with much spluttering, coughing and splashing. For this he earned an extra dunking.

Mr. Bjorgasen was the handyman for Holy Innocence. He fixed broken windows, leaky faucets and pipes. The boys loved Mr. Bjorgasen; he was their friend, their hero. He could do marvelous things with saw and hammer. He gave the boys nails and things. Best of all, he had a great vocabulary of four-letter words, especially when he hammered his finger. The older boys liked to repeat those words when they were sure none of the nuns were within earshot. It made them feel very grown up. Mr. Bjorgasen never went to church, but he was always calling on Jesus Christ for something.

Burt had a little business going with supplies scrounged from Mr. Bjorgasen. For two bent nails, he could get a ride around the yard in Archie's soapbox car. For two straight ones, he'd get two turns around the yard–fast. New nails were sold for cash only. One brought a farthing and two a halfpenny. Bolts cost a penny each, a penny and a half with nuts.

Naked In A Coat of Armor

Some nuns carried a short piece of broom handle or chair rung in their habits; the boys called them puddin' sticks. They were handy tools for getting their attention with a swift rap to the noggin'. Then there were the nuns who also carried an apple or a sweet in their pockets. The goodies were reserved for one kind of boy and the puddin' stick for another.

Each Sunday the boys filed into church in orderly fashion, like shining little saints with crewcuts. Sister Providence would position herself on the aisle at the end of the pew so that she could keep an eye on them. When she left to receive communion, the boys were free to make mischief for a moment. On one such occasion they had great fun rolling a large marble along the full length of the pew in front, its rumble hugely amplified in the quiet. When Sister returned from the altar, her veil was drawn down over her face to exemplify her solemn piety. She very solemnly drew her puddin' stick and very discreetly laid a lighting-like rap on the nearest crewcut's skull. The knock echoed over the heads of the congregation and rose high up into the vault of the chapel, at precisely the most sacred moment of the mass. The wicked louts burst into laughter and expelled other suppressed noises. This was sacrilege, and they would hear more about it before they were many days older.

Father Turner officiated for the convent. He said the masses and heard the boys' confessions and kept quiet about them. He was good to the boys, often finding time to play football with them or tell them funny stories. A parishioner gave him a Labrador puppy one day, and it grew into something resembling a Shetland pony. His housekeeper detested the animal from the start. Not that she had anything against dogs; she simply hated anything with four or more legs. She gave Father Turner an ultimatum: either she or the dog must go. The priest decided to give his beloved dog, Major, to the boys at Holy Innocence. The boys were thrilled to have this big, black, sleek animal as their mascot. Mother Superior was in shock but could not bring herself to contradict Father Turner. In time, everyone at Holy Innocence grew to love Major. Everyone, that is, but Sister Ludavena, who said, "That black beast is possessed with the Devil himself." She kicked him and threw her puddin stick at him at every opportunity.

Evening prayer was held in the classroom. The boys were made to kneel on the hard benches, probably to torture them for their sins. Or perhaps to remind them that the One they were praying to was not that comfortable either. After all, he wore a crown of thorns and carried a very heavy cross. Major would wander up and down the ranks and lick the cuts and sores of the barefooted ones. Sometimes he would join the boys and sit straight up on a bench as though he, too, was praying. When the puddin' stick came flying, three boys and the dog would duck and fall to the floor, disrupting the solemn occasion.

One time Sister Ludavena accidentally stepped on the dog's tail. Major let out a yelp, stood up on his hind legs, stretched himself to full length, and laid a massive paw on each of Sister's shoulders. The frightened woman turned to stone while the boys' mascot dragged his long tongue across her pallid face and slobbered her with much affection, truly an example of turning the other cheek.

Naked In A Coat of Armor

It was a proud day in Burt's life when he was chosen to take part in a Christmas pageant. He was to be an angel with nothing to recite. All he had to do was to stand to one side of the manger scene and look pious. He was dressed in flowing white with full-length cardboard wings and, over his head, a halo which was suspended from a wire tucked down the back of his neck. He rolled his eyes heavenward, trying to look as holy as a Protestant kid could.

After his magnificent performance, expecting long applause, he was punished, instead, for not holding his hands clasped in prayer. After all, everyone knows that angels always have their hands clasped.

Burt got along quite well with the other kids and made a couple of good friends. But somehow he felt he didn't belong in this place. He wanted to be accepted but always felt like an outsider. He had to go to mass but couldn't take communion. He wanted to be an altar boy but he wasn't allowed near the altar. How he envied those boys dressed in white, looking like little saints while they held the sacred chalice for the priest. He wanted to swing the incense around and whip up a great cloud of smelly smoke. Burt learned all the prayers and memorized the catechism, but they wouldn't let him go to confession, not that he would confess anything anyway. He decided he wanted to be a priest when he grew up. I'll show them, he thought; it will be different in America.

Two boys were assigned to prepare the bread for the evening meal. A large wooden box of sliced bread would be placed on the little table in the scullery. A bowl of tallow, skimmed off the top of the soup pots, was positioned alongside. This "butter" in place of real beef dripping, was smeared onto the bread and then two slices pressed together and dropped into a second box on the floor. The two boys' work place was adjacent to the old folks' scullery and separated by a partition, open across the top near the ceiling. If Mrs. O'Shaunessy was on duty next door, she would sometimes call out and ask, "Boys, would ye like a smidgen of bacon fart?"

"Yes, please, Mum!" the boys would answer, and one of them dashed over to collect this rare treat.

"Ye know, boy's, bacon fart makes ye fart," Mrs. O'Shaunessy informed the two as she eyed their scrawny frames. Laughing and giggling, later on, the boys skipped around the playground, chanting this new information for all to hear.

At day's end, and before bedtime, those with sore throats queued up in their nightshirts to have their tonsils swabbed with iodine. A stick with a bit of wadding wound on the end made do for an applicator. Bedtime prayer was to ask for forgiveness and for deliverance from iodine.

Tim Flannigan was a leftover from Holy Innocence. His old man came to England looking for work and, in the meantime, he put young Tim in the orphanage temporarily. Burt and he got to be good friends, perhaps on account of the great stories he'd tell. There was the one about Father Michael Mahoney, who was the rector of Ballinagh, in the county of Cavan.

Each day Father Mahoney would pick a lad to ring the Angelus, and it was young Tim's turn to ring the evening toll. It was sundown, and he had to cross the graveyard to get to the bell tower.

Naked In A Coat of Armor

Evening light and shadow in the cemetery played tricks on Tim's nerves. Eyesight may focus sharply, then dim and blur, then focus again. The three elms at the edge of the path, over there near that tombstone, seemed as though they were three men in a huddle, plotting some spooky scheme. The crackle of a dry leaf underfoot echoed as though someone were following. The earth smelled freshly turned, like at a funeral on a rainy day. The boy felt his skin prickle and crawl. It was a relief, at last, to step into the church.

Inside, the belfry seemed to rise a thousand feet. To Tim, it seemed as though the steeple had stabbed the dying sun, which now shed crimson across the darkened horizon. He grasped the bell rope and reached high to get a good first pull, and hoped he would remember the proper sequence of the toll.

The rattle of the rope caused a flutter, and several somethings scattered out of the belfry. The lad was sure they must be winged zombies come to carry him away. The bell swung on its fulcrum, lifting the boy off his feet. The tongue hammered the great casting and the reverberating sound cascaded deafening waves down on the frightened lad. As the massive pendulum swung back towards its opposite arc, it dropped poor Tim on the floor, tangled in rope.

The Angelus was rung. Tim stepped to the church door and felt the cool on his face. The Crepe Hanger had spread his black mantle over the cemetery, and the lad thought how very, very dark it was. Suddenly he made a frantic exit, skillfully dodging between the stone nametags of a thousand ghosts, demons, who seemed to be chasing him out of their ghastly domain.

Vaulting the wall that corralled the dead, he raced down the road to the safety of his home. He was grateful for the warmth and glad to be in from the eerie gloom. At supper his father asked, "Were ye a mite scared, son?"

"NO sir."

"Well now, I thought the Angelus sounded a bit different tonight."

Chapter 5

Burt's tenure at Holy Innocence, like that of other boys, came to an end at the age of fourteen. Those with parents were sent home. The orphans were scattered throughout the Colonies, where they worked off their steerage and indenture on farms and in factories until they came of age. Burt and his siblings stayed with Aunt Flo and Uncle Ernie for some weeks until their passage to New York was confirmed. Those were happy days, because they knew they would soon be reunited with their parents. But Frieda wanted to stay with her Uncle Walter in London. It was a sad day when she left. Burt and his brothers were going to miss her.

Uncle Ernie was great fun. He'd romp and laugh and play ball with the three boys. Burt noticed he had a tattoo on each upper arm; Japanese ladies they were, and when he flexed his biceps they would do a dance. This fascinated the young boys, and they'd coax him to repeat the performance again and again. Uncle Ernie was in the British Army in India, and soldiers will get tattooed. Aunt Flo, a bit more sophisticated, thought he should be setting a better example, and would tell him so.

Uncle Ernie told the boys with a sly wink, "You kids are going to have to learn to chew gum."

"Why?" Burt asked.

"Because in America everyone chews gum."

"You're making fun of us, Uncle."

"It's true," he laughed. "They even stick it on the bed post at night so that it will be within easy reach first thing in the morning."

When the SS Berengaria steamed into New York harbor on December, 1928, Burt did not look very long at the Statue of liberty. For there, on the snow-covered Brooklyn side shore was a huge red and white sign advertising spearmint gum. Now he wondered if there wasn't some truth in Uncle Ernie's story.

The Berengaria, large, powerful and luxurious, was one of Cunards Atlantic's prestige boats. Along with the Aquitania and the Mauritania, they were known as the big three. She was built in 1913 by the Bremer Vulkan Shipyards, Hamburg, Germany, and ceded to Britain following World War 1. It plied between Southampton and New York, carrying thousands of passengers, year round. Vanderbilt had a suite permanently reserved, whether he used it or not. As steerage passengers, Burt and his brothers saw little of this elegance. When they arrived at New York and prepared to disembark, they were led down the great winding stairway to the elaborate ballroom, treating them to a glimpse of the elegance. They saw the purser for the second time since they'd left Southampton, and he was now escorting them to customs. He was supposed to be in charge of the kids on the trip. However, it was a couple of young men, Harry and George, who chaperoned them and took very good care of them. They became friends quickly; perhaps the purser tipped them a few dollars to keep an eye on the boys.

Naked In A Coat of Armor

The young immigrants were ushered into the "Great Hall of Judgment" on Ellis Island. The enormous room, packed with people, was overwhelming. How will our parents ever find us? Burt wondered.

"Is this your mother?" the customs officer asked.

"I don't know," replied Roland, seven years old.

"Well, she's a pretty lady; why don't you give her a big kiss?"

The boys seemed more concerned with introducing their friends, and this embarrassed George and Harry. "Aw, we'll see you in Coney Island sometime," Harry said as they disappeared into the crowd.

At last they were reunited as a real family in a permanent home. Eight eighty-one St. John's Place, Brooklyn, N.Y., U.S.A. was called a railroad apartment, one flight up. Here they celebrated the most wonderful of all Christmases. Although Walt was a chef at the Fifth Avenue Hotel in Manhattan, he was also the custodian of the apartment house. This gave him the privilege to cultivate a small garden in the back yard. The neighbor next door, an old Italian man, would share gardening tips and advice over the fence. Best of all, he taught Walt how to make wine.

"We'll put the new boy in class 6-B until we see how well he does," instructed Mrs. Casebolt, the principal of Brooklyn Practice School. Mrs. Ingles was delighted to have the kid from England in her room. Already there were two girls from Scotland in her class. She dashed off to spread the news to the other teachers. They had made such a fuss over the girls, with their Scottish brogue, and now there was this redhead with his delightful English accent.

"She's collecting quite a menagerie," whispered Mrs. Smart to Mrs. Graph. Mrs. Burns, the music teacher, thought it would be great fun to put on a little skit. The girls could do their Highland sword dance, and Burt, the kid from England, could sing his 'Danny Boy.' How they found out that Burt sang even though he couldn't carry a tune, was a mystery. If he'd told someone to try and impress, Burt thought, he would never live it down.

"Yes," Mrs. Smart chimed in, "And we'll get Sylvia to recite her poetry."

Mary and Florence came dressed in pretty Highland kilts and lace-trimmed blouses. They wore Tamashanters with ribbons that hung down in back. Burt wore Bermuda shorts, customary in Europe, even in winter. The dance went over big with the wise guys, especially when the girls hopscotched over their swords that were crisscrossed on the floor, kicking their dresses up over their bare knees. The swords were real sabers with fancy hilts. Burt's singing certainly didn't impress the guys much. He found out later they booed and hollered and gave him the limp-wrist signal. And poor Sylvia, well, her poetry was that old dreamy mush.

Burt fell madly into some kind of feeling for Sylvia, a Jewish girl who sat across the aisle from him. She had snow-white frizzy hair and pink eyes. She looked sort of like a gollywog that had been electrocuted. She wore the prettiest dresses and patent-leather shoes. She was always polite and proper, but most of all she was nice to Burt. She never laughed at

Naked In A Coat of Armor

his funny accent or made fun of his Bermuda shorts. Burt started to carry her books, though only down the stairs and out of the building. A uniformed chauffeur met her at the curb each day.

"Good afternoon, Miss Sylvia," he would greet her as he held the door and took her hand to help her into the car, treating her like a fairy princess. It was the longest black car Burt had ever seen. He longed to go for a ride in it. It was a Pierce Arrow, he noticed, because the headlights were on the mudguards.

"Just like in da fairytale, huh?" boomed Freddie Smith, the class bully. "Ya know, where d a footman puts Ella Cinders into da pumpkin."

"I say, don't you mean Cinderella?"

"Listen to Danny Boy, will ya. You're askin' fer a fat lip."

"Whot's a fat lip?"

"Go ahead, Moose." That was Smith's nickname. "Show 'im." Auggie egged the bully on. Moose let fly, a straight to Burt's mouth.

Burt didn't know what hit him or where it came from. It caught him off guard, and he saw nothing but stars. It brought tears to his eyes, but he wasn't going to let the guys see him cry, so he ducked around them and beat it home.

"Whot 'appened, son?" Dorothea asked.

"I've got a fat lip."

"A fat whot?"

"Moose hit me in the mouth."

"My word, you'd better go and wash up for tea and put a cold cloth on that lip. "Moose. "What sort of a name is that?"

59

Eugene A. Aichroth

At the meal table Burt looked a bit out of shape. His father asked, "Whot 'appened to you, son?"

"I've got a fat lip."

"A fat whot?"

"One of the boys 'it me in the mouth."

"You 'it 'im back, I 'ope?"

"Mom says gentlemen don't fight."

"Look 'ere son, gentlemen don't start a fight, but when they're in it they let 'em 'ave it. Right? The next time that bloke gets in your way, you give 'im what for, do you 'ear?"

"Yes sir."

Gerry, walking to school the next day with Burt, asked if Burt's mouth hurt very much. Burt said, "Not half."

"Not half?" mimicked the Moose as he snuck up behind. "Look, Limey," he said, "does yer mouth hoit?"

"Yes, ta very much."

"Cheese, da guy comes from England and can't even talk English."

"Well whot do *you* say when someone gives you something?"

"Sometimes I say tanks an sometimes I don't say nutting."

"I say, Mouse, do you know whot a fat lip is?" Burt said.

"Soitny, and da name is Moose, smart ass."

With that, Burt let him have it straight to the mouth and, while the surprise was still on the bully's face, he threw another one to the stomach. He sagged as the wind went out of him like a punctured balloon.

Naked In A Coat of Armor

An audience had gathered and the excited kids jumped up and down, hooting and hollering. "You've done it, you've done it. You beat up the Moose," they chanted. "Look, now his nose is as big as a moose's."

Burt was an instant hero. He was invited to the empty lot in back of Cushman's Bakery, where they smoked cigarettes they had stolen from their fathers.

Augie offered Burt one. "Go ahead, Limey, try it," he said. Burt took in a deep drag and swallowed. They all laughed to see him coughing, spitting and spluttering. "Ya ain't suppose to swallow it, dummy." But it was just good-natured teasing. They were all friends now. Even Moose joined in, still holding his swollen nose.

Mrs. Barr was in charge of the Glee Club, and Burt soon fell very much in love with her. She was very pretty, with copper-colored hair done up in a French braid, and she smelled so good. Burt knew she liked him. He liked to watch her flit from desk to desk, listening to her songbirds while beating the rhythm, using her forefinger like a baton. When she came to him, she would bend over and bring her face ever so close to his, to listen to his tone. Her perfume would cause his blood to race. He was a shy kid and hoped that she couldn't hear his heart beating like a jungle tom-tom. When she leaned forward, her blouse billowed out and her crystal pendant swung clear. He could peek down inside and see…things. She would rub whatever it is that ladies have between their thighs on the corner of his desk…in rhythm.

Now, surely a healthy fifteen-year-old boy just can't be expected to concentrate on 'Funiculi,

Funicula,' even though it is a 'joyous song' and, yes, Burt was joyous 'and the world was made for fun and frolic.'

Burt had another true love in Brooklyn Model School. But he loved Mrs. Slater in a different way. She was the eighth-grade English teacher and librarian. She was tall, had gray hair, and was very old...at least forty. She was rather nice looking in a severe sort of way and carried herself in a regal posture. Her homeroom was lined with shelves and stacked with books. They gave the room a peculiar antique smell.

The room had three or four louts who were notorious for disrupting the classes, and now they were in the eighth grade, the graduating class. How all the children managed to get this far in academia, no one was quite sure.

Burt was the biggest of the clowns. One day he was engaged in lousing up the study period, as usual, during Mrs. Slater's momentary absence. Suddenly she reappeared at the door. The students were in hysterics but instantly fell silent. Of course, the teacher knew who was the ringleader and ordered Burt out of the room. She followed him into the hall and backed him up against the wall.

"Just what do you think you're doing?" she demanded. "Don't you think it's about time you grew up and graduated? You've been left back twice, and you're two years late to be in this class. I'm going to tell you something, young man," she continued.

Burt thought how pretty she is for an old woman, even though she was mad at him.

"You don't have what you boys call guts," she hissed.

Naked In A Coat of Armor

The word "guts," coming from a teacher startled him. Twice more the slang bashed his ears.

"It takes guts to behave in class, and it takes guts to learn."

Wow, this old biddy had us figured out. She even spoke like us, Burt thought.

"You owe the class an apology. Now get in there and show me what you're made of." After apologizing to the whole class, Burt felt like the clown he had been imitating.

"The books in this room are not here just for storage, they are here for you to read," Mrs. Slater said.

She encouraged Burt to enter an essay contest sponsored by one of the Brooklyn Fire Departments. He didn't win first prize, but he was thrilled to receive honorable mention and, best of all, Mrs. Slater was proud of him.

Fifty years slipped away before Burt had the opportunity to earn some credits in English. And not until then did it occur to him what this wonderful lady was trying to put across to him. Sure, he had been exposed to books before; Dorothea used to nag him constantly to read. But it was Mrs. Slater who taught him to appreciate the wealth in them. She made language and vocabulary alive and exciting. She taught him something about discipline, responsibility and challenge. Most important, she was a friend, who helped him grow up.

Chapter 6

They were the Sterling Street Gang. Kids came from Eastern Parkway, Lincoln Place, Sterling Street and one was from St. John's Place. Their headquarters was an empty lot behind Cushman's Bakery on Nostrand Avenue. A brick building was demolished there a long time ago. A high board fence enclosed it to keep trespassers out. The seventh board counting from the Nostrand Avenue end was loose and served as their secret entrance. 'NO TRESPASSING' was printed in large black letters across the loose board. When a member entered the lot, "PASS" was appropriately read as the board swung. This made it a lawful entry, sort of.

The count had to be changed periodically, however, and a new board loosened to ensure security. Only members were allowed to share the inner sanctum. Absolutely no girls were ever invited. Oh, they liked girls all right, make no mistake about it, but–well, you just didn't admit it.

They spent many happy hours sifting through the rubble. The great archeological digs of Egypt were no more thrilling than their local rummagings.

"Like drilling fer erl," said Doughbelly.

"Earl who?" asked Daudy.

"Motor erl, Stupid."

"Thought it come in cans."

"Soitnee it comes in cans; but ya godda drill for it foist."

It seemed that there was no end to the treasures to be found. Doorknobs, hinges, and a pipe wrench, with

Naked In A Coat of Armor

its adjustment fixed by years of rust. Smitty found a knife with a broken blade. Bits and pieces of two-by-fours, planks and sheets of tin made great building materials. Hambone found a length of stovepipe with an elbow on each end and thought it would make a neat periscope, make-believe, that is. But the gang could barely contain themselves the time Casebolt found a real arrowhead just as Augie dug up a couple of lead musket balls. Their imaginations vent wild. They heard Indian war cries, and clouds of dust seemed to rise up over their lot as cowboys galloped over the hill. The smell of Danish pastries was more like the fumes of black powder in their nostrils as the skirmish began.

They built trenches and caves, dug valleys, and piled up hills. They made castles and forts. Here, they were in their glory; they were kings and knights, cowboys and Indians, cops and robbers and highwaymen, good soldiers and bad ones. Sometimes, they were just boys, playing mumblety-peg or marbles or ring-a-lievio. Sometimes, just sitting around, talking about girls. Now, the Bergen Street Gang had been giving the gang a hard time lately, so they called a meeting to see what could be done about it. Pinky came up with the great idea to challenge them to a rock fight.

"There ain't many rocks in Brooklyn," Porky said. "Unless you went in back of the museum."

"That's too far to go," Pipsqeak piped up. "Why not have it right here on our home field?"

"Nah, that's no good, "Toni Torreli said. "They'll know our secret entrance then."

"So we'll change it," Moose announced, matter of fact.

"Ok, that's it," Abe Lipschitz agreed.

On the day of the big battle, Jody positioned himself at the loose board like a sergeant at arms and ushered the enemy, one by one, into their holy of holies. The Bergen Street Gang were a tough lot, with bigger guys than the Sterling Street Gang, but they seemed uneasy inside their rivals' fence, not knowing the lay of the land.

They noticed right off that the Sterlings were dug in and positioned to their advantage. Hambone had set up his periscope and looked very impressive as he surveyed the front lines. Henny Upshaw gave the command, and the battle was on. Bricks flew through the air like shrapnel. The melee was progressing fast and furious until a well-aimed missile entered the periscope and smacked poor Hambone in the eye. He fell back and cupped his face in his hands, hollering bloody murder.

It scared the daylights out of everyone, and Upshaw called for a cease-fire. But after Hambone calmed down and they were sure he wasn't going to die, they went back into combat with the rage of revenge. The Bergen Street Gang got a thorough thrashing and soon white flags were flying. The foe was escorted off the property. The Sterlings saluted them by thumbing their noses and sticking out their tongues. It was a long time before they heard from the Bergen Street Gang again.

Hambone showed up in school a few days later with his head bandaged. The white cloth, wound diagonally across his face, covered the damaged eye. His 'turban,' askew, gave him a jaunty look.

A couple of days later he showed up in class without the bandage and sporting the neatest shiner any of them had ever seen. They were proud of Hambone. He was their hero. Back at headquarters, after school, it was agreed that the brave warrior had earned a Purple Heart. Henney Upshaw figured a brass escutcheon, one of the treasures they'd dug up, would make a very authentic-looking medal. He got the others to fall in, and they lined up like two rows of corn. The General, very ceremoniously, tied the medal to Hambone's coat button with a piece of string. Some of the gang thought he really wasn't a big enough to deserve that big a medal. But, anyway, Wimpy Medley played something on his harmonica while Gockle beat something out on an oil drum. It was all very formal and so impressive.

After the formalities, Slinky Sloman slunk into the back window of the bakery and started to pass out about a dozen charlottes russes. They were all vanilla, but then they couldn't be choosy; after all, he wasn't supposed to be helping himself in the first place. Red Nickles and Curly O'Connor showed up with a couple of big bottles of cream soda.

"We found some deposit bottles and cashed them in," O'Connor announced proudly. But Burt suspected they more than likely snitched them off the windowsills in the neighborhood. Anyway, it was a great celebration. After changing the secret entrance to the thirteenth board, counting from Nostrand Ave., they split up and went home feeling like heroes, every one of them.

Animal

Walt taught Burt and his brothers a love of nature and the wonders of the wilderness. He had a sense of humor and laughed sometimes. He was hired as a French chef at the Fifth Avenue Hotel in New York City. A handsome German, sporting a French mustache waxed to needle points and speaking with a British accent, took quite a ribbing for that mixture.

Walt was a good-natured sort. If he playfully patted a waitress on her ass, as she sashayed past, balancing her tray, it wasn't harassment in those days. It was all in fun and quite all right, coming from him, for they all loved him. He'd slap Dorothea around periodically, probably to prove his old-world macho. But that seemed all right because he loved her very much.

Dorothea too, could swing a smart left hook and sometimes beat the stuffing out of Walt. He'd leave home about once a month but always showed up at night on the same day because making up was so sweet. That was okay, too, because she loved him dearly.

Both of them would take turns whipping the boys into shape, making them toe the mark that they thought was the proper mark to toe. If they deviated one iota from the straight and narrow, Dorothea would beat the fear of God into them and Walt would beat the devil out. But, somehow, that was all right, too, even though it didn't seem that way at the time. The boys knew Dorothea and Walt thought their three boys were just fine. Even so, Burt's teacher found it necessary to

Naked In A Coat of Armor

cane the hell out of him just because he couldn't make any sense out of going to school.

Walt brought a stray dog home. It was wandering around the Nostrand Avenue subway station. After they fed her and groomed her for a week or so, she turned out to be a sleek black Belgium Shepherd. They called her Black Beauty, after another animal they had read about.

When their cat died, they replaced him with a feisty little kitten. It was great fun watching the predator pretend to stalk imaginary prey through the jungle of chair and table legs or to see him bat a ball twice his size around the room. One day Walt was teasing the kitten by tapping the floor with his slipper. It would slink out of its hiding place and ferociously attack his foot. When Walt took his slipper off and slapped the linoleum floor with the heel, the sharp report would excite the kitten and it would make a flying leap at the noisemaker. The whole family laughed at this clowning around and marveled at the little animal's spunk. On the second try, the kitten was a lightning flash–too fast for the slipper, and the heel came down and broke the little back, killing it instantly. There was a terrible silence while the unbelievable slowly registered.

"You swine, you've killed it. How could you be so cruel? You brute!" Dorothea railed and carried on in a schizophrenic rage all the while Walt, in a daze, dressed for work. The boys went to school to tell the gruesome tale. Dorothea agonized all day over her contemptible outburst and felt ashamed and sorry. After all, it was a second hurt for Walt, to have his wife attack him so viciously, so unfairly. He must have spent a long, miserable day and probably dreaded coming home. Toward evening Dorothea said, "Come, Burt, let's go and meet your father at the station." She looked to him, her firstborn, when she was in trouble or confused or frightened. She was like that. To kiss and make up came easy for her. She could not understand that it was not natural for most people to forgive and forget quite so readily. Burt dreaded going with her. He hated his mother on that day.

Walt roomed at Mrs. Tilford's when he first came to America. She was a widow who ran a boarding house, a brownstone on Brooklyn Avenue, way down near Fulton Street. A stoop of eight or ten steps marched up to the front door. But Mrs. Tilford's front entrance was three steps down, under the stoop.

It was dark inside and it took awhile before Burt's eyes focused to see the black mahogany stairs rising to the left and the long shadowy hall extending to the back of the house. It smelled of long years. Not until he stepped into the kitchen was there light enough to distinguish familiar things. It was a very large room. A great cooking range sat on one side and a sink and tub, made of gray slate, were supported on spindly stilts in the corner. In the middle stood a long table, complete with benches, like a picnic set. The top was bleached white from many soap and water scrubbings. A high-back chair stood at each end.

Mrs. Tilford would pay Burt twenty-five cents to scrub this kitchen floor–big wages for a fourteen-year-old boy in 1929.

Every Saturday morning Burt looked forward to roller skating all the way from St. Johns' Place to his job, not only for the big money, but because Mrs.

Naked In A Coat of Armor

Tilford's kitchen was always full of exciting hoopla. It was cozy and full of laughter. It seemed the table was occupied all day by bawdy, boisterous boarders.

After he was finished with his cleaning, Burt slipped in and joined the men at the table without them noticing. He laughed at their off-color stories, though often he didn't know what was funny. There would be good-natured banter back and forth, and sometimes they teased Mrs. Tilford, too, and made her laugh, though they were always careful not to be too rude with her. Her men had to behave or they would feel a lightning flip of a wet dishcloth.

The Fels Naptha odor from the clean floor was overcome by mouthwatering smells of Danish pastries piled high and crispy poppy-seed rolls, hot so that the butter would seep down into the pores. On the stove, the coffee would be bouncing up into the glass percolator top, demanding attention. Poured steaming hot into great mugs, it was thickened with fresh cream and lots of sugar.

There was an old rocker alongside of the stove, an antique. The upholstery was long gone, and replaced with a plaid blanket. Mrs. Tilford was a Scottish lady, and someone said the pattern of the plaid had something to do with her clan. She would take a break in the afternoon and, after washing up and combing her hair, she'd take a little something from a bottle.

"Tis a smoil," she said, with a wink, when she caught Burt watching her. But the boarders called it a nip. She kept the bottle hidden in a china jug shaped like an old man's face wearing a tricornered hat. It sat on a high shelf in the china closet. Mrs. Tilford was a large woman, and when she eased herself down into the rocker for her nap, completely resigned to limbo, there was no doubt that this was her favorite chair on a winter's afternoon.

Chapter 7

It was 1932 when Burt graduated from eighth grade out of Brooklyn Practice School. No one was sure how he managed it.

Dorothea and Walt decided to move to Bay Shore out on Long Island, where they purchased a small bungalow. Actually, it was a wooden army barracks left over from World War One and was hauled from Camp Upton, Long Island to Bay Shore.

It was a year later, on one of those clear December nights, cold enough to shatter one's breath and hear it tinkle to the ground. Even the old Franklin car protested and wouldn't turn over, and now it was time to meet Walt at the station. He was still a chef at the Fifth Avenue Hotel in Manhattan, and Burt looked forward to having him home on the weekends. Besides, it gave him an excuse to drive the car. Since the ornery antique wouldn't start, Burt decided to walk the three miles to the railroad station and greet Walt anyway.

"Couldn't start the dumb car," he said, as Walt got off the train.

"That's all right. Let's walk. It's a beautiful night." Walt loved to walk. He hiked his kids all over the Palisades. They shared a little chitchat, happenings of the week. Burt liked it when Walt let him in on his gripes about work or when he bitched about something he just read in his paper. It made him feel sort of equal, as though Walt enjoyed knowing he could confide in his son.

After awhile he slowed a bit. Burt listened to the crunch of the snow underfoot and noticed the change in cadence as they marched in step. Finally they had to stop so that Walt could catch his breath. There was a little embarrassed smile on his white face. Germans were brought up to believe they were made of iron and steel, that they never rusted or broke, or tired, or aged or died.

They reached Brentwood Road, where they had to rest again. Walt clutched the cemetery fence and, struggling for breath, gasped that he too would soon be in there. They managed to get home, and Dorothea was frightened to see how ill her husband was.

Burt ran off to get Uncle George to take him to fetch a doctor, and prayed that his old model 'T' Ford would go. On the way back, Uncle George dropped Burt off on the corner of Brook and Boston so that he could direct the doctor through the woods to the house.

When they arrived, Walt was gone. "Heart failure," declared the doctor routinely, "Myocarditis." Dorothea told Burt that Walt had called for him. If that was true, Burt wondered, what would he have said to his firstborn? "So long, Dad," Burt whispered.

"You're the man of the house now," someone said to Burt after the funeral. "You're the bread winner now." Burt felt important to have inherited so much responsibility, until he realized that, if he didn't win the bread, they wouldn't eat.

A surveyor offered him a job to be his helper. Burt thought that sounded quite prestigious, but in the early thirties people couldn't afford to have anything surveyed. He managed to land a job as a butcher's

Naked In A Coat of Armor

helper in the first supermarket in Suffolk County, New York. A self-service store, it was called then.

Gus, the manager of the meat department, was all brag, boast, and bologna but had a big heart. He took a shine to Burt and was a father figure. Burt considered himself lucky to serve an apprenticeship under him, considering him the best in the business. Gus taught Burt how to weigh his thumb, how to swear and drink—and he fixed Burt up with his first date. He was a test driver for Packard in his younger days and was able to also show Burt the finer points of auto repair and maintenance.

Gus let Burt chauffeur him back and forth to work in his old 1927 Dodge until Burt nearly hit a coal truck head on at an intersection.

"You gotta get a license, kid," Gus said when he found out Burt had no permit.

Burt liked nothing better than to drive the old man's car, especially when he wasn't riding along. Three times Burt applied for his license, and three times he failed the road test.

"Something's wrong, godammit. I know you're stupid but not that stupid," boomed Gus. Sergeant Gomalsky of the local police was a customer of theirs, and Gus asked him what could be the problem. The next time Burt was to apply for a road test he was instructed to leave an envelope with a few dollars in it on the carseat. After the test, the inspector picked it up with the rest of his papers and, sure enough, Burt got his license. It was magic. Gus repaid Sergeant Gomalsky with a big fat chicken for his help, but Burt was out five dollars.

The old man lent Burt his car to go into Brooklyn to see a girl he knew. It was raining when he got to town. Of course, a country bumpkin isn't familiar with road conditions in cities, especially in the rain and especially with his girl sitting next to him. At a busy intersection, Burt slid on the wet trolley car tracks and rammed a milk truck. His girl jumped out of the car and took off. Burt never saw her again. The car chassis was badly bent, but he was able to creep all the way back to Bay Shore, crabbing into the wind.

"Did ya have a good time, kid?" his boss asked.

"Well...I'll tell you...

It was a long hike from the butcher shop on Railroad Avenue, along Montauk Highway to La Salle Military Academy. It was so cold Burt's body felt as though naked in a coat of armor. His nostrils stuck together with each breath, and it seemed his ears were gone. It was nearing the end of what would be a twelve-hour day, and he carried a heavy package for the Academy. He had trudged through town and out the west end when a car stopped, a man flung its door open and hollered over the howling wind, "Where ya goin', kid?"

"La Salle."

"Hop in." "Man, it's colder than a witch's tit out there tonight," the driver said as he skidded back onto the road.

"Yeah," Burt agreed, wondering just how cold that would be.

The driver dropped Burt off at the tree-lined approach to the main building.

"Thanks, mister," Burt shouted as he got out.

Naked In A Coat of Armor

The trees threw spooky shadows across the road, and fear added a chill to compete with the cold. After what seemed forever, Burt stepped into the huge, brightly-lit kitchen. It always dazzled him to enter this spotless inner sanctum of stainless steel and copper. This evening was different. The staff had gone home an hour ago. It was warm and very quiet. The chef, (a Frenchman, of course) was seated at a desk in the corner, memorizing his newspaper. He glanced at Burt over the top of his specs, his round face crinkling into a smile. He said, "Aha! And what does Jacque Frost have for us this evening?"

He rose and moved to the table. He was a giant of a man and his white hat, the badge of his profession, made him seem even taller. He gently took the contents out of the package, item by item, and inspected each one very carefully.

There really was no need for him to worry, Burt knew. His store sold only the very choicest cuts to the Academy. La Salle was one of their best customers. It was a consumer's market in those days of the Great Depression, and the merchant was obliged to cater to his clientele.

Burt took his gloves off and lay his hands on the steam table and felt its warmth drift into all the corners of his body. The great man checked off each item and then skewered the bill onto a pointed rod supported by a little cast-iron stand that sat in a special spot on his desk.

As Burt turned to leave, he stopped him.

"One mo-ment, young mun." He opened the door of an enormous oven and Burt remembered a story about a giant who rolled a boulder to one side to reveal a gaping cave. He withdrew a huge roast loin of pork, hot and sizzling in the process of turning golden brown. The sight and sound and fragrance of this masterpiece all combined to make Burt's tastebuds dance. He was all agog as he watched the chef carve a whole rib off the shoulder end, the end that is marbled with cholesterol and tastes the sweetest of all. He laid it on a thick slice of fresh baked bread and handed it to Burt.

"Ziz is for your commission," he announced. Burt ate as though he had been on a long fast and, when he was finished, he licked each finger so as to not waste the slightest smear of gravy. He thanked the chef very much and stepped out into the cold again.

It began to snow as he made his way out to the highway. He had hiked a mile or so when a car skidded to a stop.

"Where are you going, son?" The driver shouted.

"Railroad Avenue, Sir."

"Here, rub this piece of onion on the windshield." Theory had it that this would keep the snow from sticking to the glass. It didn't work that well, though. "Hop in, son; this is turning into a real storm."

"Yeah." Burt wondered what a real storm would be like.

The man hung onto the big wooden steering wheel with one hand and, with his free hand, he operated the windshield wiper, trying to keep a peephole clear of snow. A traffic light hung over Railroad Avenue, a blur of red swirling in the white blizzard. Burt got out and thanked the driver. As he watched the taillight disappear, he hoped that he would get safely to where he was going.

Naked In A Coat of Armor

The men were finishing cleanup for the weekend. Burt's boss handed him a flask of stuff and told him to take a swig. "It'll warn you up, kid," he said. Gus figured that a shot of booze was medicinal for any and all maladies.

Burt took a mouthful and it was a while before his gullet could decide if it was wise to swallow or not. After he got it down, he squeezed his eyes shut and shook his head like the machos do. But unlike the pros, he coughed and spit and spluttered, thinking he was about to choke. It warmed him up some, but nothing like the kitchen at La Salle.

Chapter 8

After nearing the end of his apprenticeship, Burt went to work for Big Joe, the Butcher at H.C. Bohacks self-service store on Main Street.

Joe was six feet four, three feet wide and weighed three hundred pounds. He stood ramrod straight, impeccable in his grooming, a slave driver. Rumor had it that he had been a Prussian officer, and his staff believed it. If they smiled or laughed too easily, he suspected them of not working hard enough. Whistling while they worked drove Big Joe the butcher berserk. Marching up to Burt one day, he drew himself up to full height and glared down at him.

"Junger," he roared, "If you must whistle when you are working for me, then you had better wistle that fast Yankee Doodle; never mind that slow Blue Dunoob."

Big Joe was the manager of the meat department of one of the first self-service markets on Long Island. He fancied himself as quite the ladies' man. When a pretty woman came to the counter to be waited on, he would elbow his way past the other clerks and glide up to the counter. "Good afternoon, young lady," he would greet her, in a milk-and-honey tone. "And you are looking very lovely this afternoon. What I could do for you, today?"

"Oh thank you, Joe," she would answer, reveling in his flattery, but knowing it was just that. "Do you have a nice steak for me?"

"Yaw yaw. One nice steak for one nice lady coming rrright up." Joe would dance into the refrigerator and immediately reappear with a large slab

Naked In A Coat of Armor

of meat. Holding it high, he would twist and turn it quickly so the customer couldn't examine it too closely. "Here is the finest steak in all the land, cut special for you," he would tell her. It had been hanging around for a week already.

"Is it fresh?" she would ask. The edges were so dark.

"Ach, is that steak fresh? If it was any fresher it would talk back to you."

"Joe, is it tender?"

"Tender. My dear lady, that steak is as tender as a voman's heart. You could eat it mit a spoon...der gravy."

"Is it lean?"

"Lean as a loaf of bread."

"But look at all the bone."

"Yaw, mine dear lady, but how could the animal walk without the bunes?"

While Burt was still an apprentice, he took it upon himself to wait on a customer who ordered six pork chops. Since the chops were cut and on display in the showcase, he had no problem. The next day the woman returned with two of the chops and claimed that they were bad. She demanded her money back.

"But lady," Burt said, "They were fresh out of the showcase."

"I don't care. I want my money back."

"But where are the rest of the chops? Burt asked.

"We fed them to the dog and now he's sick. I want my money back."

"I can't give your money back," Burt said. "I'll give you six more chops."

The woman left, pleased with herself for outsmarting the dumb kid. This sort of shenanigan was common practice during the hard times of the mid-thirties.

This episode jarred Big Joe. Seeing six porkchops worth of dollars and cents walk out of the door was hard to take. "Jungerrr, what are you doing to me, giving the stuff avay? How could I pay you ten dollars a veek if you give every thing avay?" He clenched a fat fist with the thumb protruding straight up. "See dot dumb, Junger? Dot ist der golden dumb. Every time you put something on the scale you put der dumb mit...Ja?

"That's stealing," Bert said.

"Stealing nothing. Somebody has to pay for all the fat and bone you throw away. That's called shrinkish."

"Anyway," Burt insisted. "The chops were bad, the lady said. What could I tell her?"

"Tell her her oven was too hot, or tell her her frying pan was not hot enough. Tell her anything, but please don't give the stuff away."

The days before Thanksgiving were chaotic in Joe's meat department. Customers lined up, two and three deep. Butchers ran to and fro, displaying plump holiday birds for sale. Everybody spoke at once and elbowed each other for the best buy. One of Joe's special customers was a little old lady who bought great quantities of meat. Only Joe could wait on this lady, but he was very busy at this time and Mrs. Abergast was in a big hurry.

"Frau Abergast, this young fellow will wait for you," Joe said, pointing to Burt. "He will take good care of you, I guarantee."

Naked In A Coat of Armor

Mrs. Abergast looked at Joe and said, what does a young vipperschnapper like him know about turkeys? At the same time, Burt thought, can you imagine letting me wait on *the* Mrs. Abergast?

Burt selected what he thought to be a fine, tender bird and held it for her to inspect. She made the purchase after he convinced her that it was a very good choice. His pride in this accomplishment didn't last long, though. The day after Thanksgiving, the lady came stomping into the store, right past Big Joe, straight to Burt.

"Junger," she said, glaring at him. "Dot was the worst turkey I ever haff in my whole life. My guests come to my house for dinner never again."

"But," he said, trying to be very professional. "It looked like a very nice turkey. Maybe your oven was too hot."

It was the hard way to learn that you must never question an old house frau's cooking and, certainly, not make mention of oven temperatures. The blood drained from the woman's face and back again to make her livid. "What did you say, you young schmart Alec? For twenty-five years I cook for mine husbund and now, now you, young schnot nose, you tell me my oven vas too hot? From you I would not buy a quarter of a pound of bologna, never mind the turkey." Mrs. Abergast left the store, never to be seen again. Joe looked as though he was about to cry.

When business was slow, Joe was miserable. It would get very quiet in the store and he was pensive in his misery. He'd take long, deliberate drags on his cigarette, when suddenly he'd bellow, "Look, an acre of lights are burning and the electric meter goes *zzzzz*, and not one customer stands by the counter." Snatching his apron off, he would announce, "Ach, I go to lunch."

When Joe returned, two hours later, it was obvious his lunch was liquid.

One of the wiseguys called from the vegetable department, "Hey Joe, you must have had fish for lunch."

"No, why?"

"I figure it took all this time to pick the bones out."

"Visenhiemer, do," the butcher answered, with a silly grin. "No, but I drink six from dem plomber's helpers."

"What's a plomber's helper?" another guy questioned.

"Ach, you know, ein schnapps and ein beer chazer."

"Oh, you mean a boiler maker."

"Yaw, boilermaker, plombers helper, what's the difference? At Martinelli's there was a big crowd. Everybody say, 'Joe, come, drink up, and they don't let me pay for nuthing. And when I tell them one from my stories, they laugh so hard. And even der girls, when they laugh they fall from the bar away."

Business continued to go downhill. Soon all the butchers were let go. Only Joe and Burt remained. He spent more and more time at the Tavern. He became surly with the few customers left, and ill tempered with the fellows.

"Is it tender, butcher?"

"How the hell would I know?" he snapped back. "I don't grow that animal."

Nothing Burt did would please him.

Naked In A Coat of Armor

Once when Big Joe and Burt were working in the refrigerator, something went wrong. The big man snatched up a knife and rushed at Burt, intent on skewering him to the wall. Burt was unable to dodge left or right, wedged between two hindquarters of beef. All he could do was shout, "Joe!"

The man went limp; the knife slipped to the floor. Fright showed on both their faces.

"Junger," he muttered, barely above a whisper, "I thank the Gott in heaven that I do not loose my head this day."

It was sad to see the troubled man leave the store that day for the last time, the great shoulders drooped, his fedora pulled over his face. Big Joe the Butcher was fired and never heard from again.

Chapter 9

It was 1937 when the American Federation of Labor came to town to organize the food handlers. By 1939 they won a seven-day vacation for the employees. Bert was suspicious. The business manager was a Hungarian communist who later ran off with the Local's funds. Imagine a company giving its workers seven days off and paying them for it! Seven whole days all their own to do with as they please.

Up until then, workers were lucky to yet Thanksgiving and Christmas off. But it was true, and Burt was determined to take a trip to some place–any place. People couldn't afford to travel much in those days. A trip to Hoboken would have been an excursion for him.

Billy the vagabond, an acquaintance of Bert's, had hitchhiked all over the country, sleeping in haystacks and jailhouses. They would be in a gin mill on a Saturday night and, come Sunday morning, Billy Boy would be missing. A few weeks later a telegram from Arizona or Montana would notify his folks that their Billy was broke. He needed funds to get back home or be locked up as a vagrant. The later part of the message was his way of getting his worried parents to rush the money order.

Burt thought, He's the guy to go on a trip with. He would know the lay of the land and all the ropes.

Louie Lindborg, Burt's stepfather, had bought a car that year. Burt twisted his arm to let him take the new Chevy on a trip. He lost no time and approached Hilly.

Naked In A Coat of Armor

"How would you like to take a trip in a car for a change, like civilized people do?" he said.

"Boy, would I! When we leavin'? Come over to the store Sunday morning and we'll make plans," he said, not waiting for an answer.

On the designated day, Bert stepped into Mr. Podlinsky's grocery store, and there was his son poring over a roadmap spread across the counter. Completely ignoring the customers and by way of greeting he said, "Ya know where we're going, Burt?"

"No, tell me."

"Mexico."

"Oh, sure." To Burt, Mexico was a foreign land too far away. Billy knew different and it was about the only spot in North America he hadn't seen.

Burt drove up to Mr. Podlinski's store on Sunday afternoon and they loaded the car down with everything edible that came in cans, then left in a cloud of dust. Billy wore a hat, a souvenir his father brought hack from Poland. It was a straw hat, military style with a peak. He wore it throughout the entire trip and even slept in it.

They went over the Brooklyn Bridge, through the Holland Tunnel, down through the garden state. It took a long time to get across Washington, Virginia, Luray Caverns and Natural Bridge. They had no time for sightseeing. They zipped through North and South Carolina, Georgia, Louisiana and Texas.

There were gigantic schooners of beer in Houston for just five cents. Burt finished his first. "Let's go, Podlinski." He was impatient to be back on the road.

"Wait, wait. A whopping beer like this? At five cents? Man, we gotta have us another."

They spent the night on the beach in Galveston. The next morning Burt asked, "What's for breakfast?"

"Sardine sandwiches," said Billy.

"For breakfast?"

"Did you ever have sardine sandwiches for breakfast, on the beach, with the Texas sun burning down on you?" asked the vagabond. "Well you're in for a treat."

Burt watched the olive oil bubbling in the can.

Finally they found themselves in Loradom on the border. "I'll be damned!" Burt yelled, "If that ain't Mexico across the bridge! We made it!"

The Mexican customs stopped us for routine questioning. When the official asked Burt where he was born, he said, "London, England."

"Aha, and you have papers, senor, si?"

"What papers?"

"For the citizen, no?"

"No."

"Then the senor must go back, if he can get back, si?"

Burt turned around and drove back, with Billy screaming and ranting. "You god damn foreigner, why didn't you tell him you were born on Long Island?"

"Yeah, and end up as an international criminal with my ass in a Mexican jail."

"How long have you boys been in Mexico?" the American customs officer asked.

"Just long enough to make a goddamn U-turn," grumbled Billy.

"How much money did you spend?"

Naked In A Coat of Armor

"How much can you spend on a "U" turn?" Billy was still fuming. "Can I walk across the border?" he said.

"Why not?" the officer said.

They ducked into a bar for a bowl of chili. The stuff cleared their sinuses, burned holes in their stomachs, and left them gasping for beer.

After he cooled off, Billy announced, "Look I came all this way to get a look at Mexico. I'm going to walk across that bridge. See you later." Burt cruised around for awhile and took a look at the southern town. He found a genuine alligator-skin belt in a souvenir shop. It had an unusual buckle and was beautifully tooled in Mexican motif. He paid three dollars for it and felt guilty for the extravagance. When he got to the town park, he lay down in the shade of a big live oak and took a nap.

When he woke he rode down to the bridge to see if Billy Boy was anywhere in sight. There was no sign of him. Every ten or fifteen minutes he'd swing by the bridge to see if he'd shown up. It was getting late and he began to worry. Finally he came into sight. His five-foot frame came strutting, weaving and tumbling across the bridge with a shit-eatin' grin on his face. Beside the enormous sombrero he was wearing, he had two gallons of tequila slung crisscross from his shoulders on colored ropes. He looked like a giant animated mushroom. The customs officers went into hysterics.

"You know you're allowed three gallons of that stuff?"

"Oh, great," said the mushroom, and made a move to go back.

"No you don't," Burt said, grabbing him by the collar and pouring him into the car. Billy was so determined to go back across the border that they decided to try again in Brownsville, a little further south. But then there was the question of money—or the lack of money. They put their heads together to try and come up with a solution, but solutions don't come up without cold cash. "I have an uncle who lives in Liberty," Billy said. "Maybe we could borrow some money from him and cross the Canadian border. Besides, we could get some good chow up on the farm."

"Where's that?" Burt wanted to know.

"Up in Indiana. From there we could cross over into Canada at Windsor, then come down through Toronto and Niagara Falls. What do you say?"

"You're out of your numb noggin. That goddamn tequila has gotten to you. That's what I say."

"All right, smartass, you come up with something better."

Bert couldn't come up with something better, so they turned due north. About thirty-six hours and fifteen hundred miles later, they surprised everyone at Uncle Jacob's farm. Aunt Bebe was all for celebrating and cooked up a storm. Great platters of chicken and pork were brought to the table. Dishes of corn and cabbage. Home-canned peaches with gallons of thick cream for dessert. They ate like pigs at the trough, and they decided to stick around for another day. The dinner conversation was loud and hilarious, as the family became reacquainted and east and west brought up to the latest news. Uncle Jacob had four children, Jake the oldest, Jody, Jill and Judy the youngest.

Naked In A Coat of Armor

"What's the Empire State Building like?" asked Judy. "Have you been up to the top?"

"Nope."

"Are all the buildings in New York City skyscrapers?"

"What's it like to ride in the subway?" Jody wanted to know.

"Something like speeding through a dark wind tunnel," Billy the world-traveler explained.

Jake was twenty-two, the same age as Billy, and a lot of fun. They were a hard working family, devout Catholics. The next day, Sunday, everyone dressed up in their Sunday-go-to-meetin' clothes to attend mass. In the afternoon, the boys were wondering what to do for excitement and decided to take a ride. "Let's get some beer," Billy said, always thirsty.

"We'll have to drive up into Michigan for that," Jake said.

"How come?"

"We have a strict blue law in Indiana."

"What does that mean?"

"All the liquor places are locked up tight on Sunday."

"That's a stupid law. Well, let's go across the border."

Returning with their refreshments, they pulled off the road and relaxed under a shade tree and sipped cool beer. Jake whispered something to Billy, who turned to Burt and asked, "Wanna get laid?"

That caught Burt off guard. He didn't know much about things like that. He hadn't given it much thought, especially on Sunday where they have a blue law. Besides, hadn't they been to church that morning? But, then, he didn't want the guys to know he was still a virgin. So he said, "Why not?"

"Why not."

After they finished their drinks, they up and took off. Jake, the wise one, navigated the group into town and pulled up to a house that had a red light on the porch. They piled out and followed Jake into the front room. It was smoke filled and dimly lit, furnished with overstuffed furniture and a bar. Ladies lounged in revealing dresses, some with gentlemen. The madam, a rather buxom wench flaunting a bit too much cleavage and bouncing her bubbles like baubles in a bay, approached them from across the room.

"Welcome," she said, in a motherly tone. Have a seat and make yourselves at home."

One of the girls slid in alongside of Burt. This made him very nervous. "What's yer name, sonny?"

Burt didn't think he liked that "sonny" bit, either, but he gave his name.

"That's a cute name. Where are you from?"

"New York."

"My, but that's a long way away. Have you been up in the Empire State Building?

"No." Burt wasn't sure he liked this gal. She put her hand on his knee. "Come along, let's have some fun."

The woman took him by the hand and led him to her room like a kid on his first day to kindergarten. The room was tiny and furnished with a bed and dresser. She let her dress slip to the floor and lay back on the bed. All that sudden nakedness scared the hell

Naked In A Coat of Armor

out of Burt, and for a moment he figured on making a run for it.

After a roll or two, the pro said, "Do me a favor, Honey. Take your belt off, the buckle is hurting me." Take my new, genuine alligator belt off? Absolutely not, he thought.

"I won't take it off for anybody, but I'11 unbuckle it," Burt said. He held the buckle in one hand and supported himself at arm's length with the other, while wishing he had a third to cover his wallet. He just didn't want to get too close to this hooker.

The boys met outside. "Well, how'd it go, Burt?" Jake asked.

"Okay, I guess," Burt answered sheepishly. He really wasn't sure, though he did feel sort of sort of grown up now. After all, hadn't he been the family breadwinner for some years? Hadn't he learned a trade? Didn't he have a job when no jobs were to be had? Hadn't he just driven hundreds of miles across country, seen and done things a lot of young people his age might never get in on? And now...well...he'd lost his cherry. Wasn't that what boys were supposed to do: sow oats? He felt that now he had become a man. Still, there was a guilty feeling. He wasn't sure it was worth two bucks. A stiff penis has no conscience. Getting laid by a whore had nothing to do with manliness.

"Well it beats playing with it." Jeff chuckled.

"Yeah," Jody chimed in. "Wasn't it Omar Khayyam who said, 'It is better to plant thy seed in the belly of a whore than to cast it upon the sands of the desert'"?

"Will you listen to the child philosopher," Jake kidded.

"Philosopher hell," said Billy the traveler. "If you ask me, he sounds more like a pimp."

The next day, Billy had to negotiate a loan from his cousin Judy. The sweetheart lent him twenty dollars, which was quite a large sum out of her budget. Burt doubted that Billy would ever reimburse her. Her sister, Jill, gave the visitors a big bag of apples when they said goodbye. Little did the travelers know how much they would appreciate that fruit later. Burt couldn't help feeling that Aunt Bebe was glad to see them go. It seemed she never saw boys who ate so much.

They reached Windsor, Canada at night. The customs officer proceeded to question them with caution. Being confronted with a mish-mash of ethnic names, he became suspicious/s. Billy Podlinski was driving the car registered in Lindborg's name, the stepfather of Eichwald the passenger. Struggling to pronounce the driver's name, he demanded, "Where were you born?" New York," Billy said. Then the officer surprised him and asked, "How long were you in Poland?"

"I've never been to Poland. My father brought this hat from Poland," Billy retorted.

"I didn't ask you about the hat. I want to know where in Poland were you?"

"I've never been out of the country."

Burt was getting nervous and wished he was home.

"And you, young man, where were you born?"

"Who me?"

Naked In A Coat of Armor

"Yes you."
"Uhm, I was born in New York, too," Burt lied.
"Will you please recite the alphabet for me?"
Burt did.
"How much money have you gentlemen got, and how long do you intend to stay in Canada?" "We have twenty dollars, Sir, and we are just driving through to Niagara Falls."
"Very good, boys. Stop at the office, and they will issue a driving permit. Welcome to Canada."
"Jesus, I was never so scared in all my life," Burt said.

Billy wanted to know what that alphabet thing was all about. Burt told him that the Europeans pronounce their "z" as "zed," and explained it was how the border patrol nabbed a foreigner sometimes.

The next day they were merrily cruising through Toronto, enjoying the sights, when they crashed into the back of a truck. The radiator of their car was pushed back onto the fan and it would cost nineteen dollars for temporary repairs.

"That's what you get for tailgating while watching the girls," moaned Billy. They spent the last dollar between them to send a telegram to his mother for money. But there was no answer all day or all the next day. They were growing desperate with nothing to eat but apples. They went down to the river to shave and tried to make themselves look presentable, hoping they wouldn't be picked up for vagrants. Billy, who had been in tight spots before in his travels, ducked into the Young Women's Christian Association and told his woeful story very woefully to a very nice lady. Could she lend him some money to send a telegram to his parents?

No, she couldn't lend him some money, but she would take him to the telegraph office and send the message for him.

Burt did not know why the kind lady thought that was necessary. He knew how cherubic Billy could look when he was begging.

They decided that she should send the message to Burt's mother this time, hoping they would have better luck. In the meantime, the nice lady took them back to the YWCA and fed them.

There was no news from home all the next day. Not until the afternoon of the third day did a money order arrive.

After paying the nice lady for her kindness and receiving her wishes for their good luck, they were off. They didn't even take a good look at Niagara Falls. All they wanted was to get home. Customs was disappointed to find no contraband on them. They zipped through, onto U.S. soil, and headed straight for Long Island.

When they got home, Burt asked Dorothea why it took her so long to answer their telegram. "I'm not used to having my children requesting money like that," she said. "I don't know anything about telegraphing funds. Besides, I don't have that kind of money. I had to go to Mrs. Podlinski and asked her what to do. 'Mrs. Lindborg,' she said, 'don't give those boys no money. Those boys just keep goink. I know my Beelee. Don't give them nothing. They will come home when they don't have no more money.'

Even though Mrs. Podlinski said not to, Dorothea, not used to such behavior, was worried and finally gave in.

Books

"Great supper, Mom," said Burt into his napkin as he pushed away from the table. "Well, gotta get going."

"Where are you going?" Dorothea said.

"Out."

"Son, you've been out every night this week. It's not good. You're going to ruin your health. Where are you off to again that's so important?"

"Aw, come on, Mom. I'm just going to meet Bottle and then we're going over to pick up Hambone and maybe go to a gin mill, Charley Nick's or Tony Cat's, depending on what's doing."

"How you talk! Gin mill. What's happened to my gentleman son?" she wailed. "Why don't you stay home once in awhile and read a good book?"

"Aw, Mom. Men don't read books. Come on."

"Son, you're wrong. All the answers to all your questions can be found in the written word. Don't ever forget that. And what do you mean, 'depending on what's doing'?"

"Well, you know, you like to see a good crowd in a place. You like to meet different guys and dolls." Burt smiled, and a smile crept across Dorothea's face.

"You're a bad boy," she called after him, though she really didn't mean it. No, he was a good boy, the breadwinner of the family since Walt was gone. She heard him rev up the Model-A, his pride and joy. The 'Blue Bird', he called it. The girls loved it, too, especially if there was a good-looking guy in the rumble seat.

Hambone, Bottle, and Burt barged in at Tony's carrying a bundle of firewood. Tony used to kid them and say they came to his bar only to come in out of the cold.

"What's with the wood?"

"We just come in to get warm. We know you're too cheap to keep the heat up." Hambone laughed.

It was a good crowd at the Viking, and of course it was late when Burt got home. He took his shoes off and tiptoed up the stairs. That damn creaky step, the second one from the top, always gave him away and, just when he thought he was home free.

Dorothea stood at the end of the hall waiting for him. "Where in the world have you been? I've been worried sick. Do you know what time it is?"

"Now, Mom, don't go into your song. Just go back to sleep. And please, Mom, don't worry so." Burt thought his mother always looked a little older when she worried about him.

"What do decent people do at this ungodly hour?"

They talk and laugh and sing and dance." Burt laughed.

"You've been drinking."

"I know." He gave her a peck on the cheek. "Go back to bed, Mom, and sleep tight."

"Don't know what I'm going to do with you, son."

Some four years later, a military draft was initiated and, soon after, President Roosevelt sent greetings to Burt, and he ended up in the Coast Artillery. Japan knocked Pearl Harbor on December seventh and badly shook the country. About a year later, some of the outfit found themselves on what was called the 'Z' roster, more commonly known as a shit list, and were scheduled to ship out to the South Pacific. Burt's buddy, Jan Manz, was on the list, and he hit Burt up for a ten-buck loan.

"Who do you think I am, J.P. Morgan?"

"Look," said Jan, "they're giving us a pass, probably the last one in the States. I'd like to go into town with the guys and hang one on, maybe get laid too."

"Yeah, but ten bucks?"

"Look, I'll leave my books for collateral."

"Books? Collateral? What the hell are you talking about?"

"You lend me the sawbuck and I'll leave my books with you till I can pay you back."

"There ain't any books worth that much."

"Listen, yardbird, those books are worth twice that much."

Burt was quiet for a long while. He liked Jan. They'd been together ever since Uncle Sam put the finger on them. Maybe they would never see each other again. This was the least he could do for his pal. And another thing: maybe men do read books...and him a sergeant. He was one of the more interesting guys at a bull session. He had a lot of knowledge and was well liked.

Jan was gone several weeks before Burt got around to thumbing through the books. He really wasn't very serious about it at first, but when he came across something, it took him a while to catch on before he realized the author was telling him things he liked to hear. He thought he was some smart apple. He was so fascinated with Lin Yutang's pagan philosophy that he went around quoting the book to his buddies, and pretty soon they nicknamed him the Mad Monk.

The fellows never heard from each other again. From then on, when Burt read a good book he sometimes wondered what Jan Manz was doing.

Chapter 10

Burt's interest in airplanes started around 1930 when he stopped being interested in trains. He would ride his bike from St. John's Place all the way to Floyd Bennett Field, N.Y. located on a peninsula jutting into Jamaica Bay. He'd hang around just to watch the planes take off and land. When landing, the pilot would cut the engine and glide to earth like a whisper. The only sound would be the wind strumming on the guy wires between the wings of the bi-planes. He liked to listen to the lingo while flyers discussed all sorts of aeronautical problems, how they pulled up into a stall or pulled out of a spin just in time.

The pilots were his heroes, especially the ones who wore jodhpurs and high brown boots, laced all the way up to the knees. It reminded him of a picture of Lindberg he'd seen. They chewed tobacco and could spit between their two front teeth. Once Burt was watching a man chomping on a cigar butt while he worked on an engine. When you do that you have to spit, especially if the butt isn't lit, and it wasn't. The guy's hands were black with oil and he needed both to do whatever he was doing. Then came time for him to spit. Well, he jockeyed the cigar, no hands, to one corner of his mouth, then simply tilted his head to the other side and let it spew out of the opposite corner, sort of like draining the dregs from a coffee mug. He glanced at Burt out of the corner of his eye and gave him a dirty-faced wink. Wow! Burt thought. That was neat. Only an aviator could do that, the kind that wore jodhpurs.

Eugene A. Aichroth

"Take me for a ride, Mister?"

"It'll cost you money, Kid."

"How much?"

"Go on home, you ain't got that kind of money." But he persisted in dreaming: If only one of these great men would give me a ride!

Burt delivered the Brooklyn Eagle and had to turn most of his money into the house, so there wasn't much left to save. But he got another route with the Brooklyn Daily Times. Now, with two papers to deliver, he was making big money. But Dorothea found out about this extra cash and he had to turn more in. Even so, he managed to accumulate a few dollars and, one day, he made his way to the airfield.

"Take me up, Mister?" he said to a pilot working on his plane. It looked like a Waco Biplane.

"Go away. I'm busy." He had sewn up a slit in the wing canvas and was now smearing airplane dope over it to pull it together and seal it. He cut a long narrow piece of canvas to cover the stitches. Smeared dope on one side of it, covered the sewing with it, and then spread more schmear over the whole patch.

"I got money," I persisted.

"Hey! Go on home and tell your mother she wants you."

"Please, Mister."

"Okay, okay. Let's see your money: five bucks for fifteen minutes," he said, wiping his hands on a piece of rag.

"Four's alls I got."

"Gimmy a few minutes to let this schmear dry, and we'll go."

Naked In A Coat of Armor

After what seemed an awful long wait, he said, "Feel that patch and see if it's dry."

"Taint sticky."

He gave me a pair of goggles and said, "What's yer name, Kid?"

"Ernst Eichwald, Sir. They call me Burt."

"Okay, Burt. Let's go." After boosting Burt up so he could climb down into the hole they call the cockpit, the pilot strapped him in tight and strolled to the front to pull the prop through. On the first pull, the engine only coughed up a cloud of smoke and blew it back over Burt. It smelled like castor oil because caster oil was used for some engines, including planes and racing cars. Burt worried that maybe they weren't going to yet started. But after a couple more pulls the engine exploded with a loud noise and the whole plane shook violently. He worried whether that was normal. But he knew everything was okay when the pilot pulled the chocks, spit a long stream through his two front teeth, checked Burt's safety belt again, and climbed into the back cockpit. They fishtailed out, taxiing over the bumpy grass. The wings flapped badly, and Burt wondered if that was normal, too. It didn't seem to bother the pilot any. The pilot turned into the wind and they sat there while he revved up the engine and checked the magnetos. This really made the wings flutter, like a bird trying to take off, somehow being held back. Burt was thinking they were never going to go, when suddenly the machine leaped forward and tore across the field, forcing Burt back up against the seat. He hung onto the leather bumper around the edge of the cockpit. Dorothea would kill him if she found out, he reflected, but he was too excited to care. Soon they were airborne; Burt could tell because it wasn't bumpy any more and they were already racing across the tops of the trees.

The pilot eased back on the stick and the plane climbed to altitude. When he leveled off, Burt ventured a peek over the side and was fascinated by the view. All things that moved down there looked like insects. A few clouds were all that moved overhead. He relaxed to the thrill. At last he was actually flying, wishing that it could go on forever when, suddenly, the plane seemed to drop out from under Burt, taking his stomach with it, but leaving the rest of him suspended in mid air. He couldn't remember ever letting go of his grip on the sides of the cockpit. Then, just as quickly, the seat came back up under him with a jolt, jarring his teeth. He found out that air-currents aloft will do funny things, things that make passengers quite nervous.

The pilot made a few lazy banks and turns, just like the hawk gliding gracefully high up and to the right of them. They circled back and entered the landing pattern, and the pilot positioned the plane into the up-wind leg and throttled back for a landing. The ground seemed to come up at them awfully fast, but they touched down gently and rattled across the rough grass and came to a stop at the edge of the field.

The pilot cut the engine, slid his goggles up onto his helmet and hollered, "You okay, Kid?"

"Yes sir."

The pilot climbed out, unstrapped Bert, and helped him onto the ground. He was a little wobbly, but every bit the hero the pilot was.

Naked In A Coat of Armor

"Wow!" was all Bert could say, and held out four crumpled dollars.

"What's this?" the pilot asked.

"Your money, Sir."

"Put it back in your pocket and get out of here." The man in the jodhpurs spit through his front teeth, wiped his mouth on his sleeve, and shook hands with Burt. "So long, Kid," he grinned.

Eugene A. Aichroth

The author during his military years in the Army Air Corps (Air Force)

Part 2

"Man survives where swine perish, and laughs where gods go mad."

Dostoyevsky

"Happiness is something that comes into our lives through doors we don't even remember leaving open."

Rose Lane

Eugene A. Aichroth

Chapter 11

1935-1945

Time moved on, though of course it's we that pass on; time is forever. It was 1937, and Bottle, Hambone and Burt were in Cosmo's Bar and Grill across the street from the firehouse. The town was a small place, dull, dead and depressed. They sipped their brews and began crying that nothing ever happened. They hated their jobs, yet were glad they had jobs to hate. "Ya know what?" announced Hambone. "Let's join the Navy."

"Yeah, not a bad idea," Burt agreed.

"You guys are nuts." Bottle was going with a girl, and it seemed like it was pretty serious. The evening wore on, and eventually they all decided to join up in the morning. It wasn't that they were patriotic. Actually, the beer was doing what beer will do, making them real brave and adventuresome. But come morning time, the three of them piled onto a train and ended up at Whitehall Street in Manhattan, eager to sign up. When they were told they had to enlist for seven years, Burt backed down. God, he thought, I'd be twenty-eight by then. Most people are dead at that age. Bottle didn't like the idea either, but Hambone went through with it and signed on the dotted line.

In 1940, the U.S. Department of Commerce, Civil Aeronautics Administration offered a civilian pilot training program free of charge. It was a way of encouraging men to enlist in the Army Air Corps. The top five in the class at the end of the course were eligible for flight training in the Army. Burt signed up and was sent to Hempstead, Long Island for a physical exam.

There, a nurse ushered him into the examining room and told him to strip. The doctor made the routine tap/feel/breathe-and-cough, then handed him a paper cup and pointed to a door, mumbling something barely audible.

Burt stepped into a lavatory and wondered what he was doing there, holding a paper cup. *Maybe he wants me to take a drink*, he thought, *but then why would I need a drink? Damn it, I didn't hear what he said.* Burt was a very shy kid in those days. Sweat began to bubble along his hairline. It took him a long time to muster the courage to open the door a crack and peek to see if the coast was clear. There he was in the middle of the room, covering his parts with one hand and holding the cup with the other. The doctor leaned back in his chair and just stared at him with a quizzical expression. He must have been wondering how Burt could be gone so long and have nothing for him. It was obvious he was going to wait for Burt to say something. "I'm sorry, Sir, but I didn't hear what you said." He shot forward in his chair and glared over the top of his glasses. "How the hell can you pilot a plane if you don't hear what people say to you? Piss in the cup, boy! Piss in the cup and leave it on the counter in there. Then, get dressed."

Cheese, Burt thought. *I didn't think doctors talked like that.*

He drove out to Westhampton Air Field three nights a week after work to learn about aerodynamics, weather, engine mechanics and Civil Aeronautics

Administration regulations. Arty Solofski, from Central Islip, was also enrolled, so they alternated the driving. It was a bitter cold winter and they got into the habit of stopping at a tavern on a lake in Moriches to yet warmed up. Floodlights lit up the lake, and the Fire Department would hose it so that there would be a smooth surface for ice-skating. One of them got the bright idea that it would be fun to drop their girlfriends off at the lake, since they both loved to skate. Then they would pick them up on their way back from classes. Perhaps it was because of this distraction that Burt was not one of the chosen few at the final exams. Art, however, made good and ended up as a major in a fighter group; flew fifty missions in Italy during WW-II.

Two years after his discharge, he was killed in an auto accident. Fate can be very spiteful. "Hattie and me are engaged," Bottle came and told Burt one day.

"Why you son of a gun," Burt said, slapping him on the back. "Congratulations. Hattie's a fine girl. She'll make you toe the mark. When's the wedding going to be?"

"August sometime, and we want you to be best man."

"Gee, that's great. I'd be honored."

Hattie was a Canadian girl, and the wedding took place in her hometown, Northbay, in 1940. It was around the time the Battle of Britain was raging. Her brother was a flight instructor in the Royal Canadian Air Force. When he heard that Burt was interested in learning to fly, he suggested he join up. Burt thought that was a great idea but was afraid to go through with it. He was in Canada illegally with no proof of citizenship. In addition, he thought his part-German background could lead to some embarrassing questions. It was wartime, a time filled with hate and prejudice. Again Burt's career in aviation was blocked.

But President Roosevelt sent greetings to Burt, and suddenly he was in the armory at Jamaica, New York taking the oath of allegiance with twenty other rookies. No sooner did they drop their right hands than a burly sergeant sounded off.

"OK men, you are now in da US Army. Look proud. I want you all to move down to da far end of da armory on da double."

When they reached the end of the building, the sergeant turned them around and bellowed. "I want you all to march back to da other end and on your way pick up all papers, cigarette buts and candy wrappers. Pick up everything dat don't grow. If it moves, salute it. If it's too heavy, paint it. Let's go! Heads down and assholes up." Burt wondered what he and the others had let themselves in for?

Soon they were six months into 1941 and had six to go before they all would be sent home again. They were the members of the first draft for one year of military training. A song was popular with the soldiers in those days, something about "I'll be home in a year, little darlin'."

Burt wound up in an artillery outfit stationed in the Georgia swamps, the only Yankee in a battalion of Alabama National Guards. He was pretty apprehensive about that. But they turned out to be a great outfit, displaying some of the southern hospitality he'd heard about. Burt lost no time inquiring about transferring to the Air Corps and soon learned that that required a three-year hitch in the regular army. *No way*, he thought. *In another six months I'll be home.*

In the meantime, the Japanese commenced to doing funny things in the South Pacific, Hitler's blitz was streaking across Europe, England was taking a beating, and the United States was beginning to realize that the skirmish over there was for real. When the boys in congress began to debate whether to keep the draftees in for another year, it became obvious to Burt that something big was going to let go soon. He dreaded ending up as a dogface in the infantry, slogging his way across the mud fields of Europe or wading through the jungle swamps of Bouganville and Guadalcanal. He looked forward to combat–that is, he was curious about the business of war, but he wanted to observe it through the eyes of the Air Corps.

The boys hated Camp Stewart, Georgia, and when the Air Corps moved a mobile office onto the property and set up a recruiting station right on the base, Burt was first on line. With one stroke of the pen and with no questions asked, he was discharged from the Coast Artillery and enlisted in the Air Corps for three years.

"He's lost his marbles," his buddies said. "What kind of a nut would sign away three years of his life to the military?" Four months later, Pearl Harbor went up in smoke and the United States declared war on Japan and Germany. It didn't occur to any of them that it would be three or four years before they would see home again.

Eugene A. Aichroth

Out of the Mud, Into the Blue

About a dozen happy Air Corps recruits were shipped out of Georgia and sent north to Jefferson Barracks, St. Louis, Missouri. There, Burt met a lovely girl, Lora. But they managed to see each other just two or three times before Burt received shipping orders to Albany. New York would have been great for Burt, a New Yorker. But no, they were sent right back to Georgia–Albany, Georgia. A brand new base, Turner Field, was an advanced flying school. They arrived on the tail end of a hurricane.

What a sorry sight greeted them: rain, wind, and red mud up to their ankles. Anything that wasn't lashed down was blown onto a pile. Burt wasn't so sure that he'd like this place, though they did have airplanes. He was assigned as a grease monkey on the flight line and soon learned how to taxi the advanced trainer. He was in his glory. One day he moved a plane out towards a runway, but then turned back.

Chuck, the line Sergeant, an old regular army man, waited for him to climb out of the cockpit and said, "Eichwald, you had me worried there for a minute. Do that again and I'll put your ass in a sling so quick you'll really think you're flying. Don't get any wild ideas, you hear?"

In order to qualify for pilot training in those days, two years of college was required and, of course, you had to be a perfect physical specimen. There was no doubt in Bert's mind as to the latter. The young men thought they could win the war all by themselves. But eighth grade was the extent of Burt's formal education. So that left him out.

Naked In A Coat of Armor

He signed up in a course for Link Trainer Instructors. Link Trainers were simulators for teaching pilots instrument flying. Up until then, that was the closest he got to flying, but the training proved valuable later on. They were an elite group and the work was rewarding. It was the beginning of a well-rounded education, complements of Uncle Sam.

Lora and Burt continued as pen pals and developed a pleasant friendship. Burt was also corresponding with his first love, Allison, the girl he left back home.

Ted Tomlinson and Burt were offered a beautiful deal. They were put on detached service as Link instructors at a Primary Flying School just outside of Albany. They took lodgings in Mrs. Tatum's rooming house, where they shared a tiny room filled with a double bed and a dresser with three legs. Although they were in uniform, they traveled back and forth to work like normal people.

A few days later, Burt was granted an emergency furlough; and he knew why. His mother had one of her convenient life-and-death seizures. This time, she even convinced the War Department that only her firstborn, standing alongside her deathbed and holding her hand, could keep her from slipping into eternity.

Burt had no objections to the unscheduled leave. After all, he wanted to see his girlfriend Allison, not his mother. Much as he loved Dorothea, she could be one big pain in the ass when the mood so inclined.

He returned late at night to Georgia and the rooming house. Trying not to wake Ted, he undressed in the dark. As he was about to climb into bed, there came a frantic tapping on the door. Their landlady, a very proper woman (although Burt knew Ted slept with her occasionally) informed Burt in a frenzied whisper that, in his absence, Ted had changed rooms and moved their belongings to larger quarters in the front of the house. Instead, a lovely girl was now curled up in what had been their bed. Fortunately, Mrs. Tatum was in the nick of time to steer Burt clear of an awkward situation–or perhaps it was unfortunate. The landlady ushered him to the new room, which was spacious, with twin beds and a desk and chairs.

As he crawled into his empty bed, weary from the rail trip from New York, he could not help fantasizing snuggling up to the lonesome girl in the other room, caressing her ever so gently so as not to frighten her when she awoke. Would she be resigned to dignified acquiescence? Or, better still, enthusiastic cooperation? The latter, of course, being much the preferred. Or, on the other hand, would she scream bloody murder, waking the whole bleeding household, bringing the male boarders, intent on kicking the door down and rescuing the damsel from obvious rape? God! What embarrassment! What fun! What a shame that Mrs. Tatum was so in the nick of time.

In the meantime, the demand for pilots fluctuated directly with the numbers lost in combat. Soon the standards for qualifying had to be lowered in order to fill the quota. A high-school diploma and a passing grade on written and oral tests were the first stipulations. Charlie, Jack, and Burt palled around together. They worked on the flight line and would go to lunch together. Sometimes the three went on pass. They grew to be pretty close friends. One day Charlie came up to the others all out of breath and said, "Hey,

Naked In A Coat of Armor

Guys! Let's take that cadet entrance exam and see what happens."

"Can't," Burt said, kicking his enthusiasm. "It comes too late."

"What are you talking about, too late?" Jack looked at Burt thinking he was being chicken. "I'm a year too old already and, besides, I don't have a high-school diploma."

"So what? Let's take it anyway, just for the fun of it," Charlie said. "What can we lose? We'll have an afternoon off."

"You yardbirds are nuts," Jack piped up. "As for me, I'm sticking to good old Terra Firma." He was easygoing, lazy, just marking time until the war was over.

They moseyed over to Operations one hot afternoon and dragged the "chicken" along with them. A noncom handed them applications to fill out.

The usual standard inquiries presented no problems. Question number four asked, "Born?" Burt put down "Yes," but then he figured they might not have a sense of humor and added, London, England. At least that made it look like he was on the good-guy's side. Another question asked, "Father's nationality?" Why do they want to know that? he wondered. Does it make a difference? Even so, Walt was dead. Burt wrote down, "German." Mother's maiden name? *Mother's maiden name*, Burt reflected, *how the hell do I know? What's that got to do with anything?* Extent of education? High School. Name of school? Burt wrote down Brooklyn Tech and hoped they didn't check on it. Seemed to have a good ring to it. That's where potential pilots would go. He sweated over that form almost as much as he did over the exam that followed. They knocked themselves out for a couple of hours on paper.

"Holy Cow," Charlie said, rubbing his eyes after they got through. "Wouldn't want to go through that again. How do you think you made out?"

"Tough exam all right." Burt laughed. He wasn't going to make it, anyway.

"You jokers asked for it," kidded Jack, the smart one.

But the following day they were ordered to report to the flight surgeon for physical checkups. Wow! They had passed the toughest part; they had it made! They laughed and danced and hugged each other. The next part would be a snap. The medics would find them to he the finest physical specimens in the land, they thought.

There was still that bit about age and, after mulling it around some, Burt decided to change the five to a six on his birth certificate, bringing him just within the age limit.

The first part of the physical was to check for twenty-twenty vision. And that was where Burt got the shock of his life. They found that his left eye was impaired.

"Can't be," he argued with the medic. "Always saw good, never had any trouble."

"Sorry, soldier. That's it."

"Wait," Burt persisted. "I've got a cold, my eyes are watery, maybe that's the trouble."

"Well come back again when you feel better."

How was it possible that he would flunk the medical? Burt was shot down. The other two guys breezed through with no problems and were good with expressions of sympathy. They got their shipping orders and moved out. The good-byes didn't come easy.

The following week Burt had another appointment for an eye exam. And, of course, the results were the same.

"I've got a hangover, Sarg." He was desperate. "Maybe that's the problem."

"Make an appointment for next week and try again," he said indifferently.

The examining room for vision was like a long narrow hall, with a screen hung on the far end. When operating the projector, the medic had his back to the patient. The next time he took the exam, Burt slipped his nose out from under the orthoscope and read over the top with both eyes. He moved along nicely this way, until the Sarg turned and caught him. "Okay, soldier, that's it. Out. Out!"

Lost out again, Burt was feeling pretty miserable as he walked back to the barracks. There must be something wrong with that machine, he thought. That afternoon the public address system ordered him to report back to the base hospital. Must be they are going to court-martial me, he thought. But no, once again, they would check his vision. By this time he had memorized the eye chart and passed the exam. Burt was ushered into the flight surgeon's office. He was a big man seated behind a big desk. The sergeant introduced Burt and the doctor glared at him for what seemed a long time.

"At ease, soldier," he said without a blink. "You must really want to fly."

"Yes sir."

"Well good luck." With that, he signed the medical report, stabbed an exaggerated period, punctuating it as final, and Burt was off. Burt pondered why the man did that for him, concluding that perhaps he was trying to get rid of him, figuring that someone else down the line, would catch up with him.

Chapter 12

San Antonio Aviation Cadet Center, here comes Burt! Sergeant Casanova, also a cadet candidate, was in charge of their shipping orders and travel arrangements. He showed up just as the train was about to pull out.

"Where the hell have you been, Sarg?" The Noncom appeared out of the morning mist, running down the station platform, his hat askew, jacket unbuttoned, tie flying and his fly open. "For chrissake, Sarg, you had us worried," Burt said.

He just stood there with a shit-eating grin on his face. But Burt and the others were relieved to see he had their papers in a manila envelope tucked under his arm.

"All aboard." They hoisted the sorry soldier up onto the train and they were off.

The testing started all over again at the Center but was much more thorough. The flight candidates were escorted through a production line of twelve doctors. The place looked like a nudist convention.

Bobby Brennan joined the Air Corps to help the war effort. Besides, he wanted to be a hero but he wasn't sure about leaving his Mom.

"Spread your cheeks," the third doctor along the line told him. Bobby pulled his face into an exaggerated grin.

"You've got a cute smile, soldier, but it's the other end I'm supposed to look at, damn it." We didn't let the kid live that one down for awhile.

"Gee, how did I know what he wanted?"

Later, when they were alone, he asked Burt, "Why do you suppose one of those doctors asked me if I like girls?"

"I don't know, maybe he's a shrink."

"What's that"?

"Bobby, I don't know, I'm no doctor. Don't worry about it." As an after thought, Burt said, "You do, don't you–like girls?"

"Oh, sure. Don't you?"

It was Burt's luck that the Sellen Chart used there for the initial eye exam was the one he had memorized, and he breezed through without suspicion. In addition to the medical, there were more written quizzes and endless oral tests. The men were subjected to a variety of exercises that incorporated special mechanical devices to determine reflex, coordination, and concentration. "The penny arcade," they called this phase.

No passes were issued during these hectic days and the flight candidates were beginning to be a pretty dull lot. Someone got wind of a rumor that promised a respite in the routine. An Air Corps medical team was conducting some research in aviation medicine and studying the effects of oxygen deprivation on the human body. Volunteers were asked to participate and were trucked to Randolph Air Base for the day.

A large steel cylinder was set up in a hanger. Portholes in it made it look like a Jules Verne submarine in dry dock. The interior was painted white and florescent lights made it very bright. A dozen of the heroes were seated on benches along the sides of the cylinder, facing each other. The uniform of the day consisted of the bare minimum. They wore only earphones and throat mikes. They looked like frogs on lily pads. An assortment of wires, tubes and electrodes were taped to their bodies to record various data such as pulse rate, temperature, and blood pressure. The men felt like marionettes waiting for the puppeteer to make them dance. Someone ignorant of what was going on would have taken them for a UFO crew from very far out.

One symptom of oxygen deprivation is an accumulation of gas. When the pressure of the cylinder was adjusted to simulate the thin air of high altitude, the passengers began to feel uncomfortable. Soon, one of the volunteers would raise up on one cheek, trying not to look too conspicuous, then lower himself again. We knew he was feeling much better because of the contented, though embarrassed look on his face. When another took a turn and was relieved, he had a silly grin on his face—and so it went until all burst into uncontrollable laughter.

The time spent on this project was good for the men. Not that they had volunteered in the interest of science, mind you. Rumor had it that if they bribed the driver a little he would drop them off in town for an hour or so before returning to base. The few minutes allotted to them to taste a drop of Texas beer was a rare treat.

Back at the Center, at last they received the little white slip they worked so hard for, waited so long for. "You have been classified by the faculty board of the Army Air Force Classification Center as Pilots," it said. This was the greatest thrill of their lives. But for now they were just plebes, qualified to commence ten rugged weeks of pre-flight school.

Pre-flight was a short distance from the induction center, and the men were marched across the street in formation, carrying all their personal belongings and gear. The new upper-classmen (plebes just the day before) were there in full force to greet the newcomers, screaming from upper balconies, howling and roaring like animals in a zoo. Burt felt as though everyone in the place had gone stark, raving mad and the outside world knew nothing of it.

They harassed the newcomers every foot of the way to their quarters. They warned them that from now on it wasn't going to be easy. They gave ridiculous commands, impossible to execute, and then gigged the plebes for not complying. "Get on the ball, Mister," the plebes heard constantly.

The Cadet Commander, a ramrod of a man, looked the new group over and glared. "Gentlemen, you are now entering one of the most important phases of your training to become a member of the fighting air crews of the United States Army Air Force. You have set a high objective for yourselves and must, in consequence, put out much effort if you are to reach that objective. You are the class of 43-k. You will be billeted in barracks number 427. You are not soldiers, nor yardbirds, nor even rookies. You are nothings, and from now on you will be addressed as Mister. You will execute the commands from your upper class. And you are expected to adhere strictly to the cadet code of honor. Is that clear?"

"Yeah," someone in the ranks answered.

"Mister, step forward one pace...NOW! On the double!"

Naked In A Coat of Armor

Kovalski looked a bit forlorn out there all by himself. The Ram marched up to him and bellowed, "The next time you sound off like that I'll make you regret taking your first breath. Do you read me, Mister?"

"Yes."

"You will hang a 'sir' onto that."

"Yes, Sir."

"Speak up, Mister and look proud."

"Yes, Sirrr," Kowalski screamed with all his might.

"You will learn to do better," the Commander said. "I'm sure your seniors will see to that. That is if you're here long enough."

The Ram turned to address the formation.

"For starters you all will memorize the chain of commands starting with President Roosevelt, your Commander in Chief, on down to yourselves—you, the lowest dregs at the bottom of the chain. But don't worry too much about that, since few of you raunchy feather merchants will last for the next ten weeks. Very soon you'll be dragging your frames out of here to go crawling back to the miserable outfits you came from." He informed the men that they would occupy the first floor of the barracks while their eager upperclassmen would be over them on the second floor. They learned that seniors wore blue nametags while the freshmen wore red.

"Dismiss the squadron, Mr. Barker," the Ram commanded the squadron Sergeant. The plebes began to saunter toward the barracks, dragging footlockers and bags, and wondering what they had let themselves in for. The sauntering was the cue for the upper class to roar in unison that all plebes move on the double whenever they move. When a room was called to attention, chairs had to be kicked over, proving that the move was fast enough. Each underclassman was assigned to a senior and. from then on was known as his little boy. Each little boy had to become famous for something. For example, Cadet Sergeant Barker, whose ego had gotten the best of him, and who thought that his place was on the right side of Jesus, asked Brennan, "And what is this 'little boy' famous for?"

Bobby, who loved to generate a laugh at all cost, answered, "Sir, I am famous for cutting toilet seats in half to accommodate half-assed upper-classmen." Burt stood alongside of Brennan, and although at rigid attention, burst into hilarious laughter. Barker stepped in front of Burt. "Well, what have we here? A laughing boy?" He pushed his crimson face into Burt's and snarled like a cur. His breath smelled like carrion.

"We do not tolerate laughing boys in this outfit, mister. I'm going to jig you till you bleed. Then I'm going to jig you for bleeding. Let's see how many pushups you can do. Burt got down and started the exercise. Fifty-one, fifty-two, fifty-three…and fell on his face. Barker walked up Burt's spine and straddled his shoulders, pinning him to the floor. "Not in very good shape, are you, mister?"

Why is it that when you put some guys into a uniform with chevrons on the sleeve and a stripe down the leg, and hang a long saber at their sides, they immediately think they're Little Caesar and become dizzy with power? Must we be bullies to be leaders? To govern, to coach, to guide, to teach?

Naked In A Coat of Armor

Burt got a letter from Charlie telling him he was on his way to radio school. They washed him out at Pre-Flight after they discovered he had deformed thumbs. It was a hard blow to take. His goal was to earn a commission to impress his father. They were often at odds with each other. Charlie was determined to prove he could make it on his own. Burt felt real sorry for him.

The plebes were lined up, all of them in the exaggerated position of attention known as a "brace" (shoulders racked back, gut sucked up and chin pressed in). Mr. Holsworth stepped in front of a freshman and asked, "Mister Hansen, can you describe a kiwi bird for us?"

"No Sir," said Hansen, looking as though his jugular was about to burst from the distorted position he was in.

"Mr. Hansen, we cannot hear you. Sound off, please."

"No, *Sir*!" screamed Hansen.

"No, Sir, what? Mr. Hansen?"

"No Sir, I cannot describe a kiwi for you, *Sir!*"

"Where are you from Mr. Hansen?"

"Sir, I am from New York, the Empire State, Sir."

"And where's that?"

"Sir, in the North-eastern part of the United States, Sirrr."

"They are not very well informed up there are they?"

"No, *Sir*!"

Holsworth turned to the plebe next to Hansen. "Mr. Kolby," he said, "perhaps you can describe the kiwi bird for this northern birdbrain."

"Sir, the kiwi bird is a small vertebrate with feathers. It inhabits the deepest darkest parts of Equatorial Africa. It is known for its unique characteristic of flying in ever-diminishing concentric circles until it flies up it's own rectum. Having achieved this astonishing performance, it can be heard to cry, 'Kee, Kee, Keeriest but it's dark up here.' Sir, that is commonly known as the kiwi bird."

"Very good, Mr. Kolby. And as for you, Stupid, you will memorize this valuable bit of information and report to me at this time tomorrow."

In the mess hall, the plebes stood at attention until the upperclassmen were seated. They were seated on command, facing them. They were privileged to sit on only four inches of the chair. The plebe on the aisle seat was dubbed the gunner. It was his duty to see that the food on the table was replenished at all times. When a platter was empty, he had to hold it aloft at arm's length until a waiter refilled it. The cadet commandant would pace up and down to insure order, or to simply rattle his saber. The table was constantly informed as to his location.

The gunner would put his knife and fork at rest, sit at attention and, announce, "Sirs, the Big Dog is now on his downwind leg." Or as the case may be, "Sirs, the Big Dog is on his upwind leg." All of it left little time for gunners to eat.

Barker singled Hansen out one evening and said, "Mr. Hansen, Mr. Holsworth regrets that he is unable to be here to hear your discourse on the kiwi bird. He suggests, therefore, that you recite it for me. Please sound off, Mr. Hansen."

Naked In A Coat of Armor

"Sir, I have been unable to find time to memorize the piece, *Sir*!"

"Time? Why, Mr. Hansen, you have all the time there is. Maybe you could find a little time to do some side-straddle-hops for me."

"Yes, Sir."

"Please commence, Mr. Hansen."

Hansen continued the exercise until he collapsed on the floor. The blood drained from his face and his eyes rolled up into his head. Barker was one frightened bastard and disappeared upstairs to his room. So were we scared. A couple of us lifted Hansen onto his bunk and applied a cold cloth to his forehead. He came around after awhile. His pulse felt normal and some color returned to his face.

"Why didn't you quit?" someone asked.

Andy said, "I wanted to punch him in the nose."

"Oh sure, you know what that would have done for you? End of short career," Burt said.

"I just wasn't going to give the son of a bitch that satisfaction," Hansen mumbled.

"Smart. Real smart. You stupid knucklehead."

Burt was shook up badly enough to go upstairs and request permission to talk to Barker. He knocked on the door.

"Who is it?" the frightened man called out.

"Aviation Cadet Eichwald, 32117417, request permission to talk to Mr. Barker." Barker opened the door and ushered him in.

"Sound off, Mister, he said, with his back to Burt.

"Sir, may I speak to you as man to man?"

"At ease, Eichwald."

"Barker," Burt started, "I can understand the disciplinary value of this hazing shit, but what I can't stomach is when an upperclassman finds himself in a crisis he turns his ass around and ducks out. God help the guy who has you for his wing man in combat." With that Burt made an about-face and left. He worried all night and all the next day. Would Barker nail him for insubordination? Why did he have to be such a hero; was this to be the end of his career?

The curriculum consisted of math, theory of flight, aerodynamics, aircraft engines, aircraft recognition, surface craft recognition, calisthenics, current events, and military etiquette. (After all, they were to become officers and gentlemen). All that, and, of course, the ceaseless hazing. The Texas sun didn't help matters, either. At times, Burt would catch himself lying in the hot sand on the obstacle course, completely wrung out. He would wonder what it was that possessed him to join an outfit like that. They were like a bunch of schoolboys playing games while there was a war going on. Why did he lie about his age? Maybe he was too old for this shit. They would break him in two. Why did he lie about the extent of his formal education? Would those lies come back to roost? Algebra worried him; it would be his death. A monomial is an expression of one term. A polynomial is an expression of more than one. $(XY)^2 + (xy)^2 =$ etc, etc. Who cared? Why couldn't the simple times tables suffice, maybe throw in a little long division.

Kowalski and Brennan tutored Burt with infinite patience. They tried to get through to him but he was running out of time. In desperation, Burt approached the math instructor with his problem. He explained

Naked In A Coat of Armor

that he had gone to school in Europe, where the curriculum was either beaten into the student or out of him.

"Sir, perhaps this created a phobia," Burt told him, though he doubted that reasoning would register with the instructor; after all, there were only three answers to a question in this outfit: Yes Sir, No Sir, and No excuse, Sir. But to his surprise, Lt. Martin proved very understanding and, for an army officer, quite compassionate. He agreed to tutor Burt a few minutes, one on one, each day. Together, Brennan, Kowalski and Lt. Martin dragged Burt through by the skin of his thick hide, and barely in time.

Those were times that tried. Burt worried about his weight, which was on the borderline of the accepted.

"Eat bananas," advised Brennan. "And drink milk. That'll put it on." So Burt drank milk and ate bananas until he began to feel like a baboon, but he didn't notice much increase on the scale. He worried about his eyes. "Exercise 'em," Kowalski suggested.

"What are you, some kind of doctor?"

"It'll strengthen the ciliary muscles."

"Whatever the hell they are," Burt mumbled. He lay in bed rolling his eyeballs up into his head. Left and right and right and left and up and down, hoping he wasn't being watched.

Suddenly, it was "turn about day," the plebes' turn to give the seniors some of what they dished out. But before they were granted this privilege, there was to be one last humiliation. A dress parade was scheduled the night before moving-up day. The uniform of the day would be jock straps and name tags. They were lined up in formation, Chessman up front playing a march on his harmonica. Nesbit, next, as the guidon, carrying a broom with toilet paper streamers.

The upperclassmen marched the plebes between lines of laughing hyenas. After passing in review, the plebes were brought to a halt and put at parade rest. Then awards were presented ceremoniously to each of them.

The upperclassmen handed the plebes the stacks of past jigs written against them–those terrible white slips that kept them in a constant state of anxiety wondering if they had accumulated enough to be disqualified.

During that previous five weeks of hell, the plebes longed for the chance to strangle certain seniors or hang them up by their thumbs. But this was the time, at last, to celebrate their great triumph. They had made it.

Upperclassmen shook hands with the new upper class. For the next five weeks it would be the new upperclassmen's turn to welcome the poor new plebes. They wished each other good luck. Burt saw Barker shake hands with Hansen, but he couldn't hear what they were saying. He sensed that things were okay between them. There was a feeling of relief.

It was a soothing atmosphere, as though the new upperclassmen had been through a cleansing process. They were in excellent shape, physically and mentally, each of them feeling they could win the war by themselves if called upon. Soon they would be leaving too.

They reported to a small flying school in Chickaskia, Oklahoma, southwest of Oklahoma City. There they finally commenced with flying instructions. The reception was incredible. The dormitory was beautiful. The beds were made up in pastel-colored blankets. Each man had his personal locker, and curtains hung at the windows. The very best food was served in great quantities, by waiters in white jackets.

"Kick me," said Brennan. "I think I'm dreaming."

"You'll get kicked later on," Chandler said in his melancholy way. "Remember, beware of Greeks carrying gifts."

The following day they met their instructors.

"This, gentlemen, is the PT-19 Primary Training Plane, a smart little aircraft powered by a 175 HP inverted inline engine, with inertia start. It has a wingspan of thirty six feet, a top cruising speed of 150 miles per hour, with a 50 mile-per-hour landing speed."

The new pilots soon learned how sweet and forgiving this craft was when they practiced acrobatics, takeoffs and landings, stalls and spins, S's across a road.

Burt was enjoying an exciting time and doing very well. His Link Trainer skill was now paying off. But you can't learn much about landing an aircraft when anchored to the floor. And so came Burt's Waterloo.

He was having difficulty learning to set the plane on the ground. The trick was to stall out when you were a couple of inches off the ground. But Burt would make a perfect landing at more like five feet off the ground.

"Jesus Christ, you'll kill us both," his instructor would cry.

Cadets were expected to solo after ten hours of instructions. If they didn't solo after thirteen hours, they were disqualified. Although the instructors were civilians, it required an Army Officer to make the final decision to wash out a student.

Burt was scheduled for an army 'Wash Ride' and, after the examining officer had him go through the routine aerobatics, he asked, "What seems to be the problem, Mr.?"

"Landings, Sir," Burt answered.

"Okay, let's go back to the field and land." As they touched down on the field he said, "I see what you mean. Try again."

After another hard landing, he said, "Your air work is good. I'm going to recommend a few more hours of landing instructions." It was a rare occasion indeed for a student to be given a second chance. Burt nearly broke his arm saluting that officer.

Jack finally wrote from Basic Flying School and told Burt he was doing pretty well. Not counting, of course, when he and his instructor had to bail out of their 'Voltare vibrator' due to engine failure. While dangling from a tree in his parachute, he wondered if this flying thing was all it was cracked up to be. He really never was that enthusiastic about flying.

McCollough, Bert's new instructor, was a no-nonsense, rough and coarse character from the old barnstorming days. He was a very patient man, Burt believed, but even a patient man will eventually run out of composure.

One day, after a particularly trying hour with Burt, he took over control of the aircraft and they raced over the countryside. They hedgehopped at breakneck speed over the treetops and bushes. Burt could see the branches rustle violently in their slipstream, as though they were shaking angry fists at the fliers.

McCollough flew down into the valleys and swooped up over the hills. After he was finished venting his steam, they gained some altitude and leveled off.

"Take hold of the stick in your left hand," he ordered. "Now, Mr. Eichwald, please reach around with your right hand and pull your head out of your ass. Was it dark up there?" he inquired seriously. "Didn't that give you a feeling of depth perception?"

On another occasion, Burt was doing pretty well and began to feel that he was mastering those confounded landings. After Burt had taxied to the end of the field for yet another try, McCollough climbed out of the cockpit. Oh God, at last, at last, Burt thought, he's going to let me solo. But no, he walked to the rear of the plane simply to relieve his bladder. Burt was beaten, shot down.

When he was finished he looked up at Burt in the cockpit and asked, "Any questions, Mr. Eichwald?"

By god, he really is going to let me go, Burt thought.

"No Sir," he answered, "Let me take it up."

McCollough looked at Burt as though he must be kidding.

"I'm sorry, mister, I'm afraid you'll kill yourself."

If the man had kicked Burt in the teeth, he couldn't have felt worse.

"Tell you what I'll do," McCollough said, after reading the hopeless expression on Burt's face. "If you do as well tomorrow as you did today, I'll let you go."

The next day, Burt was to earn his second washout ride. Even nineteen hours with excellent instructors and a second chance, it was the end of his flying career. Well, so much for memorizing the eye chart. McCollough felt pretty bad, too.

"This doesn't mean you can't fly, fellow. Army training is too hasty. There's a war going on. There's not enough time."

Yes, Burt thought, *all the courses I've taken in this man's Air Force have been too accelerated.* He promised himself that some day he would treat himself to a normal, leisurely course of study on some ivy-strewn campus.

Chapter 13

About a dozen of the group would be flyers with clipped wings. They were shipped off to Keesler Field, Wichita Falls, Texas. The place was the largest replacement center in the Air Force. Ex-cadets, once the elite and now depressed, called it the asshole of America. Here Burt would start his military career for the third time.

Rookies, feather merchants, ex-fly boys and noncoms were all thrown in together to commence basic training. It was comical to see master sergeants, with several hash marks, being instructed to salute by the numbers. The group were a disillusioned lot.

The drill sergeant, a big bear of a man, greeted them drooling with sarcasm.

"Welcome, gentlemen, to the real world. I know you ex-hotshot pilots are pissed off at this world, but it's not my fault you couldn't cut the mustard. There will be no special privileges here for you. You're nothing but yardbirds to me, and it's my job to get you all back on the ball. You will shape up and ship out, and the sooner the better."

Discouraged, depressed and bitter, Burt thought of going AWOL, maybe shooting himself. But you can't run from self. You can't hide, because the music follows, and eventually you must turn and face it. After coming all this way, his ambition and enthusiasm came to a screeching halt. One day, during calisthenics, Burt decided to simply walk off the field. He managed to get as far as the moat around the perimeter.

"Where are you going, soldier?" An officer intercepted him. Where he came from, Burt didn't see. He just popped up out of the grass like an asparagus in spring.

"To the dispensary, Sir. I feel sick."

"There are five hundred men out there, and they're all sick. Get your ass back in there."

Burt started going to the PX in the mornings and buying a cup of coffee and a newspaper. There was an excavation for a new building nearby, and he'd climb down into it, out of sight, and spend the morning reading the paper and wrestling with ugly emotions. After lunch he'd walk around the company streets carrying a clipboard with paper and pencil, looking as though he was taking a survey of some sort. They had a name for the likes of Burt. The gentlemen officers referred to them as "Gold Bricks."

Those not so gentle were more to the point. They threatened to put Burt in the stockade, and that jarred him to his senses. He really wasn't looking for an easy out. He just wanted to excel in what he chose to excel in. He knew he could, having gotten as far as he did in the cadet corps. It was his habit to blame the lack of formal education for his shortcomings. That was his excuse, his crutch. Suddenly it occurred to him that he was gaining a fine all-around education in the Air Corps, on the house, with Uncle Sam's compliments.

I'll sign up for Aircraft Mechanics School, Burt thought. *I'll qualify for that. After all, I've had a little experience on the flight line.*

One day, those accepted for various schools were given their shipping orders and told to pack their gear and fall in at the railroad siding. Potential mechanics,

Naked In A Coat of Armor

radio operators, clerks, cooks and bakers all boarded a train. They didn't know the whereabouts of the different schools, they just knew they were leaving the current chicken farm and traveling north.

It had just stopped raining in Bellville, Illinois. The train stopped at a siding and the men stepped off into mud, ankle deep. "Why we're always greeted with mud at Air Force Schools, I don't know," Pete complained.

"A prelude, maybe, to the shit that's to follow." Gerry said.

"Will you look at that," Burt said, pointing to a large sign arched across the entrance to Scott Field. "THROUGH THESE PORTALS PASS THE BEST DAMN RADIO OPERATORS IN THE WORLD."

"Propaganda. They're going to have to do better than that to boost my moral," Gerry grumbled. The whole trainload of men, looking forward to various schools of their choice, were marched through the mud to the wooden duckboards leading to the barracks of the Fourth Area. Would-be aircraft mechanics, radio operators, cooks, bakers, and clerks–all pissed off–would become "The Best Damn Radio Operators in the World," or else.

Here they would learn about radio receivers and transmitters, voice and CW transmission. In addition, they were expected to pass twenty-five words a minute, sending and receiving Morse code.

"I'm looking forward to that bit," said Pete. "We had difficulty passing a mere eight words in flying school. This is the last bit that breaks the spirit, the insult for sights set too high. This is the kick in the teeth that heralds the ultimate depression."

"Yeah," Burt said, with more sarcasm. "This ought to be a real challenge. Great for morale."

"Esprit de corps, hobbled," moaned Gerry. "All that aviation cadet stuff, cadet honor code, of officers and gentlemen, all of it, down the shit drain."

Burt empathized with him and thought, *I need a furlough. I need a break. I need to get home and see Allison. Haven't written to her in many weeks.* Allison was the home-town girl he'd left behind.

For a soldier to learn to kill or be killed he must first learn to hate, and this is probably part of the process. Burt needed a shoulder to cry on. He called Lora, his St. Louis girl. She was happy to hear from him after so many months.

"Burt," she said. "You're too late."

"Don't tell me," he thought, and then asked, "Married?"

"Oh no. It's, just that, well, I'm leaving for Columbia, Missouri tomorrow to take a class at the University. It's an accelerated course in electrical engineering." She had left General American Insurance to do her patriotic bit for the war effort.

Columbia! Why does she have to be so goddam conscientious, anyway? Burt thought. God, that's a hundred and fifty miles away.

"I'll call you sometime," he said, and he did. They managed to see each other on weekends. They planned to celebrate New Year's Eve together. Burt boarded a bus for Columbia and promptly fell asleep. He woke in time to catch a glimpse of a sign announcing," Mexico, 10 Miles." He rubbed his eyes to see that the landscape was covered in a foot of snow. Now he panicked, rushed up to the driver and asked, "Where are we?"

"Mexico."

"You're kidding, man. What's with all this snow?"

"Mexico, Missouri." He laughed, with the rest of the passengers joining in. Burt crawled back to his seat.

Lora and he went to a place where patrons were expected to bring their own spirits, while the house supplied the set-ups. A peculiar custom in the Midwest. Honky Tonks, they were called. They joined the local fun, and ate, and drank, and danced, celebrating whatever the new year had in store for them.

"Do you think a man can be in love with two women?" Burt held Lora's hand across the table. She pulled away. "Is there someone else? Don't tell me you're married?"

"I'm engaged. –Will you marry me?"

"You're joking."

"No. I'm serious."

"Do you mean to tell me that you would leave the woman you're engaged to just like that?"

"Lora, I love you. We have more in common than I ever had with Allison. Your letters were far more encouraging when I was going through a difficult time as an aviation cadet. You were far more positive and uplifting than Allison, with her morbid litanies of local gossip."

"My Dad says some soldiers forget their commitments when they're away at war."

"Lora, I want you to be my wife. Say you will. We can wait till after the war to get married, if you like."

"Yes," she said. "I love you too, Burt, very much."

Burt's pass was illegal, he having borrowed it from someone else. It couldn't be turned in at the gate.

Having taken a taxi to within a safe distance of the entrance to the base, the plan that a lot of the guys knew about was to continue on foot along a hidden path to an oak tree against the fence. The trick was to locate the path in the first place–not easy at night. Burt paid the driver and began the search, walking towards the gate as far as he dared. *Must have missed it*, he thought, and turned to retrace his weary steps. Three men appeared out of the dark and approached him.

"Where are you going, soldier?" the tall one demanded with authority.

Back to camp," he retorted with equal authority.

"Well, let's go."

Something about those fellows made Burt feel they were on his side. "Look," he confessed, "I don't want to go through the gate."

"If you're coming with us, you won't."

Burt recognized this new voice, though he couldn't see the face. It was his friend Pete. "Pete, what the hell are you doing here?"

"You want three guesses, knucklehead?" a third voice chimed in. "He's doing the same thing you are." Burt recognized Gerry and was relieved to have two friends for company, in his misery.

Naked In A Coat of Armor

"You sweethearts going to stand here till we get a Military-Police escort? Let's get out of here," said the tall one.

They moved up to where the flood from the base lights met the dark. Here, the tall one ducked off the road onto the narrow footpath winding through the brush and they followed it to the tree by the fence. They climbed up and out on a limb and dropped onto the parade grounds. The place was lit up like a ballpark for a night game. The tall one, apparently used to entering camps in roundabout ways, cautioned the others to step out nonchalantly so not to attract attention. It was then Burt noticed First Sergeant chevron's on his sleeve and thought, *I guess with a rating like that you should know all the angles.* Suddenly a whistle shrilled across the still night and the Top Kick took off like a whippet on a racetrack, with Burt and his friends as rabbits right behind him. When they reached the shadows of some buildings, they stopped to catch a breath and realized that the commotion was just the Charge of Quarter's, getting the kitchen patrols up for an early start. They slithered deeper into the shadows and, at the railroad spur, they crossed the tracks under a freight car and were home free.

"Happy New Year, you yardbirds," laughed the Top Kick. "See you around."

"Thanks, Sarg, you too."

"Man, I'm tired after that sprint," gasped Gerry.

"Yeah, and in a couple of hours we'll be in class, going dit-dah, happy again," Pete said.

"Got myself engaged," Burt told the fellows.

"Why you son of a gun, congratulations!" Pete shook Burt's hand.

"I'd buy you a drink if it wasn't so late, or early, and if I had the price," added Gerry.

They were good people. Both married. Pete was from Ohio and had a little girl. Gerry hailed from Wisconsin, and his pride and joy were two fine boys. He was resentful at having his life interrupted by the damn war. All he wanted, like most Italian family men, was to get back to his family and his old job. Pete was thinking of breeding racehorses after the war. He was a giant whose stature belied his gentle, thoughtful nature.

Mulling over his resume, it occurred to Burt that with so many varied experiences, he was gaining a marvelous education, albeit one informal and piecemeal. Even if being interested in everything and master of nothing was undesirable, it made for an absorbing life, and a good remedy for boredom, he decided.

Both Radio Theory and Mechanics proved to be interesting classes, but Code was something else. They had a young and pretty WAC as their instructor.

"All right you F.O.s, now settle down," she'd call out, to get their attention. Sgt. Mary Osborne was told F.O.s stood for Flight Officers, but the young louts knew it meant Fuck Offs.

She told the men that those who were musically inclined would have no trouble passing code. "Samuel Morse's song," she said, "is sweet rhythm, transmitted on waves of ether." But she had no patience with those endowed with tin ears.

Naked In A Coat of Armor

The morning after New Year's Day, the C.O. decided to have a midnight muster. He sprung that on the men when they least expected it, to see if anyone was AWOL. Sometimes these roll calls included a short arm inspection. The Charge of Quarters, a buck sergeant, ordered the men to "Grab yer socks...up and out."

Burt rolled over and went back to sleep. He came back and shook the hell out of him. "Up, up, the Major's waiting for you."

"Oh fuck the Major," Burt said.

"What did you say, soldier? We'll see about that. I'm going to tell the Major." He left but soon returned to shake this sleepy lump again.

"The C.O. wants to see you."

"What for?"

"You'll see."

Burt was awake, but his brain was slow in bringing up the rear. "Are you telling me you told him what I said?"

"You're damn right I did."

"Why you goddam kindergarten kid."

"Let's, go. Let's go, before I turn you in for insubordination." He marched Burt down to the Commander, who demanded, "What's this all about, soldier?"

"Sir I made a disrespectful remark about the Commanding Officer," Burt said.

"Oh you did, did you? What was this remark?"

Embarrassed, Burt hesitated, shifting first from one foot then to the other.

"Sound off, Soldier," the C.O. demanded.

"Sir, I said, fuck the Major."

The man backed up a step. As a ripple drifted through the formation, he bit his lip, not knowing whether to laugh or cry. He turned away to scowl at the twittering in the ranks. After he regained his composure, he asked, "What's your name, Soldier?"

"Sergeant Ernst Eichwald, Sir."

"I can't have my people talking like that about me. You will march your ass around the base perimeter for the rest of the night. You will report to Sergeant Kinder on the hour every hour. Is that clear?"

"Yes Sir. May I address the Commanding Officer, Sir?"

"What is it?"

"Sir, there was nothing personal intended in my remark."

"I know goddam well there was nothing personal, or I'd have your ass court-marshaled right now. Dismissed."

Burt got a letter from Charlie telling him to stick with it and that things would get better when he least expected it. His words of encouragement paid off, and soon after he got the letter, Burt passed required code words per minute. Charlie's letter was a long one, pouring his heart out. He was a serious man. A deep thinker, intelligent, and Burt liked him a lot.

Of course, the big news," he wrote, "*is your engagement to Lora. Congratulations, Burt, to both of you. I'd like to repeat a line from your letter and agree with you that it is unfortunate that we can't see in advance what life has in store; it would make things easier. In any event, Burt, I know you've given much thought to your decision and have done what you think is best. I'd like to wish you both all the luck and happiness in the world. If you are truly happy, you will need nothing more. I think you know how much I'd like to be there for the big event. As for things on this side of the Atlantic, I'm finally getting into the home stretch. Have just two more missions to fly, and I'm really sweating them out. I need just a little more of the kind of luck we've been having and all of us will be through before long. I know it sounds a bit screwy, but I might decide to stay in England a bit longer. They have offered me a commission as communications officer if I stay. Thanks for keeping your fingers crossed and etc. I can assure you a minor reason for my wanting to get through over here is to bend an elbow with you and get a look at that ugly pan of yours.*

Charlie

P.S. Don't forget to let me know the date. Also let me know if you need any money. I've saved up a few shekels. C.

In answering, Burt mentioned for him to get his tour over with. Hell, Burt thought, I'm sweating out his last two missions almost as much as he is. Burt's letter was returned, with one stark word stamped on it: "MISSING" and dated 4-25-44. The bold letters in black stared up at Burt, matter of fact and so terribly final. He and his friends knew things like this happen, but the shock is different when it's close to home.

Eugene A. Aichroth

They buried him in Ardennes American Cemetery, Neuville-en-Condroz, Belgium. Burt decided that maybe it is a blessing that we are unable to see in advance what life has in store for us.

Chapter 14

April 29th, 1944 found Burt's unit bound for Yuma, Arizona and to gunnery school. It was a new phase in training, designed exclusively for "The Best Damn Radio Operators In the World." The mood was more relaxed. The food was excellent: chicken-a-la-king on Wednesday, and ice cream for dessert. No passes were issued, but they had their own beer garden on the base. True, they were stationed in the desert, where the temperature was 102 degrees and the work was intense, but the evenings were cool, with clear skies and the pleasant scent of orange blossoms drifting across their tent city.

They were taken up in an old war-weary B-17 Bomber for an orientation flight, to see the gunnery range. The pilot spread out a bit and gave them a view of the surrounding countryside. The state was conducting a major experiment in irrigation. From 5,000 feet, the orange groves appeared as a green mosaic in the bleached desert.

"The desert shall rejoice," Pete recited, "and blossom, as the rose."

"Beautiful," Bert said. "Where'd you learn that?"

"It's in the Bible, you heathen," Gerry butted in, disgusted with Bert's ignorance. "Don't you know nuttin'?"

"Look Einstein," Bert said, "if you know it all, there's nothing left for me to know. It must be awful to end up with absolutely nothing left to learn."

"Go to hell, Eichwald."

"I'll meet you there. Don't you 'heathen' me. I've forgotten more about that book than you'll ever learn. I've had that book rammed down my throat till I'm nauseous. Agnostic, yes. Heathen, no."

Gerry backed off from this tirade. He raised his hand to baffle his mouth and whispered to Pete, "What's agnostic?"

Pete told him and added, "It's when you haven't been convinced whether there is a God or not. Some would call you a coward for not making up your mind. Actually, it takes some courage to admit it. As for me, I don't worry about such things. See, there's always something to learn. Now will you jokers simmer down and be glad we can always argue the point without getting too carried away." He looked out over the fifty-caliber at the waist-gunner's position, took a deep breath and breathed, "What a beautiful day. Wonder how my Lucial is and what is she and our little girl doing on a day like this."

They were schooled in a variety of firearms in general and the fifty-caliber machine gun in particular. The final test on this piece was to fieldstrip it and put it back together again, blindfolded. The curricula included a continuous practicing of Morse code and radio procedure. Gunnery was exciting, with a great deal of skeet shooting, air to ground firing, and air to air firing at towed targets. One boy, (that's what they were, just boys) was carried away with enthusiasm and one day fired a couple of rounds at the tow plane. They never saw him again. *They probably gave him a Section-8,* Burt speculated. Luckily, no one was hurt.

Hattie wrote to say Bottle was on infantry maneuvers in the Laguna desert, just north of their own location. Burt got in touch with him and invited him to stop in at the Air Base when he was finished. Sure enough, when Burt got back from a flight one day, there he was his long frame stretched out on Burt's bunk, fast asleep. Burt looked down on this soldier and could see he'd been through a tough time. It was Wednesday, chicken-a-la king and ice cream day.

Bottle made up for all the C-Rations he'd been living on for the past few weeks. In the evening, Burt introduced him to the beer garden, and they downed a few 13.2 brews. Bottle was impressed.

"Even this weak beer beats drinking the water we caught in truck tarps. You goddamn fly boys don't know there's a war on. You've got it made."

Their good-byes didn't come easy. They both knew that in a couple of weeks Bottle would be in the European theatre. How he managed to drag his skinny frame all the way across the continent in some of the fiercest fighting from D-day to VE-day was a mystery.

After finishing up in the Technical Training Command Burt's unit was to get ten days' delay enroute to Westover Field, Massachusetts. Burt wrote to Lora and suggested that they could get married, then, in St. Louis, her hometown. But the Army changed its mind, as the Army will, and all furloughs were cancelled.

Westover Field was an overseas training unit. There, Burt would meet his pilot and the rest of the crew. That was the way it was supposed to happen. But it didn't. Most men were assigned to crews, but Burt was not. He hung around, wondering if he had some mysterious disease.

He wrote to Lora in Ohio to ask her if she'd want to get married in New York. "There's some talk about them giving us seven-day furloughs," he told her. "Seven days isn't much, but do you think you could come arunning on a minute's notice? I had hoped that we could spend some time planning," he wrote. "I don't quite know how to put this, but do you still want to marry a soldier just before he goes overseas? Are you sure you understand what sort of work I'll be doing and what the future might have in store for us? Does it occur to you that we might be together just for seven days, and that I might be gone for the duration of the war? And there will be days when you'll feel lonesome and wish you weren't tied down." Was he trying to talk himself out of getting married? he wondered.

The rector of New York's Little Church Around the Corner, Dr. Randolph Ray, discouraged wartime marriages. He thought the majority of them were hurried, impulsive affairs in which little reasoning had been given. He didn't convince Lora and Burt. They had given the matter a great deal of serious thought and felt that it was important that they shared some happiness, given those fragile times.

A radio operator stationed at Chatham Field, Georgia became ill, and Burt was the lucky replacement to go–but not before he managed to wrangle a leave out of the CO first. He made a hurried call to Lora.

"When you arrive at Penn Station," he instructed, "call my mother and she will give you particulars about getting out to Long Island. See you soon."

Naked In A Coat of Armor

Burt didn't see her soon. A student bombardier dropped a practice bomb into the woods and set half of the Massachusetts countryside on fire. All hands were recruited to go wandering around with Indian pumps in an effort to contain the mess. Three days later they had it under control. In the meantime, Lora called Dorothea, who, of course, knew nothing about their plan.

"Lora, What are you doing in New York?" Dorothea said.

"Haven't you heard from Burt?" Now both were confused.

Lora was embarrassed. She couldn't very well tell her future mother-in-law, "I'm here to marry your son." Finally, after a long pause, Dorothea said, "No, I haven't heard, Dear, but catch the Long Island train to Bay Shore and Burt's brother Rolland will meet you." After Dorothea hung up, she turned to Rolland and gasped, "My word, what am I going to do?"

"Well, for starters," said Rolland, ever the comedian, "where's your pill box?" He hoped that the old lady would not succumb to one of her convenient seizures.

Burt planned to catch the first train out of Springfield but had the presence of mind to call home first, only to learn that Lora was already on her way to meet him in Massachusetts. The poor girl arrived at the station tired, a bit bedraggled, and thoroughly confused. It didn't help to tell her they were to make an about-face and go back to Long Island. He felt so sorry for her. There was time before train time. "Come," he said, taking her suitcase. "Let's get a drink at the hotel lounge."

Eugene A. Aichroth

"I'd like that," she said, happy now that they were together.

Burt ordered a rum and coke for each of them. They held hands and chatted happily over their drinks. They ordered another. There was so much to say and so little time. The rum and cokes were smooth, and they were in love. They decided to stay in the hotel and return to the Island in the morning. They registered as Corporal and Mrs. and, carrying Lora's suitcase, appeared quite legitimate. "Mr. and Mrs. has a nice ring to it," giggled Lora.

The room was old but clean and neat, the bed inviting.

"Do you mind if I sleep in the nude? I don't want to look rumpled in the morning," Lora said timidly.

"No, Honey," Burt answered, equally as bashful, but wishing she would.

What an amorous sensation, all their nakedness so close together. He felt the coolness of her flesh and thought of a quote he'd read somewhere: "Let me lie upon thy cool breasts until the fires of passion begin to burn."

They made violent love, and Burt was premature. Lora slapped him, and he learned that the female of the species also needs orgasm.

He wondered why it's called, 'making love.' A tumble in bed for a few minutes doesn't make it. It takes a whole lifetime to really make love.

The second time was better, and when she whispered, "Don't stop now," Burt managed to stay. "A little more–more–more. Ooooh–ooooooh…aaaaah."

Naked In A Coat of Armor

They lay in each other's arms, damp, drained and content. The room was sensual with the smell of sweat, cologne and semen. They slept. In the morning, he turned to touch the softness of the sleeping girl beside him, hoping for an encore.

"No, we mustn't; we have to catch the train to New York. Besides, what will your mother think?"

"My mother will let her imagination run ugly. If I were engaged to be married to the Virgin Mary herself, she would do all in her power to prevent a wedding. She would use all her cunning to block it. My mother thinks no one is good enough for her gentleman son."

"Don't be unkind to her."

"I hate her...well, not really. Actually, I love her...I think. But I warn you, she is a Jekell-and-Hyde."

"She seemed such a gracious lady on the phone, and she writes sweet letters."

"Ah, that's just what I mean; there in lies the catch. She can be sweetly engaging when luring one into her web to torment. I warn you, stand your ground and I'll back you up."

"Oh, go on with you. Take your shower. Better make it a cold one." She giggled as she dodged Burt's lunge.

Wartime rationing wouldn't allow for all the fine regalia and hoopla customary for weddings. Lora's grandmother gave her her engagement ring. But they shopped for a wedding band, there in Springfield, before boarding the train. Later, they dashed off for a Wasserman test, a prenuptial regulation. They were married in a little church in Sayville, with Burt's brother Roland and his wife, Marie, standing up for them. Dorothea witnessed the ceremony, conducted by Reverend Dr. Bland. It was a pretty day, and the dogwoods were in full bloom.

Seven days were short, though sweet. Lindborg, Dorothea's husband, was upset because the couple did not postpone the wedding until he could get away from defense work in Washington, D.C. It didn't occur to him that a corporal couldn't dictate his furloughs.

Most of their courting had been done in railroad stations or bus terminals, saying hello and good-bye. Now it seemed that their marriage would commence in the same manner. Lora left to return to Wright Field, Ohio, and Burt went back to Massachusetts.

Pete, the lucky stiff, stayed in Massachusetts for his overseas training, while Gerry and Burt were shipped back once again to Savanna, Georgia. Burt was introduced to his pilot and crew, and they seemed like good people.

Noncommissioned officers were given quarters and rations to live off the base. Gerry and Burt lost no time inviting their wives to join them. They made do with the tiny cinder-block billet the government supplied. For the newlyweds, a castle wouldn't have been much better.

A few wonderful weeks slipped by, and Lora and Burt were at the station once again. Their good-byes were different this time. "Don't cry; dry those tears. We're going to have Thanksgiving dinner together in 1945, and I'll be in civilian clothes," Burt said. You watch." He voiced this prediction impulsively, feeling the need to say something reassuring...for both of them.

Naked In A Coat of Armor

Dorothea, Burt's mother, was an angel, a saint on earth, a martyr. She was a beautiful woman–tall, statuesque, commanding. Her golden hair cascaded to her waist. She had steel-gray eyes, the skin of the Anglo-Saxon, and the red cheeks of England's roses. An intelligence radiated from this well-informed woman. She derived great pleasure from debating with the intellectually curious.

Prominent people sought her out for her philosophy, her theories and teachings. She delved into most of the major religions and dabbled in the unorthodox. She possessed an uncanny, sanctimonious influence that mesmerized people.

Dorothea would exchange opinions on any subject from pornography to politics. She was kind and gracious, understanding and compassionate. No one in need of nourishment for body or soul was ever turned from her door. She had a vast store of advice, encouragement and guidance for any who would listen to her. The woman loved animals and harbored all sorts of strays, cripples and misfits, both human and beast. She was a gentle and loving woman. This indeed was Dorothea. But there were terms. She expected her doctrine to be accepted without any reluctance, without any doubt or question.

And woe to the poor devil who dared to stand and challenge her. It was then that the Jekyll became Hyde. The change was as if the alcohol she swallowed was like the fictional doctor's mysterious potion. The talons unsheathed and the eyes seared like hot irons, registering her seething anger. Revenge was the ultimate. Now she was poised for the attack, to be pursued with ruthless drive.

All the ugly human characteristics that she professed to abhor would surface like sediment disturbed in a clear brook. Determined to stop at nothing, she would commence to torment her prey, in cat-and-mouse fashion, vicious and cunning.

She was a master of deceit and malicious gossip. For some mysterious reason, her cussedness was directed toward her so-called loved ones. She believed that people are most cruel to the ones they are most fond of. Yet she did not mellow.

Dorothea left a long wake of grief and broken lives and, on her deathbed, the transformation was complete. The golden hair, now like dirty snow, framed the face that was now furrowed like gray corduroy. Rigor mortis curled her lip into a fixed smile.

Burt drew the sheet to cover the dreadful features and wished he could bury his woeful reflections, too. He wondered if his mother was enjoying her last laugh. There are reasons, he thought, why human beings behave the way they do. He wondered what it was that warped this unhappy woman's character.

Burt's next stop was to be some theater of war, east or west. He was hoping they'd send him to England, and he would look forward to seeing his grandmother and other relatives again. Pete and Gerry went to Italy. They flew missions out of Cerignola, to strike Austria and Southern Germany. Burt's letter to Pete was returned to him, marked with that ominous word: MISSING. The print looked too big and black on the tiny "V MAIL" envelope.

Their wives kept up a correspondence with each other so to maintain a link between the couples. Pete's wife wrote to say that the War Department notified her that he was killed in action over Yugoslavia. So many dreams shot down.

November 9th, 1944, was a pretty autumn day. The mailman had just one small envelope to deliver. Lora watched for him each morning and, now, sauntered out to the mailbox. She felt happy and pleased, as though everything must be right on this sunny day. She drew the letter out of the box and saw only the ugly black stamp on the back of it. Her pulse raced through her body as she ran back into the house.

Not until she collapsed into a chair was she able to turn the envelope over and see that it was her letter addressed to Gerry. The relief she felt was almost as shocking as the initial trauma. The crumpled letter fell to the floor as she let her tears flow free for what seemed a long, long time. Many years later, Gerry told them his story. He was shot down on a mission to Vienna. Flack tore his back open, but he managed to bail out. He lost consciousness soon after he hit the ground. A German motorcycle patrol draped him across their sidecar and took him to a hospital. After being patched up, he was taken to a Stalag, where he spent the rest of the war.

Gerry later met Bill, their bombardier, and spent several hours reminiscing and telling war stories. That's what veterans do when they haven't seen each other in a long time.

"What happened to you after we were hit?

"Well, when you dove out of the camera hatch and I saw how you banged your head on the edge, I decided to go back and jump out the front. There was a big hole through the flight deck and I saw Harvie slumped across his chart table. That delay was enough to put me behind Russian lines. They fired a few stray shots at me as I was drifting down, so I thought they were Germans."

"That must have made you a bit nervous," said Gerry.

"Boy, was I! I was never so scared in all my life. Remember the armband they issued us, with the American flag on it?"

"Yeah, it had "Ya Amerikanits" printed on it."

"Well, that convinced the Russians that I was on their side, and they piled me into a horse-drawn wagon smelling of manure and hauled me to their headquarters. After interrogating me, they took me to what was left of a bombed-out hotel, and there was Chet, Eddie and Joe. Wow! Were we glad to see each other! The Russians brought bread, sausage and vodka, and I tell you, we had one hell of a party.

"I don't think I'm a fatalist, exactly," Gerry went on, "but it sure looks like the cards dictate the who, when and what."

"How'd you get out of there?"

"Well, the next day they hauled us in a truck to some airfield where a U.S. Air Force plane was waiting to fly us back to Cerignola."

Chapter 15

It was 0400 and Burt's company was in the mess hall eating shell eggs and bacon and flushing it down with great mugs of GI coffee. The company was fed fresh eggs when they were scheduled to fly a combat mission, a welcomed change from powdered eggs.

After they finished eating, the men tumbled out into the raw British night and climbed into the black hole of a ten-wheeler. The driver bumped them across the darkness, following the tiny slits of his blackout lights, and dumped them off at Operations. The light hurt their eyes as they pushed past the blackout curtain and into the ready room.

It was warm inside, warm from the body heat of many men in various stages of dress and undress. Animal smells irritated the men's nostrils. They were like cattle milling around at an auction.

Dressing for a mission was a ritual. First the Long Johns, then the olive drab uniform, (flying togs didn't look military, so unless they were wearing a uniform underneath, the enemy could shoot the men for spies if they had to bail out behind their lines), then nylon coveralls embroidered with wire to keep them warm electrically. Felt booties were snapped to the cuffs and leather gloves pulled over silk gloves to complete the electrical circuit. The silk was to protect the hands if it was necessary to remove the heated leather gloves to attend to a jammed gun. A lump of bare flesh would stick to cold steel at forty below zero.

They called Burt Pappy because at twenty-eight he was the oldest one on the crew. He plugged into a test receptacle to see if his suit would really keep him warm. Satisfied, he covered all with fleece-lined leather pants & jacket, lined boots, leather helmet, and parachute harness. Completely decked out in ceremonial regalia, and after picking up the headsets for the crew, now he got the urge for a bowel movement. Stepping out into the dark mist, he felt his way to a cold privy and commenced to peel off like an onion. Afterwards, he ambled out to the hard stand where the big bird sat. The rest of the crew were lying under her great wings like the rood of a mother hen, hoping that they could catch just a few more winks of sleep. Zeke stood by quietly. He was always on hand to send the crews off and wish them luck. He would be there again to count the aircraft as the formation appeared over the control tower on its return.

He was a tall mountain man from Tennessee, one of those "southern highlanders" Kephart sometimes spoke of. Once Zeke built a still and hid it deep in a rhododendron patch on the west side of the Smoky Mountains. It was a beautiful piece of work. When once he put his hands into a project, he stuffed his mind and heart in with it too. As a mechanic, he was an artist. When Uncle Sam tapped him on the shoulder, he joined the Air Force. He left his high-crown black fedora at home, and regulations made him wear shoes. His overalls, well marinated in oil, seemed to be the only connection between his hands and feet and his basketball head. He looked like a life-sized manikin. He seemed to sparkle in the sun and glisten in the rain, like a knight in stainless steel. Red, who seldom had much to say, once remarked, "God, if Zeke fell down he'd be halfway home."

Naked In A Coat of Armor

"Yeah," laughed Marty, "he sure is a long drink of water."

"She's in fahn shape, sah." Zeke would report, saluting the pilot and scratching his scalp by holding the peak of his hat in place while rotating his head. It reminded one of a pitcher twisting the ball in his glove. Then he would spit a chaw and follow the brown stream with his eyes as though he had aimed at a specific object. Wiping his mouth with his greasy sleeve, he would look around to see if we noticed that he was, indeed, on target. Then he would add, positively, in that smoky drawl of his, "Ah shit yo not, sah." That was Zeke's way of emphasizing the truth and nothing but, so help him.

Burt had a feeling Zeke loved the 'Monster' more than he did her crew. It would break him in two if they didn't bring her safely back to him. Tech Sgt. Zeke Milsap, the crew chief, was the best mechanic in the Eighth Air Force.

A signal flare exploded over the control tower. Someone yelled, "Green!" The mission would go. The crew cursed because they were briefed for "Big B." Berlin worried them. Four hundred anti-aircraft guns surrounding the city could throw up more flak than they did at Schweinfurt or at the submarine pens in Kiel. The operations officer had unveiled the map on the wall, and a groan rippled across the audience. On it, a red ribbon traced the route to the target. Some were tempted to go on sick call.

If the flare had been red, that would have meant the mission was scrubbed. Then the men would have had mixed feelings, glad they didn't have to go but bitching because all the preparations would have been a dry run. Then they would make a mad dash back to the mess hall, and if they managed to get back before the mess Sergeant was notified that the mission was cancelled, they might be lucky enough to yet a second helping of "combat eggs."

But the signal showed Green and the engines began to protest with their piercing whine. One, Four, Two, Three. Four silver disks where the idle propellers were, now showed they had revved up to speed. The lumbering bombers moved slowly into the fog, like prehistoric bulls, snorting their reluctance to go. Soon the planes were milling around in the mist over Great Yarmouth, trying to get into some sort of formation; this could be frightening. It was a time when pilot skill was really tested. Col. Drobar, in his P-47, broke through the overcast and began to herd the others like a busy sheep dog.

"Tighten it up," he screamed over the air.

"Squeeze in there, goddamit, close it in."

They knew the importance of a tight formation. Then there would be less chance of a bandit cutting one of the bombers out for individual attention. But sensing a four-engine bomber off your wing in the fog makes for tightening buttocks and bulging eyes. Finally, "Tail End Charley" caught up and they formed into a long "V," like twenty migrating prehistoric birds, and took up an Easterly heading for Berlin. Fifteen thousand feet over the North Sea, the gunners fired off a few rounds to test their machines.

"Co-pilot to crew," Dan's voice suddenly crackled over the intercom. "Oxygen check."

"Top turret OK."

"Radio OK."

"Right waist OK."
"Left waist OK."
"Tail OK."
"Nose OK."
"Navigator, sound off." No answer.
"Will, go see if Jim is okay."
"Roger."

Will climbed down and worked his way past the front wheel well to get to the navigator's compartment. He found Jim sitting on the floor, leaning up against the bulkhead. He had a silly grin on his face and looked as though he didn't care if school kept or not. Oxygen starvation puts people into a lethargic state, something like a cheap drunk, and the victim is unaware of the seriousness. Will gave Jim a quick shot of pure oxygen. Jim came out of it instantly, and wondered what Will was doing in there by the chart table.

"Co-pilot to Navigator, you all right, Jim?"

"Yeah, Dan. I guess Will saved my ass."

McNealy, suspended out over the water in the nose turret, felt drowsy in the warm sunshine. His thoughts drifted to home. "Man," he said into the intercom, "if I get out of here alive and get back to the good ol' U.S. of A., I'm going to lay on the beach in Galveston, and drink sof' wine and screw sof' women."

Martyr answered, "Someday, I'd like to collect me an acre of tits and dance on them in my bare feet."

"Cut out the shit," the pilot cut in. "We're on radio silence now."

They made landfall along the coast of Holland somewhere. Then, moving into Germany, they avoided Osnabruck. Magdebury would be coming up soon. Those were major industrial cities well fortified with anti aircraft guns. Over rural areas, Red noticed that fields were plowed in peculiar patterns and then realized the plowing was done by tanks during a recent ferocious contest. Slit trenches came into view and appeared like split-rail fences zigzagging across a Virginia landscape.

As they approached Magdaburg, about eighty miles west of Berlin, they received orders to change course, southeasterly to Dresden.

The air was clear over the target, and they were moving up to the "IF," the initial point of the bomb run. Then it started: first one click, then another, followed by click...click...click...click. The crew was fingering their mike switches. The intercom nerve system bound them together. It afforded a confidence, a feeling that each one would survive.

The rhythm of the clicking increased with the pulse of the men as they neared the place where all hell would spill over. McNealy soon broke radio silence with his "Bombs away" announcement. Between the US Air Force and the RAF, successive waves of heavy bombers set one of Europe's loveliest cultural cities ablaze, killed some thirty-to-sixty-thousand people, and smashed a lot of fine china. The Germans retained some American prisoners in an abandoned slaughterhouse within the target area, but slaughterhouse five was somehow spared.

That was a raid for spite in retaliation for Germany's spite bombings of Coventry, England. Burt had relatives in both countries. People often had their shopping interrupted when whole shops were blown

Naked In A Coat of Armor

away from under them. They, too, knew all about air raids.

Burt's Grandmother lived in Southend-on-Sea, situated on the mouth of the Thames. Enemy navigators used the town as a checkpoint on their way to London. Housewives would come running out of their kitchens, wiping their hands on their aprons, to watch a dogfight overhead. They would cheer when one fighter dove to the ground in flames and, if the other did a victory roll for them, they knew their side had won.

One sunny afternoon while Burt was visiting his grandmother, the air-raid siren let go and they all made a dash into the garden. But Granny beat them to it; she wasn't going to miss the show. Two Messersmits and three Hurricanes, engaged in serious business, marred the unblemished sky with their deadly acrobatics. Spent brass rained down on the group like hailstones. They saw a long black streak of smoke as one of the fighters dived to earth and burst into flames across the street in South Church Park. Burt ran to the smoldering wreck and saw that the explosion blew the pilot clear.

The body lay spread-eagle with arms and legs flung outwards, creating an impression in the soft soil. For an instant a thought crossed Burt's mind, remembering how as kids they'd fall backwards into soft snow and sweep their limbs outward to create angel impressions. The clothing of the flyer was burned off his back from head to heel. Burt rolled him over to see the left side was scorched and all that remained of the fruit salad were the bare wires that held the colored ribbons together. In the place where the face had been, there was only a black cavity. As he stood wondering, *What is this madness about?* an uncanny feeling seeped into him and a familiar face seemed to appear to fill the void. At his throat, the flyer wore the Knights Cross with clusters, the highest honor for an ace in the Luftwaffe. The nametag over his right breast read, Major Hans Schnyder.

Burt felt confused, but then he'd come a long way through a lot of confusion. *Mustn't try to dope out this lunacy*, he thought, shaking his head; *it could get me a section eight.*

Dan complained over the intercom, "Can't close the bomb bay doors. Pappy, see if you can work them with the hand pump."

Burt climbed back down into the well and flipped the lever of the hydraulic pump a couple of times. The doors would travel about a foot, then fetch up.

"If we don't get those goddamn doors shut, the formation will leave us behind," Marve said to no one in particular.

Burt walked out onto the catwalk a bit and spotted a fifty-caliber casing caught in the door track. He disconnected his oxygen supply and the lines that connected him to the intercom and made his way back to where he could get at the problem. He hooked an arm around a strut and leaned out over Stuttgart and yanked the brass out. He worked his way back to the radio corner but by then was feeling pretty lightheaded. He managed to plug into his oxygen supply and turn the knob of the regulator for a full blast. The shot revived him and he called to Dan, "Try it now."

Naked In A Coat of Armor

"Beautiful," he said, as the doors closed like a roll-top desk.

"You know, Pappy, you shouldn't stay off oxygen so long."

"Yeah," Burt answered. "Besides, I could have been sucked out for a nosedive into the Fatherland. Imagine the explaining I'd have to do, to both sides, after parachuting into a town I went to school in."

Puffs of flak began to appear. It made the sky look as if an artist flicked a brushful of black paint onto a blue canvas. Suddenly the bomber off their left wing seemed to come apart, in slow motion, as a gift package does when a child tears the wrapping off and spills the contents on the floor. Pieces of wings and fuselage, mingled with parts of bodies, pinwheeled across the sky like spent fireworks celebrating some grisly hit. Wilson looked out the port window and his buttocks clamped together.

One parachute blossomed like a toadstool after a summer shower. "Good," he said. "At least one guy made it." But the billowing silk caught fire, ignited by burning debris. Will's face showed the terror, rage and the frustration that must have been tearing through the parachutist's mind. Well, you don't go till your number's up. But what about the pain and anguish that rips the heart of the one that gets the routine War Department notice, "Missing in Action" or "Posthumously Awarded"?

An explosion rocked the men a bit and, at about the same time, Forester announced that number two engine was on fire and streaking a trail of oil and smoke. Burt missed a lot of the chatter on the intercom. He had to monitor the radio. The pilot, a calm kid from

Massachusetts with a lot of discipline for a nineteen-year-old, managed to put the fire out and feathered the prop.

Dan was a bit more shaken up than Marv and looked as though he was trying to strangle the control column. The co-pilot would rather be winning the war in the local pubs.

"All positions, check in on damage," Marv ordered the crew.

"There're some cables sagging down over my gun," Red said without a trace of emotion. The waist-gunner was a nice, easy-going kid from South Dakota.

"Go see what that's all about, Will." Marv knew it must be something, for Red to report; he'd once said Red wouldn't say pooh if he had a mouthful of shit. The engineer hiked through the bomb bay to the waist and reported that a couple of cables to the trim tabs were cut.

"Yeah," Marv complained. "This bitch is flying like a tractor-trailer."

They lagged behind a bit but managed to keep up. It was quiet for awhile. Burt looked out across the formation serenely suspended in the cold blue sky. How could it be possible that they'd unloaded tons of death and destruction just a few minutes earlier, or was it a year ago? It was hard to believe that three aircraft were missing from the group.

The view to the outside was clear, though distorted, as if one was seeing through a tumbler of water. Black specks, with the sun bouncing off them, came toward them like fireflies cavorting on a summer's eve. They came closer and went into their graceful aerial acrobatics. Burt and the others watched as if the specks were clowns showing off in the center ring. Burt mused that it wasn't their turn, yet, to be convinced that the enemy were not clowning but intent on blasting them out of the sky. The tranquil scene appeared like something etched in glass rather than anything animated and deadly.

Marty, the tail gunner, and Plack, the nosegunner, were buddies, though different as salt and pepper. If they were looking for one, the other was sure to be with him. Heads and Tails, the others called them.

Mack, a Texas boy, worked as a ranch hand for his father, who owned some fifteen-hundred head of cattle. He was sure of himself and had all the answers. Marty was a little more easy-going; he'd "yes" everybody to death. He seldom got mad about anything. Once, though, he burst into the barracks after a training mission hopping mad. "The next time you clowns piss out of the chaff chute," he warned, "I'm going to kick your teeth in." When the crew heard that, they went into hysterics. The chute was used to throw out shredded aluminum foil in an effort to louse up enemy radar. If it was used for relieving bladders, the urine had a tendency to follow the contour of the fuselage and would work its way into the tail turret.

"Too bad it wasn't maiden pee," Forester hollered across the room. "They say it's great for growing hair."

Marty's folks owned several acres of wheat in the Judith Basin in Montana. They operated huge combines with a spread almost as wide as the wingspan of a B-24. Marty was an only son and was looking forward to getting back home to run the family business.

Suddenly Ekland called out, "Three o'clock, coming in at three o'clock." Phom phom phom... phom phom. Every time the top turret gunner swung around, he nudged Burt's shoulder with his toe, and Burt knew that Ekland was keeping busy. He was a young fellow from California. Burt saw him admiring his hands when he'd finished cleaning his guns after a mission and asked, "Did you hurt yourself?" He looked at Burt as though he wanted to cry. "I worry about my hands. I wanted to be a surgeon. Got credit for two years of pre-med, so they gave me a job as gunner on a bomber. You figure it out."

"Don't try," Burt said, wishing he could come up with a better answer.

Someone hollered, "Marty! Lookout! He's on our ass. Fire, Marty...for Chrissake, fire!" The tailgunner never squeezed off a round, nor would he ever again.

Funny, isn't it, Burt thought, *it doesn't make much difference who is enjoying the performance at the Semper Opera House of Dresden or who is basking in the warmth of the sun streaming into the tail turret of a bomber. We are at once friend and foe. The god of war presides on both sides.*

Wilson had to pee and did it in his helmet. He set it to one side, where it promptly froze. The plane cane out of a tight turn and they bucked for home. The clowns followed them for a while, then peeled off to refuel. They let down over France and, in the lower altitude, the urine began to thaw. Wilson figured this was a good time to dump it overboard and cracked the bomb bay doors open just enough to let it go. But the back draft picked it up and the surprised Wilson got a faceful of slush. The men didn't let him live that one

Naked In A Coat of Armor

down for a while. The Channel, like a silver snake, stretched below them. They tapped off a request over the air for a weather report. Burt looked out over the formation and saw that the golden rays of the late sun appeared as fingers strumming the silver strings of vapor trails dancing along the trailing edge of the wings. After a few minutes, they were over England and on their approach leg. Marv stood the monster B-24 up on one wing and slid into a Rackheath peel off to get them on the ground in a hurry. Once an enemy fighter followed the formation home and dropped a bomb on each end of the runway. That made for some quick shittin' 'n agittin' by those not on the ground yet.

Somehow they were not the cocksure wiseguys after that trip. They piled out and draped themselves onto a Jeep. On their way to Base Operations, the ambulance flashed by. "There goes the meat wagon," Mack mumbled, "Going to pick up Marty."

They slumped down at a table, after an eight-hour Cook's tour of Germany. The smell of the rubber oxygen mask was still in their nostrils, and they were beat. The interrogation officer motioned toward the traditional bottle of Scotch and told the men to help themselves. Burt poured a large dollop into a paper cup and drew a long, long slug of the scarce liquid and let it burn his throat. Marty usually pushed his share to; he didn't like the stuff. Somehow, today Burt couldn't bring himself to drink to Marty.

"Rough trip, men?" asked the kid that was the interrogation officer. "How many were there?"

"About four, maybe six."

"What kind were they?"

"Oh, for Christ sake," Burt snarled. "What kind were they? They were the kind that shoot at people."

"What's your name, sergeant?"

"Ernst Eichwald. Sir."

"Look sergeant," said the kid, in a menacing tone, "We want to know, understand?"

"Then ask someone else. Ask Marty. Maybe we weren't there."

"Listen to me, men. The Krauts have come out with a new fighter plane with a propless engine. ME-262 jet, they call it, so keep your eyes open and look for it on your next trip. It's a real fast sucker, and we want to know more about it."

Forester grabbed the half-empty bottle and they filed out of the building and walked to their Nissen hut.

"Who the hell ever heard of an airplane without a propeller?" Even though Wilson was a good mechanic and up on aircraft development, he had to mull that one around for a while.

The men were glad to find that the off-duty crew had kept the stove stoked. The tiny heater glowed red, trying to keep so much space warm. They dropped onto their sacks, grateful that they were one more mission closer to stateside.

Ekland burst in, his nose red and running. He breathed into his hands for a little warmth before moving toward the stove. "Got the aerial photos up on the bullboard already," he said. "Looks like we hit them on the nose again–the best record for accuracy in the Eighth Air Force."

"Cheese, makes ya proud of the outfit, donnit? Makes ya proud to be an American." Wilson glowed.

Naked In A Coat of Armor

"Oh, for Chrissake, knock it off, Willie; how corny can you get?" Mack groaned, feeling more embarrassed than disgusted. "All we did was deliver some freight to the Krauts, period."

Delivering a lethal load from high altitude is detached, impersonal combat. It's not like the infantryman, who sees a man fall after he aims his rifle. Or the Commando who feels the warm blood trickle over his fingers after he's cut a throat in hand-to-hand combat. Bombers weren't sent out to kill people. Their targets were marshalling yards, factories, airfields, oil storage dumps and the like. They simply delivered a cargo.

Maybe during quiet time the thought would creep to mind that people were indeed hurt. "This is London," Edward R. Murrow would announce over the radio and jar them into realization with details and statistics. Churchill expressed apprehension over bombing so many French railway centers, in view of the fact that scores of thousands of French civilians–men, women and children–would lose their lives. Considering they were our friends, this might be held to be an act of very great severity, bringing much hatred on the Allied Air Forces.

Burt was stretched out on his bunk, his hands behind his head, staring up at the curved corrugated ceiling. Thinking seemed to come easier from up there. He rolled over and propped himself up on one elbow. "Listen, all you guys. Don't be proud of being an American or a German or a Jew or Black or White. And don't you ever be ashamed of it either, 'cause you had absolutely nothing to do with it. Just make damn sure you can always be proud of being a man."

"Amen," growled Mack. "All ya need to know about the other guy is, is he prick or prince. Now will you guys shut the fuck up so I call get some sleep?" His voice was muffled because he always slept with his big nose buried in the covers.

The CQ came in without knocking. "You jokers are up for a practice mission at oh-five hundred; sleep tight," he said with an exaggerated grin on his face. A shoe hit the door as he slammed it behind him.

"Here we go again," grumbled Ekland. "Colonel Scharp's School of Aeronautics; that's us. We ain't never going to get our asses back home, flyin' dem damn practice missions."

"Listen, cry-baby," Wilson instructed. "Every time you're up on a practice mission, the real thing is taking off somewhere else, see? It's a way of screwing up Hitler's radar and Goering's clowns. And, anyway, the crying towels are all in the laundry—so cheer up, Sad Sack."

"La de da," hollered Forester. "Enough of this bullshit."

Forester was a loner. After he pulled one tour of duty overseas, he volunteered to do another twenty-five missions. Some thought him to be a patriot, a hero, but there were those of us who figured his gears didn't mesh.

Jim Forester wasn't for God and country, nor had he lost his marbles. He was a compulsive gambler. He volunteered so as to get in on the high stakes over there. He didn't care if school kept or not, so long as there was a poker game or a hot crap game going on somewhere.

Chapter 16

The Germans were on a steady retreat and had vacated Frankfurt the week before. Some Brass were scheduled to go on an inspection tour of the city. Marv and his crew were selected to fly them to the continent. It was a rare opportunity for Air Force Personnel to see bombing results first hand.

They slid into the field just outside of the city and overshot the runway a little bit and nearly tore down the chain-link perimeter. No one had any remarks, so maybe no one was watching. Trucks transported them along a good highway through pleasant countryside. Old men and buxom women were working prosperous-looking farms. The peaceful landscape belied the terrible conflict that raged there just a few days earlier.

The men would have felt like carefree tourists, if they hadn't been armed and wearing steel helmets. Allied vehicles traveling in every direction were proof that something exciting had taken place.

As they approached Frankfurt, the roads were clogged for miles with refugees leaving the city, their belongings hurriedly piled into carts, wagons and onto bicycles. Convoys of raunchy-looking prisoners of the Imperial Riech were being transported west from the front lines: elderly men and boys grown old in ragged uniforms. They were cold, sick, and hungry, no longer resembling the master race. Even so, some looked proud and defiant, and others were relieved that it was all over for them.

As they entered the once beautiful city, they saw an appalling site. The silence draped over it was uncanny.

The feeling was like seeing a shroud and knowing that it covered a cadaver. Something happened here.

The first building to come into view was the once-magnificent railroad station. The front entrance was blown out, the glass roof and sides were shattered. There were whole trains thrown in a heap, like toys by a bored child. The annealed girders of the ornate building looked serpentine, like cobras weaving to and fro. Whole blocks of brick and stone and debris were piled upwards from the curb. Bathtubs, radiators, pipes and cables were strewn on top. There didn't seen to be a l living thing anywhere. Burt felt like an intruder in a morgue.

An armored tank appeared. The links of its ponderous tracks' rattling and squeaking seemed too loud as it rudely bore into the quiet and moved down to patrol the main street. A lone woman looked forlorn as she stood at the intersection, confused and unsure whether to cross the Kaiser Strasse. Her long black hair and masculine overcoat made her appear taller than she really was. Her face, very beautiful, very pale, was too old for her age. Burt wondered what the past had done to her and what the future had in store for her.

On another offbeat assignment, Burt's crew flew to Belgium to haul gasoline back from a fighter base that was being recalled. They installed a neoprene bag in the Monster's bomb bay for the project. It wasn't routine, and they worried about it. Any deviation from the conventional had the men sitting up and taking particular notice. After all, this kind of flying didn't count, and they had only a couple of missions to go to get back to the good old U.S. of A.

Naked In A Coat of Armor

They had fun, though, wandering around Antwerp. They found a bakery that had some real baguettes and at a bar they had some drinks. In a mood, Marv and Jim kicked their high-school French around a bit, though it didn't impress the proprietor much. He sold them each a bottle of the "finest cognac."

Later, they posed to have their pictures taken in front of the Monster, proudly displaying their contraband. Burt wrote Lora to say that he would not open the bottle until their anniversary, their first. Come May 12th, he wandered off by himself and opened the bottle very ceremoniously, wishing his love was there to celebrate with him. He raised the bottle in a toast to a happy future, only to find that this "finest cognac" was nothing but a cheap cherry-flavored soda.

They were sent on a mission to deliver a special cargo of a new type of incendiary bombs, to flush out a pocket of Germans holed up in Royan, near Bordaux, France. Napalm, it was called, a mixture of polystyrene, benzene and gasoline that made a hot jelly. The containers looked more like depth charges than bombs, something different, and again they were nervous.

On another occasion they carried a top-secret load—two enormous bombs slung one on each side of the catwalk—which took up the full length of the bomb bay. It was frightening sight to foggy heads in the early morning darkness. Blockbusters of some sort, they thought. Burt lay his hand on the casing to steady himself as he climbed aboard. "That's peculiar," he thought; it feels like cardboard. The mysterious load turned out to be nothing more than propaganda leaflets.

Later, over Germany, Burt watched the sky become littered with paper, like some tickertape parade. Guess we're telling Jerry to knock it off, he thought.

That was their last business trip. He wondered if there would be tickertape when they got home.

The Germans quit on May 8th, 1945, VE Day; that meant their job was done in the E.T.O. They were confined to the base, on this victory day in Europe, for fear that they would tangle with their allies in the frenzy of celebration. They had their own celebration with beer and sandwiches on the base.

In the early days after the armistice, they had flying assignments known as "Trolley Missions." They flew ground personnel over the continent at low altitudes to show them the results of the part they, too, played in the recent ugly fracas. Some infantrymen with minor disabilities were brought to air bases to recuperate. "Any chance to get a ride with you guys sometime?" one fellow asked.

"Sure," Burt told him. "The next time we go on a trolley mission, we'll take you along." But when the time came, he backed off.

"I don't think I ought to push my luck," he said, embarrassed. Burt knew how he felt after all that he had been through.

Burt couldn't imagine himself changing places with a foot soldier for a day, even in peacetime.

The navigator did a great job as tour guide. He would point out places of interest and points of significance, where great armored battles were fought–places where front lines jockeyed back and forth in desperate struggles to gain ground. They circled Cologne and saw the famous cathedral standing

Naked In A Coat of Armor

tall and undamaged, though surrounded by rubble–a tribute to precision bombing. It was strange how explosives sometimes left the outer walls of a building standing intact while the insides were scooped out like a boiled egg from its shell.

Back when they had a couple of weeks to go to finish their training as a bomber crew, prior to being shipped out to some theater of war, Mack, the nose gunner, thought it would be great to take a mascot overseas with them. Since they were the elite, or so they liked to think, it had to be something really macho, like a lion or tiger or maybe a panther. They were hard to come by, though.

The discussion drifted to Great Danes, St Bernards and Labrador Retrievers–ridiculous, and against regulations. Burt got in touch with Louie Lindborg, his stepfather, and asked him to see if he could get them a Toy Fox Terrier, preferably one with a pedigree to be sure that it would not grow into a Great Dane.

A small black and white something, the so-called best of the litter, was purchased in Washington, D.C. Louie told Burt that he stuffed the dog into his coat pocket and boarded a train for New York. When the conductor approached to collect tickets, the pup stuck his nose out and let the startled man know he didn't like being disturbed. Louie was informed that animals were not allowed on passenger trains, and the dog had to be put off at the next stop. When the train slowed for the station and the conductor came stalking down the aisle, the woman seated next to Louie whispered, "Let me have the little fellow." She took the dog and passed him to the passenger behind her, who in turn handed him onto the next person, and so on down the length of the car. This juggling so confused the conductor that he soon gave up the chase.

Their training completed, the men were ordered to report to Mitchell Air Force Base on Long Island. This was good news. It meant they would be flying to Europe instead of going by troop ship. There would be no problem with stowaways and, besides, some of them could dash home for a weekend or two, last chance before leaving the States.

Burt met the mascot, which was about the size of a softball, all charged up and raring to go. He had some doubts about taking him back to the base. It was going to take some guts to introduce him to the crew.

Friends and family went into a huddle to choose an appropriate name for the little question mark. They took it very seriously, going through all sorts of eloquent monikers out of Greek mythology and Roman gods of war and thunder. Burt had a name for him, but he didn't mention it. Lora, however, thought of the most fitting label of all.

"Frank Buck is his name," she announced. Buck was a famous adventurer who searched the world's jungles for rare animals and brought them back alive for zoos, game farms and the circus. He was known as "Frank Buck bring 'em back alive."

"What the hell is that?" bellowed Mack when Burt brought fuck into the barracks. "Don't tell me that's our mascot."

"Mascot!" sneered Marty. "'Tain't even a dog."

It took awhile, but the guys had to admit the little whelp seemed sort of special. Buck took to military life like any other rookie. He followed the men

Naked In A Coat of Armor

everywhere, attending all the training sessions, lectures and exercises. Of course his favorite was chow time.

The machos wouldn't admit it, but they all grew to love him. Each day, more and more, he grew out of that baseball shape and began to look more like a respectable miniature of the real thing. It was a delight to see him run and jump and bark and growl. The men wondered how such a small bundle could be so feisty. He'd passed basic training.

The military changed its mind and ordered the group to New Jersey. That meant they were to go overseas in one of those sardine cans they'd heard so much about. One miserable night, they were piled up on a dock waiting to board a ship. Buck was crammed into Burt's gas mask bag with the mask. USO girls served hot coffee and donuts, which eased the chill before they filed on board. The S.S. Uuraqua, of South American registry, was painted in the morbid gray of war. It loomed up out of a ghostly mist and seemed to be a part of it. Weary of bananas, it was now hauling a different cargo. Olive drab uniforms crowded the fantail.

The pup, slung in the bag, hung from his shoulder close to Burt, shared a tiny bit of warmth. There is something special between a man and his dog, something different than between a man and his horse or a man and his woman.

The cold and the damp, the dark, and the apprehension, made Burt shudder. His eyes clung to the blacked-out shoreline as they tugged further apart. "So long, old girl," One of the huddled masses called in a shaky bravado voice as they slid past the lady of the harbor, "Hope I get back to see you again."

Eugene A. Aichroth

Burt had heard about life on a troopship, but he found he had to be on one to really feel it. Hammocks were strung the full length of the hold, in tiers of three high. If the hammock above was occupied, the man underneath had to sound off if he wanted to turn, as both had to execute the maneuver together. There wasn't enough room to hide a pair of socks, let alone a dog.

Burt mentioned this to the navigator, Jim. "No problem. We'll take Buck in with us; we have a state room." That fancy accommodation was a cubbyhole for four and now was crammed with eight men. But there was a closet in which to hide a dog. Two days out to sea, the officers learned that there was to be a daily inspection of quarters. Buck couldn't stand inspections, nor did he like being shoved into a closet. When the inspecting officer heard him whine and whimper, he suggested that they get rid of whatever that was. They contacted a member of the ship's crew, who agreed to take custody of the dog. And so Buck was transferred temporarily to the Merchant Marines. They were granted visiting rights, and every day one of them would slink off to some prearranged spot and renew their acquaintance with the mascot.

On one of those visits Burt noticed that the pup was still growing. Pedigree…hell. He was no longer a miniature. To get him into England on the QT, Burt now had to stuff him into his musette bag. They managed to wade through the confusion of disembarking without being discovered and were soon settled in an Air Force base in Norwich.

The weather was typically English—miserable— and their pal became quite ill. A base employee took

Naked In A Coat of Armor

him to a veterinarian, who soon snapped him back to his old feisty self. Odd as it seems, grown men become very attached to their pets. Some believe the English think more of their dogs than they do of their children.

Buck seemed to tighten the bond among the crew. Also, he was a link to home. But he wasn't a hero to everyone. Harry disliked all animals, especially dogs, and especially small dogs. He was downright nasty to the animal and Burt suspected he'd kick him once in awhile when nobody was looking. Buck sensed his dislike, too, and every chance he got, he'd pee on Harry's bunk.

The mascot accompanied them on low-altitude training flights and on pub missions, too. He'd ride with one of them on their bikes to "The Green Man" or to the "Heart's Ease" and drink beer with anyone who was buying. Burt took him on a tour of London's Trafalgar Square, Piccadilly Circus, and all the places tourists are supposed to see—well, nearly all. Once they were thrown out of the famous Servicemen's Center at Rainbow Corner. One weekend Buck and Burt took a train to visit relatives at Southend-on-Sea.

After what seemed too long, Burt asked a fellow traveler, "How much further to South-end, sir?

"Next stop, Yank."

When the train slid into the station, Burt spilled out onto the platform in complete darkness. The blackout seemed more intense there. He stumbled along, trying to keep from crashing into a stanchion. A hand took hold of his arm. "This way, Yank." It was the old gentleman he'd spoken to on the train, the one wearing a bowler and carrying the ever-present umbrella.

"Where are you off to?"

"York Road."

The older man led Burt to the taxi stand and asked a cabby, "'Ow much to York Road?"

"Four bob."

"That's four shilling, Yank. Cheerio," said the man with the bowler. Burt climbed into the cab.

"Did that Bloke think I was going to rob you?" the driver asked.

"How should I know?"

"Bloody cheek." The cabby was indignant because, yes, he would have overcharged Burt if it weren't for the man in the bowler. The way the driver managed to weave in and out of traffic with visibility almost zero, and still find the address, was miraculous. He let Burt out onto the black sidewalk. The house was even blacker. All the windows were covered, showing not a sliver of light. Burt wondered if anyone lived on the whole block.

"Better wait till I get into the house," he told the driver.

A nine-year-old boy, Burt's cousin John, let him into a black vestibule and shut the front door before he opened the inside one and revealed the fact that there was some light in Southend-on-Sea. Burt's grandmother looked exactly like she did when he'd said good-bye to her sixteen years ago.

"Good gawd, boy, but you're thin" was the way she greeted him.

"They're keeping me pretty busy these days, Granny. Burt gave her a kiss and they shared a big sixteen-year hug.

Naked In A Coat of Armor

On one of those visits, Buck and Burt were arrested for taking pictures of the famous pier, a place Burt remembered as a kid, and now a military installation. A raunchy deputy on a dilapidated bicycle escorted Burt to the station house on High Street–the same station where Dorothea had to report every week when Walt was interned for the duration of the First World War.

The buggers kept Burt for most of the afternoon, while they developed his film and scrutinized the pictures. They did, however, return them to him. His Aunt and Grandmother, meanwhile, were frantic when he didn't show up for tea.

After finishing their tour of duty, they were ordered to fly back to the States. Their route took them from Norwich to Connecticut via Wales, the Azores and Newfoundland. Each time they landed at these bases, they would let the dog run free so that it would appear he belonged to the local field rather than to them. They were able to smuggle him back home unnoticed. While waiting to board a train at Bradley Air Force Base in Connecticut, a soldier remarked, "I see Buck got home okay."

"I wondered," another GI said, "why I kept seeing a little black-and-white dog everywhere we landed."

After their furloughs, they were sent to Sioux Falls, South Dakota. They had a two-or-three-hour layover en route, in Philadelphia, and the GI's, eager to stretch their legs, dashed off to pay respects to the city of brotherly love. Buck, of course, joined them to check out the local taverns. But soon he got the urge to wander off on his own in search of canine interests.

When the men reported back to the station, he was missing. Buck was lost. They paced up and down the train, frantically inquiring after the dog. They were a miserable lot as the engineer blew the whistle and moved out, bound for the Midwest. After arriving at their destination, Burt sent a note to the Philadelphia Bulletin, explaining that their mascot was AWOL in their city.

Soon he received a letter from a woman in charge of the Philadelphia Hospitality Center for Servicemen, telling him that Buck had been turned in at the Center and that she was making reservations to have him flown to South Dakota, compliments of United Airlines.

In the meantime, Burt received papers verifying that they had made him an honorary member of the USO, the American Legion, and the Philadelphia Chamber of Commerce. He found out that the base band was called out to serenade him upon his arrival.

But alas, Burt's crew had been sent to Great Bend, Kansas, for training in B-29s, and then to Japan. MacArthur signed the Japanese surrender on August 8, 1945, and their trip to the Orient was cancelled. Their friend finally caught up with them. They were discharged soon after, and Burt brought Buck home to Long Island.

July 11, 1957 was a pleasant day, not proper for death. But gloom chilled Buck's home because Buck died. Some said he was a Toy Fox Terrier, but it didn't really matter. What he lacked in size and pedigree he made up in companionship. Burt's children's tears dampened Buck's grave at the foot of the flagstaff in front of the house. Buck, World War II veteran, mascot of the 467th Bomb Group, Eighth Air Force, Rackheath, England. On that day, the family flag flew at half-mast.

Eugene A. Aichroth

Naked In A Coat of Armor

Gene with his daughter, Gail, opposite page, and above with the love of his life, his wife, Lillian

Eugene A. Aichroth

Part 3

"There are two things in life to aim at: first, to get what you want; and, after that, to enjoy it. Only the wisest of mankind achieves the second."

Logan Pearsall Smith

"Wonder, rather than doubt, is the root of knowledge."

Abraham Heschel

Eugene A. Aichroth

Chapter 17

Burt was discharged from the U.S Air Force at Jefferson Barracks, St. Louis, Missouri on October 4, 1945–the same place, four years after, when he enlisted in the Army Air Corps, and where he met his Lora. After visiting her folks, they left for Long Island. They had purchased a little old stucco bungalow situated on a patch of scrub oak in Bay Shore, a place that snooty folk called "Rabbit Town." No, it wasn't a little old bungalow, it was a castle, because they were newlyweds, and they were together, and this was their home. They were lucky because returning veterans found there was a severe shortage of housing. They had some money for new curtains and a fancy linen tablecloth with napkins to match for Thanksgiving dinner. On this day they would dress for dinner.

Lora wasn't yet the marvelous cook that she became, and the baked chicken may have looked a bit scrawny to a Julia Child. To Burt, however, it was the most tempting, brown, crisp bird he'd ever seen on any dinner table. She served it with stuffing and sweet potatoes and white potatoes; also cauliflower and gravy–and even pumpkin pie. Burt struggled with the first bottle of wine he ever tried to uncork. There were flowers...wild ones, and even a candle in a rickety holder. They were kids. God, Burt thought, what wealth; how right the world is, now that the fighting is finished and there will never be another war.

Many happy hours were spent remodeling the interior of their home and re-landscaping the exterior.

Lora and Burt spent exciting days drawing up plans, discussing structural changes, colors and furnishings. They planned rock gardens, rose gardens and vegetable gardens. Something else they planned on was children. They wanted a boy and a girl. Burt wanted the boy to be born first, even if they were twins. Why? He didn't know why. Probably some subconscious macho brainwashing instilled in him somewhere along the way. But it wasn't to be, not then, anyway. The doctor told them that they were both healthy specimens and to be patient. After two years of being patient and doing what comes naturally, they contacted an adoption agency. But negotiations were cut short a week later when they found out that Lora was pregnant. Hallelujah!

Their son, John, was born March 28, 1948. The card accompanying the flowers read, "Sweetheart, the gods have blessed us on this Easter morning." They were to be blessed again when their daughter, Susanne, was born Oct. 14, 1949. A typical American family, someone commented. They were very happy. Burt had found work with the local utility company and embarked on a new career.

Time moved them through the coming years, with sadness and joy, tears and laughter. Through kindergarten, the grades, and on to high school. Into sports and music, Girl Scouts and Boy Scouts. When John was in high school, he and Burt planned on hiking the Appalachian Trail in the White Mountains National Forest of New Hampshire. They made a fuss about assembling their gear and making plans until late

Naked In A Coat of Armor

at night. Each day the excitement of adventure grew as they came closer to the date of departure.

One evening after work, Burt found John on the couch taking a nap. "Hi son, what's up? Let's go."

"I'm tired, Dad."

"Tired, from what?"

"I walked home from school."

"Big deal. If you have trouble walking four miles how are you going to manage five days of hiking in the mountains?"

"I'll do all right," he mumbled. He seemed sure of himself.

The next morning at the breakfast table Burt noticed that the boy's carotid pulse was pounding out the side of his neck. He and Lora took him straight to the doctor, who told them they had a very sick boy. Arrangements were made to have him admitted to St. Francis Hospital.

Time moved again, but horribly slow for ten days. At five in the morning, the phone exploded, and a foreign voice with an urgent message, commanded, "Come quickleee, Johneee vereee seeek."

It was snowing that morning, not hard, just big feathery lakes, gently drifting down into a somber hush, like snow will do sometimes, in the early hours, before a spiteful wind whips it into a blizzard. The flakes were so big you'd expect them to make some sound, but they didn't. They reflected the lights from the buildings around the courtyard and sparked and flickered as though some signalman was flashing an urgent message by code. It was one of those gray mornings that put the damper on all the world.

Lora and Burt sat in the chill of the waiting room. The wait seemed like hours...days. Burt got up and stepped out into the weather to have a cigarette and stood at the foot of a stone image, the patron saint of the hospital.

It was still snowing, leaving a white yarmulke and shawl on the statue. Looking up into the passive face, he pleaded, "Let there be a happy ending to this ugly time, and I will do whatever you command. I'll say whatever you want me to say. I'll go to wherever you send me; I will learn whatever it is that you teach." He wasn't praying. He was begging. Forgetting to light the cigarette clamped between his fingers, he went back in, to Lora. A nun presently ushered them into the surgeon's office. They'd been there before, and again Burt admired the richness of the solid wood paneling in the room; the elegance seemed to make the certificates and diplomas on the walls the more impressive. Strange that he should be preoccupied with this interior décor, he reflected. Perhaps he was stalling for time, time to run far away from this place, so far that he could not hear the terrible news that their son had died. Myocarditis, the doctor called it and requested permission to perform an autopsy. So much for begging from St. Francis.

They drove home, Lora and he, unable to exchange a single word, each of them sharing their grief and yet grieving alone. Sorrow is a very private, very selfish emotion, jealously guarded, not to be shared with everyone. Still, he wanted to climb to the rooftops and scream out his anguish for all to hear. When they arrived, they sat together and held each other tight, as if the only thing left in the world was each other. Then the dawn seemed to turn a bit lighter, through the tears, and it occurred to them that they were neglecting their daughter, who also needed comforting, and they included her in their desperate embrace.

On the table nearby, Burt noticed the little heartshaped porcelain dish filled with chocolates. The card with it read, "Happy Valentines Day, Mom and Dad, loving you, from Susanne and John." The boy's wrinkled signature, like an erratic cardiogram, recorded how very sick he was. Oh, how Burt envied the Orthodox, the Jews, the Catholics, the bible punchers. They harbored such an unshakable faith in their belief, in their Priests, Rabbis, and Ministers, in their churches, synagogues, and mosques. They had got it made, they were covered; they enjoyed a peace that he couldn't feel.

A man must hide to shed his tears. It was Burt's barber who offered fellow feelings as he sat in his chair while he groomed him for the funeral. Dominick was awkward and embarrassed, as men are with such things, but his compassion was no less genuine.

"My gooda friend," he whispered, "I donn'a know what to say. I'm-a pray for you in my church."

There were a lot of people in the room at the funeral home, little groups giggling and chattering like sparrows about their particular interests. There were people in the hall and men in the lounge at the other end, talking shop and telling jokes. The room was decorated, the mood jovial though austere.

A register, ornamented in fancy calligraphy, was positioned appropriately for visitors to prove that they had attended this occasion. An unusual clock sat on the mantle in the lounge, its face numbered counterclockwise, reflecting someone's wishful thinking.

Burt and Lora, on the receiving line, felt frightened, confused and angry. What had they done to warrant such ruthless discipline? This mixture of human emotions left them detached and numb. They held each other's hands tight, needing support through this ugly fog. Faces stepped before us and mumbled uneasy condolences, embarrassed for the want of knowing what to say.

Men and women, old and young, Boy Scouts and school chums appeared and disappeared. What could they say?

"It's God's will," a kindly old lady said.

"God needs him," said a gentleman.

"We must not question the good Lord," admonished a clergyman.

"Time," said a friend, "will heal your sorrow."

"Sorry," murmured a young girl, self-consciously.

A sixteen-year-old boy told them, "He was my best friend."

Who are these people who intrude? Burt thought. *Why are we compelled to share our sorrow? Is this not a time for solitude? And is it possible that their God would "will" to snatch a child from our family? Do they really believe that their God can "need" this child more than his father or the mother who cared for him, or the sister who loved him so? If it's true that this Lord is responsible for everything, why cannot he be questioned?*

"Time," they said, "will heal your sorrow." But no one told them how much time.

Naked In A Coat of Armor

Is this the reason they decorate the parlor and the mood is made to seem carefree and jovial? Burt asked himself. *Are we not whistling in the dark, as though we are afraid to accept the end? We're awkward in the presence of another's grief, especially when we are faced with it suddenly.*

He was grateful to all the good friends and relatives and the strangers, too, who meant well and thought they had to say something. Still, a visit to the funeral parlor was a visit too late.

Chapter 18

Cappy came walking across the lawn with that seaman's roll of his, a six-pack under his arm and carrying a bag of clams. Freddy nudged Burt. "Look," he said, "two years before the mast, you'd think the deck was heaving under him."

"Happy birthday, old timer, how does it feel, you old goat?" called Cappy as he began to lay the clams carefully on the Bar-B-Q.

"Don't give me that old timer bit; I'm only sixty. You should live so long. Anyway, I'm content to have come all this way, having done every thing wrong."

"What do you mean, done everything wrong?" Cappy asked.

"Well, if you take any stock in what the electronic dictator tells us every day, we've done everything wrong. We've eaten the wrong food. We've drunk the wrong stuff. We haven't exercised enough or else we've exercised too much. It blares at us everyday telling us we've voted for the wrong people, visited the wrong places; you should have done this instead of that, or that instead of this."

"Yeah, I suppose that's right." Cappy was quiet for a minute. Then he said, "Tell me, Burt, did anything ever happen in your lifetime to influence you? I mean, that sort of left a mark on you, really nicked you?"

"Listen, Cappy, everything in life leaves a mark on you, brands you, influences you. I think we end up as the product, or the sum total of all the people that

Naked In A Coat of Armor

touch our lives. The things that have happened affected us either consciously or subconsciously.

Burt took a long pull of his drink, settled back into his chair, and looked at Cappy. "You know, I was born in England, around the time when men had doped out a new way to clobber their fellow men. World War I had just begun its second year. The Germans flew over London and dropped things that tore down buildings and blew up people and babies. A newborn doesn't understand what's going on, but he must feel the concussions and hear the noise and see the panic. And he probably figures that's the way it is in this new place and rolls over and goes to sleep. But when his mother snatches him up out of his sleep and races in a panic to an air-raid shelter, all he feels is that something is happening to him that he doesn't like, and he starts to bawl. He doesn't know that maybe his psyche has been branded or nicked."

"I haven't given it that much thought, but I bet the shrinks could make a big deal out of that," Cappy chimed in.

"Now we know why he acts kinda wacky sometimes," laughed Freddy. "Shell shocked before he was born."

"Well, Cappy asked," Burt said, "so I'm telling him like it is. No...wait, I'll take that back. I'm telling him like I *think* it is. All I know is what someone told me. Help yourself to another beer.

"Yeah," Freddy said, "It's a long time between drinks around here."

"Anyway," Burt continued, ignoring his buddy's dig. "First thing you know, you're fourteen. That's the time for your confirmation, or bar mitzva, when some priest or rabbi or minister tells you you're a man now and you can start forgetting all that kid stuff. Time to undo yourself from your mother's apron strings. And the old man figures you ought to get a job. I had a paper route, the Brooklyn Daily Times. Then I got another one and delivered the Brooklyn Eagle. Each one had a ball team, and I waited to see which one was the best before I joined them. Then they threw me off the team because I was playing with some limey rules for stick ball."

Freddy laughed. "I remember I got a job in a Jewish delicatessen—dairy, they called it back then. When old man Krieger fired me and I told my Dad, he said, 'Son, don't worry about it. Don't be in a hurry to go to work. When once you start working, remember, you'll have to work for the rest of your life.' A week later he wanted to know when I was going to get another job. Pop died when I was eighteen. Don't think that wasn't a shocker...I mean, to lose the breadwinner all of a sudden."

"There we have something in common," Burt said. "I lost my Dad when I was seventeen. After awhile, I got a job, in a butcher shop, trimming bones and making chopped meat, ten hours a day, six days a week, for ten bucks. A year or so later, a union organized the shop and we got a vacation. Imagine, a week off and with pay. Billy Podlinsky and I packed up and drove all the way down to Laredo, Texas. Man, did we have a ball. But that's another story."

Cappy dropped a fresh can of beer and aimed it at Freddy when he opened it. "You don't care how you waste that stuff." Freddy wiped the suds off his face.

"Were you guys in the service?" Burt asked.

Naked In A Coat of Armor

"You know we were," Freddy retorted. "Cheez, he thinks he won the war all by himself. I was in the Marines, the first outfit to hit the beach on Guadalcanal. I was one scared kid. While I was wading ashore holding my rifle over my head, something went POW near me and knocked me ass over teacups. Funny, with all the commotion going on around me, the one thing I remember was thinking how cool it was, lying there on the sand soaking wet. After the noncom was satisfied that I was in one piece, he roared over the noise of the artillery. 'Where the hell do you think you are soldier, Miami Beach? Get your ass in gear and move out.' To move on command, I guess, comes from being brainwashed. I moved out."

"I was in the Eighth Air Force," Burt said. "Ironic, isn't it? Born in a bloody air raid and went back to participate in a couple more, only the stuff we dropped was a little more sophisticated. I'm glad I wasn't sent to the South Pacific Theater. That way I had an opportunity to get reacquainted with some of my relatives in Europe. When I got back, I went to work for a utility."

"Well," said Cappy, figuring that it was his turn to sound off. "I was in the Navy, pulled a few Atlantic convoys while you jokers were still in bootcamp. He looked at Burt. "Made two runs to Murmansk. But you fly boys wouldn't know much about that. The air was black with German fighter planes over the North Sea. It was like sailing into a hornet's nest.

"I enlisted in the reserves, a nice deal," Cappy continued. "I kept my rating and stayed in communications. Did enough flying to qualify for flight pay. But then who would have thought we'd be back in a war again a lousy five years after the one that was supposed to end all wars. We never learn, do we?"

"No, and we never will," said Freddie. "Will Durant, historian, figures that only 268 of the previous 3,449 years have been free of war, and none since Christ."

"Yeah," Burt said, "Who was it that said blessed are the peace keepers, for they shall forever have a job.

Freddie took it all in for awhile and then said, "How come every Christmas we sing something about peace on earth, good will towards men? I guess we really don't mean it."

"Give the man a drink. He needs it after that spiel," moaned Cappy. "Now we're retired and living off the fat of our efforts, except Hungry here; he's still in his butcher shop. When are you going to knock it off, Freddy?"

"Ain't much to look forward to, now that my Myrtle's gone. There isn't much sense to anything, anymore. She wanted to travel a bit, but I kept putting it off, and now it's too late."

"I know what you're saying," Burt said sympathetically. "We had the wind kicked out of us when we lost our boy. These things just don't make sense...I mean, a sixteen-year-old live-wire at the top of his class, on the wrestling team and soccer team, and suddenly in ten days he's gone."

"Yeah," Cappy said after awhile. "We've all had our lumps. Freddy knows when we lost our boy I went to pieces. We just couldn't face it. Ruthie began to blame me, and I couldn't justify the tragedy, so I started to blame her. Surely I wasn't bastard enough to deserve that. She finally l left me and took our girl with her. We ended up with a divorce, and I'm still trying to figure out what happened. It was different with you, Burt; you had a woman that stood by you. She shared the grief and was there when you needed her, dammit, if only to hold your hand. You also had a fifteen-year-old daughter who needed you. Of course, all these things nick a man, leave a mark on him or brand him or whatever."

The fellows were quiet for a time, each going over his resume'. Then, thinking out loud, Burt said, "Getting back to the idiot box and all the media, we hear how the whole world is going crazy, people are running scared. The rich are scared of the poor and the poor are scared of the rich, the blacks are scared of the whites and the whites are scared of the blacks. The Catholics are scared of the Protestants and the Protestants are scared of the Jews and the Jews are scared of everyone. And what about the relationship between men and women? That's really frightening. I wonder sometimes if that won't even end up in bloodshed. I'm quite content to be at the countdown of my life. I don't think I'd care to start out now, in this day and age."

"Women," said Cappy, "they're different."

"What was your first clue?"

"No, seriously, they share intimate things with each other. They talk about deep-down inner feelings together. Men don't trust each other like that; they have to play the macho bit. There's a lot of talk these days about male bonding. A rallying of the troops, so to speak."

"Hell, males don't bond; they just boast, brag and bullshit and play 'Can you top this? What do you think, Freddy?"

"You wanna know what I think? I think this bull session is too goddam morbid. It's like a visit to the cemetery on a rainy day. Those clams ought to be ready now. Let's eat. Don't forget, we've had some highlights in our time, too, and we've made lots of good friends."

"Don't know about lots, but I've made two real ones. You, Cappy, are one of them and Freddy the other."

"That was a pretty decent thing to say, Burt."

"Yeah, a lot of drivel." Freddy walked over and hugged Burt, and lifted him like he would lift a hind of beef off the hook.

"You old son of a bitch, you're not so bad yourself."

Burt grinned, embarrassed, and thought, *Men are shy about throwing bouquets; it isn't macho. Perhaps that's why they save them for the funeral parlor. Then it's too late, and that's a shame.*

Chapter 19

Lora had her wash hung out to soak up the morning sun. Now she decided to walk down and pay a visit to Dorothea. She banged the heavy brass knocker on the door of the big house. "Good morning dear," said Dorothea as she swung the door wide. "Come in, come in, you're just in time for tea. You'll have a cuppa, won't you? Of course you will." Of course Lora would.

Lora would never live it down if she dared to decline. No matter who knocked on Dorothea's door, they were always just in time for tea. Either she was just putting the kettle on or just taking the kettle off. The damn pot never had a chance to cool off. It was the old girl's subtle way of detaining the caller to share a bit of fresh gossip or to roast one of her other daughters-in-law.

Lora eyed the senior woman watching the kettle and wondered what spicy tidbit she was brewing to make their chitchat worthwhile.

"Now tell me, dear, to what do I owe this early morning visit?" Dorothea asked as she set out the cups and saucers.

"Well, I'm going to fly home to visit my folks, and I thought you would like to come with me and get acquainted with some of my St. Louis relatives."

"Oh what a marvelous idea. I'd love to."

"Then it's agreed. I'll arrange for the tickets and we'll be off."

The evening before the trip, Dorothea came down with one of her chronic attacks. Burt's brothers and he knew about these attacks; they were hangovers or a cunning scheme to louse up a scheduled plan. A cussed habit of hers!

"Mom isn't going with me after all," Lora said.

"What!" Burt said. "We'll see about that." He and his brother Rolph ganged up on the old girl.

"Now, look here, Mom. Stop trying your damn nonsense on us. Now get your bonnet and shawl on and get cracking."

"I'm too weak to travel," she moaned.

"It'll do you good to get away for awhile. Now get, get."

Early next morning, the boys bundled her into the car and drove the two women to the airport. Lora called to say Mom thoroughly enjoyed the flight and had great fun meeting all the relatives and friends and getting used to the slower pace of the Midwest. But soon it was time for the trip back home.

"Do you mind if I take the window seat?" Dorothea asked as they bearded the plane.

"Not at all," Lora said. "Make yourself comfortable and kick your shoes off." They were both glad to be seated and off their tired feet. They settled back to relax and enjoy the flight. A young woman sat at the windowseat across the aisle. She looked pretty in her bright red, wide-brimmed hat.

It was the next day, when a farmer and his friend took the old army surplus jeep and rode out into the fields. He wanted to show off the rich new growth of the money crop. After riding for about twenty minutes, Carl spotted something. "What's that out there?"

"What, where?"

Naked In A Coat of Armor

"Way off to the south, that red spot."

"Yeah, I see it. Let's go take a look." They got out of the rattletrap and hiked across the field, being careful not to trample the new shoots. They reached the object in a few minutes and looked at each other in disbelief.

"I'll be damned, would you believe, a woman's hat."

"How is it possible for a gal's chapeau to end up smack dab in the middle of a thousand-acre cornfield?" Carl laughed.

Abe picked the hat up gingerly as though it might be booby-trapped. The fellows walked back to the jeep in silence, straining their brains to dope that one out. Carl had a silly grin on his face.

"What's so funny?"

"Well, the way you picked that hat up reminded me of a story." Abe raised his pleading eyes to heaven, but Carl persisted. "This guy is walking along downtown and suddenly he's caught short and has to relieve himself and does so right on the sidewalk. When he spies a cop coming towards him, he quick takes his hat off and covers the evidence.

'You there, what are you up to?' demands the policeman.

'I've caught a rare bird, officer. I think it escaped from the pet shop down the street. Will you hold my hat over it while I go see if they have a cage for it?' The cop agrees, and the fellow takes off. After what seems a long while, the policeman's patience gives out and he decides to lift the hat and make a grab for whatever is under it. Quite a number of pedestrians have gathered, by now, and a roar of laughter goes up when they see the surprised look on the lawman's face."

"You and your damn stories. What I want to know is how did the hat get out here?"

"Which hat?"

"This one, damn you." Abe was getting touchy and waved the red hat in his buddy's grinning face.

"Bet I know what happened. That boy of mine probably took that gal he's paling around with for a ride on the cultivator yesterday. I'll have to talk to him."

"If we found a brassiere and a pair of panties, you'd really have something to worry about."

Abe didn't answer that one. Instead, he mumbled, "Or worse yet, maybe some guys buried a body out there. Come to think of it, did you notice all those footprints in the area?"

"Come on, Abe; those were our prints from all the milling around the millinery we did. Take hold of that wild imagination of yours and let's get out of here."

They climbed into the jeep and headed for home.

"Found a hat this afternoon," Abe announced at the dinner table.

"So what?" answered his wife, thinking, *It doesn't take much to excite him.*

"A woman's hat, a red one, out in the middle of nowhere. I mean, out there in the middle of a thousand acres of corn? I bet that gentleman son of yours had that bimbo out there with him." "Now just one minute, Abe Maddox; she's not what you think. She's a very nice, intelligent girl, so get that small, dirty brain of yours out of the gutter." He left the table and sat in his corner to sulk.

Just then Bobby came in, scaled his hat onto the rack in the hall, and walked over to give his mom a peck on the cheek.

"Your father is knocking himself out trying to figure out how a woman's hat ended up out in the south corn field."

Her son thought for a long minute. "Cheez, yeah, that is a strange one."

"Well," Carl said, gloating, "there goes another theory." He flashed a glance at his buddy and knew the timing wasn't right to needle him.

After the flight was airborne for perhaps an hour, the woman with the hat began to fidget. Lora thought she was fumbling with the ashtray but then was horrified to see she was actually manipulating the handle to the emergency exit. The door flew open, someone let out a scream, and the steward made a dive for the woman and pinned her to the floor. Her upper torso was already out of the plane. A uniform with sergeant's stripes lunged forward and grabbed her ankle and the two men managed to drag her back into the plane. Lora had braced her feet against the bulkhead and hung onto the soldier's coattail while he wrestled to close the door and secure it. Two passengers kept the would-be suicide pinned down in the aisle, while the steward said soothing wards to calm her. It was a horrible trip. The turbulence was so rough that Lora felt she was riding in a rodeo. The stifling heat in the cabin didn't help, and most of the passengers were sick.

"That door latch fascinates me," Dorothea mused as she bent over to retrieve her shoes. The remark was meant to keep things stirred up; the old lady was like that. Good God, not you too, thought Lora, terrified, not realizing that it was the shoes her mother-in-law was fumbling with. The plane made an unscheduled landing at Baltimore, and the hapless woman was escorted to a waiting ambulance.

"My hat," the woman cried as she stepped from the plane. "I've lost my hat!"

"She's goddam lucky she didn't lose her…everything," drawled the sergeant, at ease now in his seat. "You know, when her dress was flapping in the slipstream, that picture of Marilyn Monroe flashed to mind, you know, the one where she's standing over the subway grill."

Lora lost her lunch.

"How can anyone let their imagination drift so unconcerned from such a terrible situation?" Lora said.

"I don't know, comes naturally I guess. We kept her from pulling that stupid stunt, didn't we? Whadda you want? The gal's OK, ain't she?" The uniform gave a helpless shrug.

"Men!" Lora said, her voice loaded with contempt. "OK? Lucky? What are you talking about? Maybe the poor woman has taken some nasty knocks and finds she can't cope. She probably doesn't know much about luck…I mean good luck."

Aaron, one of the farm hands, came in the back door with a gust of wind, washed up, and took his place at the table. "Just heard on the radio, some woman tried to jump out of an airplane yesterday."

Carl nearly choked on a piece of pork chop. "Man, it's windy out there today."

Naked In A Coat of Armor

"Yeah hang on to yer hat." Carl had to get that last jab in.

Uncle Otto called. Could Burt install an electric outlet in the basement for him? Burt went to survey the area in question, a cellar with a low ceiling, dark and dungeon-like. Cautiously following his flashlight, Burt spotted the large face of a clock lying on a rickety workbench. Time had draped it with cobwebs. Its works, weights and chains were carelessly dumped on the bench like so much mechanical viscera spilled from a wooden cadaver. A three-foot pendulum was flung to one side like a severed limb. Its face, splattered with numbers, seemed to plead for help.

"That's no way to treat a delicate apparatus, Otto."

"Vot you vont I should do? I am a cook. Not a vatchmaker. You vent dat chunk, take it oud of here."

Burt picked the mess up and carried it tenderly in his arms. When he got it home, it was apparent that it would have to be hung high somewhere so that the long pendulum and weights could swing clear before he could do a diagnostic inspection. It then occurred to him that there must have been a cabinet to support these innards. He called Otto to inquire.

"Ja sure dere waar eine box. Shelves I put in dere for Tante's jellies."

"Shelves," Burt said and asked if he could take a look. He zipped back to the dungeon and there, in a dark corner, stood the elegant black-walnut cabinet, complete with beveled-glass door. Crude shelves had been installed and supported with eight-penny spikes, bashed through the beautiful grain. The case was too tall for the low ceiling in the ancient cellar, so the cook, turned cabinetmaker, lopped off about twelve inches from the bottom and on such a bias that it could no longer stand free. It had to be lashed to an overhead water pipe to keep it upright. Burt stared in disbelief, almost in tears, and sat down on a box to contemplate. He could take the cabinet for what it night be worth, if only as temporary dust cover for his precious possession.

"Otto, tell Tante I'll build new shelves for her jellies."

Now, of course, Burt was not a watchmaker, either, but to see this intricate assembly of gears, cogs, clicks, springs, ratchets and pawls, presented a fascinating challenge. After studying this puzzle for a couple of days and locating a supply house for parts, he commenced to repair, replace, adjust, clean and oil the works.

Eventually he got the tired old timekeeper to go tock...tic, tock...tic. Somehow, it didn't sound right. After all, everyone knows a healthy clock is supposed to go tic...tock, tic...tock. After some trial-and-error adjustments, Burt got the fibrillations smoothed out to a normal pulse. The old-timer's face looked happy to be telling about time once more. In fact, the quarterly announcements and the beautiful chimes on the hour proclaimed that it was good to be running again and making up for time lost.

Chapter 20

Rigor Mortis seemed to be getting impatient with me, standing over in one corner and leaning against the wall. I ignored him and took a little time to reflect, letting my mind go where it would.

I've said it before and I'll say it again: I can't help feeling that a visit to the funeral parlor is a visit too late. The guy in the box usually doesn't say much. People just mill around looking to see who they know, and who they haven't seen since the last wake...or was it a wedding? Emma notices that cousin Alma has put on a lot of weight. "She always was heavy," Chuck reminds his wife, annoyed with her observation.

"Gokle's gotten to look much older."

"So have you. Five years have disappeared since you saw him last."

The visitors "oooh and aaah" at the spectacular floral display. The curious check the cards to see who's who and whose cost the most.

"I wouldn't have thought that Stella would spend that much on flowers. There wasn't that much love lost between them."

Emma knows Chuck couldn't care less about such things. Men are like that...hopeless. She leaves him, circulates a bit and sidles up to Aggie. "He looks good, don't you think?" Emma asks, for openers, as she nods toward the coffin.

"He ought to, he just got back from Florida."

Aggie's husband, Moose, hears them and glances at Ziggy. "Looks good? Hell the guy's dead! How can dead look good?"

"Yeah," Ziggy agrees, embarrassed at his friend's callous remark and wishing he hadn't said it so loud.

"What do you think that box is worth?"

"I don't know, maybe four thousand."

"Four thousand bucks just to occupy it for two days? He's going to be cremated, anyway, and the ashes dumped into his beloved Great South Bay."

Chuck feels miserable; he is going to miss his buddy, and all this chit-chat is getting to him.

A flag draped on the coffin is proof that the stiff was a veteran. He had requested that it be flown from his front yard, but it's too big for the average homeowner's flagpole. Several days later, after the cremation, they hold the final services. The urn containing the ashes stands on a pedestal in the parlor so that the guests can pay their last respects and attend the memorial service.

His good friend, Hambone, is last on line and feels awkward kneeling before the urn all by himself. But then that's what you're supposed to do, isn't it? As he gets up to leave, he thinks he hears someone call him and turns to see who it is.

"Hambone, over here."

He turns back and stares at the urn.

Nah, he thinks, it can't be. It can't be coming from there.

"Hambone, it's me, Bottle."

Hambone flashes a look out of the corner of his eye to be sure no one is watching him. I mean, after all, how do you explain holding a conversation with a can of ashes? "What the hell are you doing in here?" he whispers. "You're supposed to be in the parlor across the hall."

Naked In A Coat of Armor

"Well no wonder I don't recognize anyone," Bottle says.

"What happened? Who's over there in my place?"

"Izzy."

"Izzy Lapinsky? No kidding. Who would have thought Izzy and I would be swapping places at this time in life...life, what am I saying!"

"Cheez, I've heard of babies being swapped in the maternity ward, but this is something else," laughs Hambone.

"It ain't funny," snaps Bottle. "I made arrangements to be buried at sea and now it looks as though they're gonna drop me in a posthole along with the common landlubbers. They can't do that to me. What would it look like, a Navy man with seven years on the pig boats, disposed of like a lousy note?"

A holy man enters, wearing a prayer shawl and a yarmulke.

"Who's that?" asks Bottle, nervously.

"Shh, that's Rabbi Ben Moishe."

A groan from the urn sounds like, "Oh no."

The Rabbi gives a beautiful eulogy–you know, the usual stuff about how the deceased attended the synagogue faithfully every Sabbath, how he gave generously to the temple and that he was always very good to his neighbors.

"I'll say one thing, Bottle, the good Rabbi wasn't talking about you, that's for sure," Hambone says. "He doesn't know you that well."

In the meantime, in the next room, Father Roar is giving the last rights to Izzy and saying nice things about him. In fact he is saying almost the same things, word for word.

"God what a snafu."

"Speaking of God, I think if you guys have half a chance of going up to Him, He'll welcome you both no matter who anointed whom or where. On second thought, you clowns are probably going in the other direction, anyway."

"Listen, Hambone, I can't talk too good with what's left of me."

"I know. You sound like you've got a mouthful of peanut butter or something."

"Shut up and listen to me. Do me a favor; see if you can switch me back again. In fact, I wish I could go all the way back to the maternity ward, you know, start all over again."

"You're out of your mind, Bottle, old buddy."

"That ain't all I'm out of."

"How do you think I'm going to cart your can across the hall to the other parlor and bring Izzy's can back in here, without anyone seeing me?"

"You can do it. I know you can. You've pulled some pretty fancy capers in your time. Remember when–?"

"Will you shut up, Bottle, people are beginning to stare at me as though I'm the one that's crazy. I'll see what I can do. I'll yet back to you."

"But hurry. There ain't much time."

Hambone sees an opportunity when most of the people have left the room and the mortician is already busy arranging a future for a prospective client. He takes the urn from the pedestal and quickly tiptoes across the hall. As he is about to enter the room, he trips on the edge of the rug. The container flies out of his hands, ass-over-teacups, spilling ashes all over the immaculate carpet.

Bottle's voice, now pretty well thinned out, ricochets around the room like an echo. "You clumsy knucklehead, look what you've done. Now I'm going to end up in a damned vacuum cleaner cleaner cleaner.

Hambone makes a dignified exit. Once outside, he races across the parking lot calling out, "So long, fellow."

There was a party, and Burt was awkwardly standing in the middle of a room full of chirping women, with his hat in his hand and wondering if someone was going to tell him where to put his coat. Relatives had invited relatives of relatives, and he knew that he was expected to know all of them. But he wasn't sure if he was supposed to kiss all of them. Some would be offended if he didn't; some couldn't care less if he did. *I'm at an age*, he thought, *that if I like to kiss the girls I'm considered a dirty old man and if I don't, I'm an old snob.* His head was teaming with names and faces but somehow none of them matched.

The men were crowded into the kitchen and doing what men do at parties–boast, brag, bullshit, and play can you top this. Several of them were watching a hot game on the little TV that sat on the kitchen counter. Suddenly they broke out with a loud hooting and hollering after someone hit a homerun with bases loaded. Another was telling a joke and had to fall silent as the hostess sailed in to retrieve the hot hors d'oeuvres from the microwave. She made believe she hadn't been listening to the naughty story but wondered how it ends.

In the meantime, Burt was still in the middle of the room, still awkward. He wondered if he dropped his coat on the floor whether anyone would notice. He worried who was expecting to be kissed and who was not. Wouldn't a wave in the general direction and a large "Hallow" suffice? But, no, he wouldn't get away that easily.

The hostess flitted by and gushed how happy she was that he was able to come. Burt wasn't so sure of that, but he was sure he didn't have to kiss her because she was juggling a large tray of goodies.

"Helen, Darling, take Burt's hat and coat. That's a dear."

Helen did, and told him how nice it was to see him again. She puckered her mouth for a kiss, and he obliged. He was left with a warm feeling, even though he couldn't seem to remember who she was.

He was pleased to see Aunt Ethel settled in the big easy chair, like a dowager, and went over to give her a peck on the cheek. "Don't get up Auntie. Say, you're looking good for an old girl."

"Don't you give me that 'old girl' bit. And don't worry, I wasn't going to get up. Another thing, you're not that debonair yourself, you old goat." She flashed a wink at him. She was his favorite.

The woman seated next to Aunt Ethel laughed, and Burt got the feeling he must kiss her too, if only to be polite.

The woman on the folding chair glanced at him out of the corner of her eye, then quickly turned away and back to her partner in gossip. He was sure she was hoping the old codger wasn't going to kiss her; he probably smelled like a whiskey-soaked cigar.

Naked In A Coat of Armor

Besides, she'd much rather be kissed by the handsome guy who was leaning in the kitchen doorway. She seemed to like the way he sized up the ladies who were dancing back and forth, helping with the refreshments.

A youngster dashed up and threw her arms around his neck. "Uncle Burt," she squealed, and planted a big smack on his lips. "How are you? You look great. I love your silk hankie." He liked that, even though she wasn't his niece, because he knew her salutation was genuine.

Barnie's wife sauntered up to him only because she felt she was expected to oblige. So he moved...to oblige...because he thought it was expected. She rose up on her toes, dropped her eyes, and just at the last minute quickly turned her head so his aim landed high on her cheek and his glasses somehow became entangled in hers. He stood there wondering what it was that caused her to change her mind. Did she suddenly notice egg on his mustache, or was it just the nicotine stain? Actually, it was not a kiss at all; it was a facsimile, a farce, what the kids call an air kiss. It was simply to demonstrate to the audience what a loving sister-in-law she was, when in fact she had a syrupy-subtle way of kicking the wind out of you. She was still pretty and cute in her old age. She corseted her torso very tightly, desperately trying to control her uncontrollable lumps. But all it did for her was give her a permanent blush and a peculiar waddle. She'd drift from guest to guest sprinkling her thorny barbs and spikes like Tinkerbell broadcasting sunbeams.

"Sorry about that, Enid, but then we always tangle when we see each other."

"Oh, go to hell, Burt."

"Yes, Dear. I'll meet you there."

There was a tall, elegant woman standing near the fireplace. Her satin dress reflected flashes of light from the fire, which complimented her lovely contours. Her hair, done up in a French braid, was characteristic of good grooming. Burt liked it that way. She caught his eye and approached him from across the room in a sleek movement.

"Mr. Eichwald," she declared in a voice genuinely pleasant. "I am Susan Parker. Charles has spoken so often of you." She extended her hand in a very gracious manner, indicative of good breeding. "In so pleased to have met you."

"Thank you, likewise," he said, still awkward, though with an impulse to kiss her. But, he felt, that would be presumptuous. Instead, and for the want of something more profound to utter, he offered, "And congratulations to you both, on your engagement."

He wandered into the kitchen. "Hey Burt, where've you been?" the fellows called in unison. "Entertaining the girls, I bet."

He poured himself a drink and thought, *Susan will be good for Charles. I like his taste.*

Observation

Sitting by the waterfall in the garden, reading his paper and sipping a dollop of bourbon, Burt felt something on his arm. A tiny spider was struggling through the forest of hair. Its color attracted him, an iridescent emerald green. He watched it for a moment, then eased it over the edge and let it rappel down to a blade of grass. He was amazed that so much line could

Naked In A Coat of Armor

he stored in such a wee body. It was now about three feet from his eyes and, although the backdrop was also green, he could still distinguish it clearly.

Donald C. Peattie shares a similar observation beautifully when he writes, "Outside your kitchen window there may be a spider spinning his web. Lift up your child to see it, and tell him this shining silk drawn from the spider's body has a greater tensile strength than steel. If he learns admiration instead of disgust for the tiny spinner, he will have learned one of the greatest lessons in nature...that all life is sacred."

Burt was given an opportunity to demonstrate just that. A spider was beginning to spin her web outside his study. He called his neighbor's six-year-old and told him to come over, that he had something to show him, and to bring Jennifer, too. They soon came running up the driveway with Pudgy from across the street, Clifford and Curly from two doors down. Something in a diaper brought up the rear.

They crowded into Burt's study, and it looked as though the walls would bulge. The kids climbed up onto his bookcase, getting peanut butter and jelly on his papers as they pushed and squeezed for the best view. The poor little diaper was nearly trampled. Burt picked him/her up for the best look of all. He was as excited as the kids to hear them squeal with wonder and see their eyes pop with awe as the spider finished weaving her hammock.

Once Burt watched a mosquito trying to pierce his skin. First she moved about in search of a tender spot on the back of his hand. Then she lowered her drill, raised her hind legs and rear-end high to gain more leverage, and punctured the tough hide. He could see a sample of blood being drawn into her transparent body and watched it balloon like the bulb at the bottom of a thermometer.

Satisfied with its fill, the greedy little free-loader withdrew her syringe and took off like an overloaded blimp, leaving Burt to scratch a bump. *Shouldn't have let the little beggar get away with it*, he thought, *but at least I did take time to observe her before I thought of swat, splat and stomp.*

Burt was distracted by something frantically treading water in the fishpond. He bent to scoop it up and laid it on a rock. Its yellow jacket glistened in the sun as it rested. After it caught its breath, it preened itself, stretched its wings, and took off. *What's his name?—Androcles—has nothing on him*, Burt thought. *A monarch, on its way to Mexico, dips to steal a drink as it skims across the surface of the pond without interrupting its flight.*

A golden flash in the sunlight broke the surface of the water and swiftly snapped up a sorry gnat.

A little round, gray head, with ears pricked, peeked over the top of a rock. He wasn't sure if he could trust Burt. He crawled on his belly as he inched to the edge of the pond, not once taking his eye off the man. He then hung over the side but not before he gave Burt another suspicious look as he helped himself to a drink. When he had enough, the brazen little bugger sat bolt upright, looked Burt straight in the eye as though to say, "Well, I did it. What are you going to do about it?" Burt rustled his paper and, with a flip of his bushy tail, the creature dashed off. Burt figured the squirrel was laughing, thinking to himself, "I got a rise out of the old boy."

Naked In A Coat of Armor

Once Burt counted five goldfinches parading into the shallow where the water flowed over a flat rock, just before the falls. After the first shock of cool and wet, they splashed about, flapping their wings and ruffling their feathers enthusiastically, much like rollicking nymphs in yellow bathing suits.

Why bother with the ugly news? Burt decided, laying his newspaper aside. *I'll finish my drink while reading my garden.*

Chapter 21

Dan Russel, Burt's neighbor, had left the farm in Ireland when he was fifteen. Still, there was a bit of the farmer left in his heart, and he longed to grow a potato his way, as they did in the ol' Sod.

"Go ahead," Burt coaxed, always ready with plenty of "go ahead." *After all*, he mused, *when you get to be my age you know all about everything.*

"Another thing," said Dan, "O'id loike the kids to have some pets, oi mean beside that dumb slinky cat of theirs that snoops around wearing a silly collar with a bell on it."

"What you need is some bantams."

"What're buntums?"

"They're miniature chickens. Every kid should have a couple of bantams."

"Do ye think we could?" asked Dan, skeptical that Burt might be kidding him. "Mustn't have a rooster; they're too noisy."

"Oh, you've got to have a rooster; they're the prettiest. If the neighbor complains, just drop him in the soup pot–the rooster I mean."

Burt could see that Dan wondered if he was really serious, but he could tell Dan was really interested, now, and so was he; he was about as excited with the idea as he was. The thought of bantams brought back memories. Of course back then he had his livestock. He was the only one living up here, in the woods, before the population explosion.

Dan got busy and built a cute little hen house complete with fenced-in yard. One day he called Burt

Naked In A Coat of Armor

over to see the five chicks that had come all the way from Oklahoma. Four of them looked like little yellow powder puffs on tiny stilts, but the fifth one was was brown and looked more like a wobbly chestnut on stilts. Dan was a little concerned about that.

"So you've got a fifth wheel. It looks healthy enough; don't worry about it."

Burt ducked over every once in a while to see how the brood was coming along. He could understand how the ugly duckling felt, as he watched the four snubbing the oddball.

The first thing Dan did when he got home from work every evening was to check his chicks and try to distinguish a rooster. He was so afraid that perhaps he'd end up with all hens. Each day he'd ask Burt what he thought.

"Hey, look fellow, calm down," Burt told him. "You have to wait till these little guys grow some feathers and fill out a bit before you can tell anything." In the meantime, a friend pawned a rabbit off on him, and the kids went wild. The potatoes grew, the chicks grew, and the rabbit grew beautifully. The neighborhood farmer was real proud.

Eventually Dan and Burt recognized one chick would turn out to be a beautiful rooster. His breast was like black velvet, and he wore a white cape over his back. His tail was long, and when it caught the light it was dark green. His comb was straight and bright red. He looked as cocky as the one on the Kellogg's corn flakes box, and as conceited. Boy, was he a show-off, and he hadn't even learned to crow yet.

Lora and Burt listened to him every morning, practicing his song. Finally he mastered the appropriate tune and volume. How proud he was, and macho too. He lost no time in announcing that he was indeed the ruler of the roost. Every morning he flew up onto his perch and stretched his neck to the sky, billowed out his chest to cock-a-doodle-do his little heart out. "Up, up all you sleepy-heads, see the gorgeous sunrise."

This noisy heralding didn't do much for Burt. He'd roll over in bed and mutter, "Shut up, you fool, it's only five A.M."

They named this actor 'Chanticleer.' He was every bit as vain and haughty as Chaucer's hero. He acted as though he was the gift to the girls and let them know it. He'd strut around the yard, lower one wing and ruffle his hackles as he went into his mating dance. He loved them all, but Pertelote was his favorite. She was a pretty little hen, gray and white, and she'd always snuggle close to him when they were on the perch.

Burt noticed that the lordly Chanticleer didn't like the brown oddball much, and one time Burt caught them sparring with each other. By god, Burt thought, it looks like Dan has him another cockerel. He couldn't be sure, and Dan wouldn't hear of it...yet. It was a big, raunchy lout with a broad chest and a funny splash of white on the end of it's tail that looked as though someone had flung a gob of paint at him.

Now, one morning, after Chanticleer had finished with his reveille, there was the sound of some terrible hoarse croaking, something like a rope starter on a reluctant lawnmower. *Maybe the hens are learning to cackle*, Burt told himself. But, no, it didn't sound quite like that, either.

He got up early one morning to see what that noise was all about and, sure enough, there was the fifth wheel up on the perch, alongside of Chanticleer, trying his damndest to crow like he did. Every morning he'd join the cockalorum and dare to compete with him. Chanticleer would grab him by the neck and shoe him off the perch. But the next morning he'd be right back up there, stretching his neck and puffing his lungs, trying to bring up a cock-a-doodle do. Burt began to think he was queer and the hens would have nothing to do with a cock who could not crow like any self-respecting rooster should. They named the fifth wheel Canticleer because, with all his practice, he never learned the sound of reveille.

He did get to ruffle Chanticleer's feathers and beat him up now and then, and the girls began to respect him for that.

"That stuffed shirt," they said, "was all dance and little action. Besides, Canticleer was a gentleman and a much better lover." Even Pertelote sensed some fowl play and soon ditched the crowhard. Poor Chanticleer was left to dream and do the reveille while our hero, Canticleer, took care of the ladies.

The Kid Next Door

The kid next door was more like a pit bull than a four-year-old. When he burst out into the backyard, he came apart and flew in four directions at once. That's because he was undecided which to smash first, the cat, the dog, the rooster or his new battery-powered car. The cat sometimes was too fast for him even though the kid's speed rivaled that of light. He and the dog would gang up together and chase the chickens around and around the pen, stirring up a cloud of dust with feathers and fur flying. The only way to tell who was who was by the screaming, barking, and cackling.

When he was bored, instead of kicking a can he would sneak up and kick the rooster. Of course, the feisty bantam didn't like that too much, and one day he ran after the surprised kid and gave him a well-aimed peck. The kid screamed as though he'd been stabbed and ran off to his mother, holding his butt. He didn't bother that bird for a couple of days, but the rooster would chase the kid around the yard at every opportunity. He'd lie in wait for him till he stepped out of the back door. Then it was a question of who got his licks in first. Sometimes it was the fowl chasing the brat, and sometimes it was the brat chasing the fowl. It was comical to see that little bit of lightning streaking across the yard after the kid, it's hackles flared and neck stretched full length like an arrow.

"What was all that hollering about?" Burt said over the fence.

"That wooster bit me, Mr. 'E.'"

"Well no wonder; if you kicked me I would take a bite out of you, too."

He stood looking up at Burt with tears on his apple cheeks, as though he had lost his best friend, and probably wondering why Burt wasn't more sympathetic, wondering how Burt knew about that, anyway?

Wiping his nose on his sleeve, he whimpered, "Only kicked him once't."

Naked In A Coat of Armor

"Roosters are like elephants, son; they remember when boys are mean to them."

"Yeah, well I'm gonna kick that wooster again, real hard, see?"

He changed his mind, though, when the bird stood its ground and glared at him. It lowered its head, flared its hackles and dropped its wings to signal a charge. The kid kicked the dog instead.

"How come you're not wearing anything green for St. Pat's day?" Burt asked.

"Mr. 'E,' ya know what?"

"Did you hear what I asked you?" Burt could see he blew his trend of thought.

"Taint St. Pat's, it's St. Pater-ric, you know. And how come you're not wearing the Irish hat I brought for you when I went to see my grandma?"

Burt ignored that bit.

"Mr. 'E,' ya know what?"

"What?"

"We're going to church today."

"It's good to go to church, especially on St. Pater-ric's Day," Burt told him.

One day Burt heard a furious ruckus. The kid was up on top of the chicken yard cage hollering for his mother, who didn't hear him when she didn't want to. Burt took a look through the bushes and saw he had his roller skates on and was hopelessly tangled up in the chicken wire. Several days later, he stood still long enough for Burt to ask, "How did you get off the chicken cage the other day?"

"Took my shoes off...Mr. 'E,' ya know what?"

"No, what?"

"Member the thing you gave me and Jennifer a long time ago to grow? Where did you get that, have ya got any more?"

"No, those you have to plant in the springtime." Burt had taken a couple of yogurt cups that had plastic, dome-shaped lids and used them as handy miniature greenhouses. He planted a bean in each and gave one to the kid and the other to his sister, with instructions to water every day. He included an eyedropper so the watering wouldn't be overdone. But that process was too slow for the hyper kid, and of course he drowned his bean.

"Mr. 'E,' ya know what?"

"No, what?"

"Nothing is happening in my cup."

"Give it time."

A few days later he cornered Burt in the front yard.

"Mr. 'E,' Mr. 'E,' ya know what?" Burt was afraid he'd burst something, he was that excited.

"What now?"

"My sister's plant is growing a teeny bit."

"Holy mackerel! But how about yours?"

"Taint doin' nuttin'."

Burt didn't hear much from the kid for a while. Then one day he called to him. "How's your plant coming?"

"My sister's is this high," he said showing Burt an exaggerated height.

"Is that so? But how about yours?

"Ya know what?"

"No, What?"

"My mother said I watered it too much."

Naked In A Coat of Armor

"I told you to be careful. Never mind, maybe we can try it again some time, OK?"

"OK, Mr. E." He waved as he tore off in his plastic car zigzagging through a yard full of toys, rode over the cat's tail, and crashed into his mother's pot of impatiens.

The kid had quite a memory, and as long he brought the subject up, Burt figured he'd spring another one on him. He called his neighbor to see if the kid was busy.

"He's washing dishes," said Mrs. Kelly.

"You're kidding. God, don't disturb him." Burt figured it must be a miracle. Either that or she must have nailed him to the floor in front of the sink. "Chase him over when he's finished."

He came running up the driveway with his sister close behind. She had to see to it that he wouldn't get lost on the way over. Someone had to stand on that kid or he would climb the chimney to get up onto the roof. Or, worse, he'd likely make a sudden detour and fall into the fishpond.

"What are you doing, Mr. 'E'?"

"Here, take this."

"What is it? he asked, turning the tool over in his hand.

"Those are called pruning shears."

"Yeah, my mom cuts the roses." Burt gave each one an empty milk carton and took them back and showed them how to cut snips off the dormant forsythia bush.

"Now, put the clippings in the cartons and take them home and fill them with water. Watch them every day, and tell me what happens."

235

"I gotta go to school."

"So, take them to school and let the whole class watch them. Promise?"

"Mr. 'E'..."

"Did you hear me?" Burt interrupted.

"That ain't much fun." His attention span couldn't crowd much of this; he was getting bored. He got set to make a mad dash for home, when suddenly he remembered something.

"Mr. 'E'."

"What?"

"Is Smiley the possum still in the compo?" Burt didn't want the kid to go mucking around in his compost, so he told him, "No. He left, and you know what? He didn't even say goodbye." The kid thought that was funny and let out one of those deep-down belly laughs that Burt loved to hear when little children are really tickled.

"So long, Mr. 'E'," he shouted as he streaked across the lawn to show his mother the clippings, even though he thought they weren't that big a deal.

It wasn't long after when the kid approached Burt, all wound up again. Running across the yard, he tripped over the dog. He picked himself up and mumbled, "Dumb dog." After he caught his wind and direction, he said, "Mr. 'E', ya know what? My twigs have got little yellow flowers all over. My teacher said they're from a Cynthia bush, and she said I'm very good."

"Well that's great! I think you're pretty good, too."

"I know it," he said in his matter-of-fact way. "See ya, Mr. 'E'."

Naked In A Coat of Armor

Jerry was a spoiled brat if there ever was one–that is, if a parakeet can be a brat. He had the run of the house. His cage door was left open so he could fly and go as he pleased. He had almost as many toys as the children had. Among them were a swing, his favorite rocking chair, and a wagon.

The little clown loved to show off, especially if he sensed the visitor was a newcomer. He'd climb onto the swing and do his thing until he got the recognition that he reveled in. Then he would rock in his chair for awhile. His favorite stunt was to pull his wagon around the room, to everyone's delight. When he became bored, he would fly from room to room and sometimes perch up on a curtain rod where he could better survey the scene.

Monday, May was busy in the basement with the wash and Jerry decided to fly down the stairwell and see what that was all about. Just as May had transferred wash from the tub to the spin drier, smart-Alec Jerry made a low pass over the spinning machine and, sooof, was sucked out of the air and into the tub. By the time May realized what had happened and shut the spinner down, the bird had his feathers ruffled somewhat. But what wasn't so funny was that his head was twisted a hundred and eighty degrees on his shoulders and it was hard to tell whether he was coming or going.

When Matt came home from work, his wife and two girls met him in tears as they told him the terrible story. The poor bird lay on its belly, spread eagle on the kitchen counter, looking up at the ceiling. Matt couldn't help but burst into a fit of laughter.

"Boy, that must have been some merry-go-round," he said, with tears running down his face. This didn't amuse the girls one bit. He picked Jerry up and unwound him gently so that now he was pointing in the right direction and put him down on the carpet. The bird wobbled over to his chair, using his wings like a pair of crutches, and commenced to rock and sulk. After all, that was a pretty humiliating way to treat a member of the family. It does nothing at all for the ego.

He fully recovered after a day or so, during which time he would turn his head left and right ever so gingerly. But unlike a cat I know, who enjoyed an unexpected tumble in the clothes dryer and who would sit by the door waiting for another go at it, Jerry never went near that washing machine again, nor anywhere near the basement door.

Chapter 22

The library sponsored a nature walk and tour of the newly renovated Fire Island Lighthouse. The weather was just right for such things. Lora and Burt enjoyed the ferry ride to Kismet. The walk commenced from the Kismet Inn, west along the North shore at the edge of the Great South Bay, and then crossed the dunes to the South shore along the Atlantic coastline.

Their guide and naturalist, a pleasant woman in her fifties, was tall and statuesque. Her long legs in shorts made her look ten years younger. A red bandanna kept her hair from blowing in the gentle breeze. She was brown, as all beach dwellers are, and her stride was assertive. She seemed to take great pleasure in sharing her abundant knowledge of the environment.

She prompted the group to look and listen and see and smell the things they had trampled for granted in the past. Crossing the dunes to the south, the group passed a freshwater pond, an unusual discovery in the Fire Island sand. Their escort pointed out that it was an important watering hole for wildlife, including deer, and was protected by the government, since the area was part of the National Sea Shore.

As they neared the south shore, the sound of the surf was at full force. Rounding a rise in the dunes, they were surprised to see a couple and their small offspring sunbathing on the beach. They were naked.

Bert heard that some areas of the beaches were designated for nude bathing, but to suddenly intrude like this left him feeling awkward…uncomfortable.

His male eyes, of course, focused on the female form, though he tried not to make his peeking too obvious.

She's beautiful, he thought, not just because of feminine contours (on the contrary, she was a bit overfed, more like a Rubens subject); it was the natural way she reclined to absorb the warmth of the sun she worshipped. Therein lay her real beauty. The man lay alongside his woman, not touching her but being caressed by the same sun and breeze. The little boy amused himself, turning sand pots up, molded with a Styrofoam cup. He seemed unaware that life was different in his nudity. When the man got up, his paunch indicated too much pasta. He took the child's hand and led him to the water's edge, where the boy began to bail the ocean with his little bucket. As the surf nibbled at his toes, he squealed with delight like only the tiny ones can. He danced and jumped and pressed his eyes and laughed, always keeping a tight grip on his father's hand. This, too, was good to see. The only thing unnatural in the scene was Burt's embarrassment and the Styrofoam litter.

It was if the guide had prepared them for such an encounter—subconsciously, perhaps. It seemed simply a continuation of the nature walk. Lora shared similar thoughts. She was not conscious of the nudity until they were well past. Then, when it registered, she said, "Burt, now that you've seen the nudist portion of Fire Island, what did you think? I'm not sure whether I can accept it or not. We know that beauty is in the eye of the beholder, and so is ugly. Then isn't obscenity in the mind of the obscene?" Lora witnessed only a family enjoying wholesome leisure...their way...naturally.

Shower

Burt's first experience with a pay shower came when Lora and he were camping in Jackson, Wyoming. After a long day's drive, they looked forward to a nice shower before dinner. Burt ambled down to the public washroom and prepared himself for this treat. When he stepped into the booth, there on the wall was a coin box glaring at him and demanding a deposit, or else–or else no water.

He stepped back out into a cold draft and commenced to root around in his pants pockets for a coin. Luck was with him. He promptly deposited it. The greedy contraption meshed its gears and gnashed its teeth and, presto, wonderful hot water.

Burt soaped himself diligently with great gobs of lather and clouds of shampoo. Suddenly, while reveling in this luxury, presto! no water. What rotten timing! A body has to rinse. He had no choice but to step out into the wind tunnel and feverishly fumble for another coin. Again he was in luck. Of course, now he had a pocketful of suds and soap in his eyes, and he couldn't find where to deposit the bloody copper. After what seemed to be too long to be fiddling and especially while in the nude, he managed to satisfy the coin box and, presto! marvelous hot water. He rinsed off quickly–very quickly.

In the meantime, a gentleman stepped into the stall next door and, although Burt couldn't see him, he sensed that he, too, was taken aback when he spied the domineering box on the wall. Burt heard him mumbling to himself as he read the instructions. Then he stepped into the draft to rummage for a coin, and he too was lucky. After depositing it, delicious hot water began to flow as if by magic. Burt visualized his neighbor, coated in lather and wearing a turban of shampoo, who apparently liked to sing in the shower. The hot water lifted his spirits, and he burst into a robust baritone.

"On the road to Mandalayeee where the flying fishes playeee, and the sun comes up like–"Suddenly the baritone stopped in mid-aria, and the water stopped...and there was a silence, then, "Oh shit!"

Burt couldn't control his laughter. Of course he knew just what cut his song so short. The singer stepped out to hunt around in his pocket and, judging by the variety of four letter words he was using, there was no more change. He wrapped his suds in a towel, opened the washroom door cautiously to check that no one was in the street, and made a mad dash to his campsite. Bursting into his trailer, he demanded a quarter from his wife, who, poor thing, must've thought her loved-one had gone berserk. But, after he explained his problem, she laughed until the tears flowed. By this time, her loving husband threatened to kill her if she didn't produce some change in a hurry. Clutching the coin, our hero dashed out into the street and sprinted back to the washroom. But now both sides of the street were lined with fans, cheering and egging him on to the finish line. The story-swap around the community campfire that night featured our friend's episode. He knew they wouldn't let him live that one down for awhile.

Nightmare

One early morning, while still asleep, Burt felt a something in the lean-to with him. He opened his eyes a fraction and peered through slits–and saw an enormous black bear outside, with a cub snuffing around inside. Burt played dead. He was stretched full-length and rigid in his sleeping bag; ice flowed through his veins. Holy cow, he thought, not only am I confronted by a bear staring me in the face, but it has to be a mother with her cub. I've been told never get between a bear and her cub.

Burt's Big Beam spotlight stood ready to flip on. He thought he could blind her temporarily with the bright glare and shoo her little one out, then execute a graceful retreat, but fast. That's it! Quick–on with the light. Suddenly the darkness was gone, and so was the bear. In its place stood a great stone fireplace, which Burt had mistaken for a dangerous intruder. But what was this beside him? As he swung the light in the direction of what he thought was the cub, there, instead, was a twenty-or-thirty-pound porcupine. Much relieved, Burt began to breathe again. He would have kissed this friendly creature had he not looked so prickly. Instead, he ordered him out...out, out! But a porcupine is afraid of no animal, including man. He just blinked at Burt, who banged his hiking stick on the floor, thinking the sharp sound would convince his friend he had better leave. The porcupine slowly turned and reluctantly waddled out of the lean-to. Burt was sure he read in his sad expression, "OK, OK, if you'll have no truck with me, the heck with you."

Eugene A. Aichroth

Poetry

Their instructor was a very sophisticated lady. She was distinguished in the literary field and had several books of poetry published. Of course she spoke and read at great length about the subject. But Burt was afraid she was disappointed to see that he was not very enthusiastic to learn the mechanics of writing poetry. He did, however, doodle and dabble with pen and paper one day in his evening adult class and came up with the following:

"Kid Stuff."

Can'tcha remember when we were boys?
We'd run and dance and dash across the meadow
Barefoot on a sunny morning
The dew still cool on the grass?
Remember when we stepped into something
Where cows had been? The sun had baked a crust
And now, when we broke through, we felt the warm
Smooth between our wriggly toes.
How we'd squeal and laugh and run some more
To let the wet grass wash our feet?
Can'tcha remember how we'd stop
And lie on our backs to catch our breath?
We'd pull a stalk of grass and chew the sweet end
Where it parted. We'd close our eyes just for a moment
Looking up at the blue sea, watching the billowing ships
Go by on their way to somewhere. Remember we were boarded

Naked In A Coat of Armor

By pirates, the skull and crossbones emblem on their hats,
Long wooden swords in their belts?
Can'tcha remember when we caught a fly
And threw him into a web
Waited for the spider to come out
To see what all the wriggling was about
Then watched him settle down for a juicy snack?
Remember the time we pulled the legs off a fly,
Watched it come in for a belly landing?
Once we pulled the stinger out of a fat, round
Bumble bee and let him go, unarmed.
Remember when we found where horses had been?
We had a snowball fight with "summer snowballs."
Remember how we laughed and laughed,
'Cause Aunt Vashtie called them "meadow muffins"?
Can'tcha remember when we had to go real bad
And we sat in some poison ivy?
Mom had to dab something on our bottoms.
Oooh how we screamed and hollered, jumped and danced,
A couple of Indians at a pow wow.
Mom laughed and clapped her hands as though
We were performing just for her.
How miserable we were all that week.
Can'tcha remember? I can.

"Why, Burt", his gracious mentor bubbled, "how marvelous! You've written a poem for us, and you've told us a lot about shit."

Eugene A. Aichroth

Id

Burt's friend Jucob Stephan Wille was from Holland and was married to Hurta. Since Jack had no driving license when he first came to our country, Queenie would drive him to and from work at the Universal Wire and Cable Company.

One cold morning, Queenie called to say he could not get his car started and they wouldn't be able to get to work.

"Stand right where you are. I'll be right over," Jack said and hung up.

When Jack came driving up, Queenie asked, "What are you doing? You can't drive without a license. They'll hang you."

"Ja, well, if you think that I'm going to loose a day's work because you can't get your jallopy going, then you have another guess coming. Come, we are already too late."

Speeding down the street and going through a traffic signal, they were pulled over by a policeman who demanded to see Jack's license.

"Officer, do you not have anything to do but stop working people from going to work in the morning? Is there not a rape or robbery going on around the corner that you should be investigating?"

"Let me see your license, sir," repeated the cop in a menacing tone.

Jack reached into his pocket for his wallet while poor Queenie was thinking of making a run for it. The policeman took a long look at the paper Jack handed to him and finally asked, "What kind of a name is Hurta Wille?"

"Ja, well, I don't know, but it was good enough for my father so it's good enough for me."

"Go on, get out of here," said the exasperated cop, "before I lock you up."

Aud

Burt got to thumbing through his and Lora's old guest book and came across a note dated June 15, 1967. The seven was crossed as in the typical European fashion. His memory was refreshed as he recalled the familiar foreign accent:

> *I do not like to write in this book because this is a guest book and you have all become to mean much more than merely my hosts in this year. Mom and Dad, you have become my second parents, and you, Suzanne, I think of you as my third sister. Saxon Place 515 has become my home, and what do you write in a guest-book in your own home? The only thing I can say now, when I am looking back, is I am forever in debt to the American Field Service, which brought me here. They certainly picked out the loveliest family in the United States just for me.*
>
> *Aud*

Burt remembered thinking, *The day we dread, yet the day Aud must be looking forward to, will soon be here.* She left that morning for a tour of the northeastern states. They took her into the city to catch a bus with several other foreign students, some of whom she knew. Parting was difficult for all of them. There was so much they wanted to say, but thought it better left unsaid.

The ten months had proved to be a very enriching experience for the family. Aud was a lovely girl, a credit to her family; she was an ambassador of good will from Norway. She and their daughter became close companions. Aud was popular in school and made many friends, both young and old. They missed her very much, and she would always be welcome in their home.

Foreign exchange is a two-way experience, rewarding for both the guest and the host. Perhaps the exchange of students and teachers, scientists and intellectuals, would do more for overcoming prejudice and improving foreign relations than all the political bickering and sale of arms could ever do.

In 1989, Aud brought her family over to introduce them: Johan, her husband, Ellen Henrikke, her daughter, and two-year-old Petter, her son—a lovely family. Burt enjoyed speaking with Johan, though his English was not quite as good as Aud's. However, the so-called language barrier did not keep them from comparing notes across the sea. All had a wonderful holiday, much too short.

Lottery

Burt pulled into the mall and parked in the fire zone. He had the exact change for his paper and lottery ticket. He wouldn't be illegal very long.

Naked In A Coat of Armor

"Good morning, Gerhard," he called, as he stepped into the store and threaded past the regular loafers waiting for the OTB next door to open.

"Und a very good morning to you too, Burt," the proprietor answered. "Und what do you mean by disturbing the sub culture at this hour?"

I've come to collect my winnings but I forgot to bring a bag." Burt flashed a wink at one of the men studying a racing form.

"Ja, but you would take a check, no?"

"I would want to feel that kind of money, Gerhard. Imagine, both hands in a bag, up to my elbows in forty million dollars. Wow!"

"Well, und what would you do mit all that gelt?"

"I'd be happy to show him what to do with it," one of the flies chimed in.

"You know, I haven't time enough to spend that much cash."

"Who's he kidding?"

"I've only six years to go."

"Six years to live?" Gerhard looked puzzled. "How do you know all this?"

"I have a contract."

"Ach, pardon me, you know someone, ja?"

"No, seriously, all I need is one million."

"Ja sure, und what would you do mit eine million dollars?"

"I would sit in my easy chair and get on the phone and call the plumber to come and fix the leaky faucet. I would call to have my lawn cut, the leaves raked, the house painted. You name it. I would enjoy doing my thing at my leisure and watch someone else do the ugly chores."

"Will you listen to our new gentleman of lazy, country squire, Lord ouf der manor. Burt, I think you would go crazy, yet."

"You wouldn't like to take a trip to Hawaii? a customer with a fistful of lottery tickets asked.

"Nah, I've been there. I'm through traveling. I've done all the things I was told to do. If there's something I've forgotten, it's too late. I'm content to sit on the sidelines and watch the stampede go thundering by. I just want to be left alone and pray that some politician doesn't run off with my apple cart."

"Ja, ja, leave our gentleman alone, so now he could schmell der roses, yet."

When Burt got back to his car, he found a white slip under the windshield wiper.

Halloween

He was sitting on the stoop, dozing in what was left of the season's sun. The summer's dregs were strewn on the ground, and it occurred to Burt that he ought to do a bit of raking, but he dismissed that idea quickly, thinking he would get the kid next door to do the job, maybe tomorrow. Anyway, something came galloping down Main Street on a huge white stallion. The animal was so big the rider could hardly straddle him.

The guy, or whatever it was, looked as though he had fallen into a chromium vat. He wore a steel helmet with slits cut into it to see through and a group of holes drilled where his mouth would be. It looked like one of those strainers the bartender uses to strain a martini.

Naked In A Coat of Armor

A white banner with a red cross on it fluttered on the end of a long staff he carried. A three-foot sword hung from his belt, heavy enough to cause the rider to list to starboard. He reined to a stop in front of Burt' house and threw the face piece of his tin suit up over his head and called, "My good man, can you direct me to the castle?"

Burt wasn't sure whether to take this guy seriously. You can't always sometimes tell what you're letting yourself in for. Then again, maybe he's just going to a Halloween party.

"No castle around here," Burt told him.

"Oh but look 'ere Governor, there must be. You see, the king pinpointed it out on the map. It's on a river near a village called Albany."

"The King? What are you talking about? And I'm not the Governor."

"King Arthur, of course."

Now Burt was getting suspicious. This guy's gears were not meshing. "What's your name, bud," he asked, "and where are you from?"

"I'm known as George. I'm from Camelot."

"Yeah? How'd you get over here?"

"I booked passage on the Mayflower. Mind you, they had to bump that pompous peacock Sir Waiter Raleigh, but I suppose it was a matter of priority. You see, the King commissioned me t to come and rescue the damsel from the wicked ogre."

"Damn what?"

"Damsel. Princess."

"Yeah, and who is this okra guy?"

"He's a mean hairy giant, very strong, and he keeps a dragon to guard the castle. It is very ferocious and breathes fire."

"Well, I don't know of any castles or dragons or even okras around here, 'cept maybe in Albany, Burt said. "There are some big mansions up on the river. Some of the rich maharajahs like the Vanderbilts and Harrimans and Roosevelts put up some pretty fancy shanties along the river, and they've probably got some damsels there, too. Incidentally, for your information, Albany is not a village, it's a large city and it's the capital of our state."

"Oh dear, I do beg your pardon, old chap."

"There's a glitzy mall there that some people call a white elephant. There's some okras there, and they're pretty hairy too.

"Ogres, my good man, ogres."

"Whatever. I bet you'll even find a dragon or two, and I know there's some damn cells there. Anyway, that's probably where Arty wants you to go."

"Oh dear, how disrespectful. One must never address his majesty in such a cheeky manner, you know. But, ta very much for your help. Jolly good of you. Cheerio," he called as he spurred off down the street.

Cheese, it's a wacky world, ain't it?

Chapter 23

The old man threaded his way between the noisy tables, clutched his overloaded plate, and wondered why it wobbled so. The place was crowded with senior citizens attending the church's annual potluck dinner. "Mind if I join you?" he said to a poker-faced old timer sitting on the end of a crowded table.

"Help yourself; it's a free country. But please, no chit chat."

"You mad at the world or something?"

"Look, if you're going to start reciting your dull resume, I'm going to have to move. Look around; where can I move to?"

"OK, no chit chat." The old man dipped into his bowl. "Soup's good!"

The grouch next to him thought, *Oh boy, here it comes, the opening remarks.*

The old man wiped his mustache and dug into the vegetable casserole that shared the plate with homemade baked beans, turkey, ham and scalloped potatoes. You'd think this guy hadn't eaten in a month. He topped off with a great slab of chocolate layer cake and a cup of coffee. "These people sure put out a nice spread," he said, belching. "And you know, I don't even belong to this outfit."

"You mean you sit there and put a plate like that away and you don't belong to the church?" complained the old grouch.

Burt, nearby, hadn't seen any signs when he came in saying, No Jews, No Gentiles, No Catholics. He could be a Shiite for all they cared. *That's what's so good about these people,* he thought, t*hey put out a generous luncheon and invite folks to come and enjoy. It never occurs to them to 'sound their trumpets before them.' They don't ask you to sign a pledge; they're just practicing some of what they preach—which is more than a lot of them so-called holy men, do.* He took his handkerchief out and blew his nose and then tucked it back into his pocket and brought out his wallet. He slipped a plastic folder to the old grouch and said, with much pride, "My grandchildren—twins, a boy and a girl."

"I can see that. So what?"

"Great kids. I live with my son and his wife. They worry about me. My daughter-in-law is a sweetheart. Every drive out of their driveway, she crosses herself. She's Catholic. Catholics worry. Now she has me wondering if I'm really that bad behind the wheel. If so I'd rather have an air bag in the car than a rosary hanging from the mirror, obstructing my view.

"How do you stand those kids every day?" the old crab asked.

"It isn't easy. They try to wear me out and I try to wear them down. First thing you know, all three of us are in a heap on the floor, fast asleep. When we wake up, refreshed, it goes something like this:

> *'Grandpa, tell us a story.'*
> *'Told you one yesterday.'*
> *'Tell us another one.'*
> *'Well, OK. There was this big dog with dark brown silky hair.'*
> *'Yeah, a chocolate retriever,' Jeff says in disgust.*

'How did you know?' I ask him.

'You told us that story,' Jenny chimes in, and rolls her pretty eyes to heaven.

'Well how about the one about the pitbull?'

'What's a pitbull?'

'Well that's another breed of dog. Smaller with a barrel chest and muscles like steel.

Men train them to fight. They drop a couple of them into a pit and watch them tear each other apart.'

'Grandpa! That's terrible! You're teasing.'

'Nope, they egg them on and shout and wave money around and use nasty language.

First thing you know they're fighting among themselves.'

'You mean like the grownups do at our little-league games?'

'Well...yes, something like that.'

The old man looked at the grouch and said, "Ever notice how kids can embarrass you?"

'That's sick, Jenny says. Why do they do things like that?'

'Because they're sick,' Jeff says with authority.

'Anyway,' I go on, *'sometimes they use chickens to fight like that. Cock fights they're called. They strap sharp steel spurs to the rooster's legs and watch them slice each other up.'*

'How do they tell who won?'

'When one stops moving the other one is the winner.'

"Those are fine stories to be telling the kids," the old grouch said.

"Not much different than the Grimm fairy tales they tell in kindergarten," the old man said, "like fattening up little boys and girls to be eaten and pushing wicked witches into ovens. I think it's one way of showing them what good and evil looks like. Right and wrong. We can't shield them from the world we brought them to. They have to learn to distinguish the ugly from the beautiful."

"Our little Jenny climbed up on my lap the other day and said, 'Grandpa, tell us a nice story like King Arthur and the Knights of the Roundtable.' I said, 'Did I ever tell you about the Knights of the Square Table?'

'Oh Grandpa, you're teasing again, aren't you?' she says.

'No, no, the knights of the square table were the bad ones. They never polished their armor. They always looked dirty, tarnished and rusty. And when they walked, their tin suits made squeaky, raspy noises. The good knights of the roundtable could hear them coming when they were still a long way off and would ride out to clobber them before they could get too close to the castle. And they always won. They rescued the pretty ladies and made the rusty knights take all their garbage and litter with them, when they retreated. They had to drag their slain dragons out, along with the dead ogres. The shining knights would then

make sure that everything was left neat and clean before they rode off to report to King Arthur.'

The old crab put his fork down and took a sip of coffee. "What church you belong to?"

"Don't belong to any, though I'm interested in all of them. My son married a Catholic."

"So your grandchildren are being brought up in the Church?"

"Well, not really. Sometimes they go to a Synagogue."

"A Synagogue!" gasped the old grouch, not sure that he heard right. "What does your daughter-in-law say to that?"

"She doesn't mind; in fact she attended a Bar Mitzvah the other day."

"What's that?"

"It's similar to the Christian Confirmation. Then there's the time that young Jeff came home and asked if he could go to Sunday school with his friend Stinky. They're Presbyterians or something.

'Go', his mother told him, 'and learn something new and come back and tell us all about it.'

"You people are all balled up. Don't you think it's about time you established your priorities and made up your mind where you're headin'?"

"Look, old timer, there are nine different ways to go to Chicago, and everybody eventually gets there, by whatever way they choose. See you around," the old man said, standing to leave. "I gotta be getting back."

"Wait." The old grouch protested, shaking his head.

The man turned around, a quizzical look on his face.

"You forgot to finish your dessert."

Adventure

Burt's friend Phil used to commute all the way to Jersey, where he was employed as an accountant for a shipping corporation. For forty years, he'd walk to the station every morning, buy a container of coffee and a newspaper and catch the 5:45 out of Babylon. Later, the company moved to Manhattan, downtown near Battery Park. After he retired he'd walk to the station every morning, buy a container of coffee and a newspaper, and wave to the guys pulling out on the 5:45. Burt saw that Phil couldn't get used to being left behind. Either that, or he couldn't or didn't want to let go.

Phil and Burt were chatting one day and got around to the subject of retirement. Phil was trying to tell Burt that he was glad, not that he was retired but that he didn't have to catch that train any more.

"Did you ever try to get to downtown Manhattan when the city buses were onstrike?" Phil asked. "Or when the railroad people walked out, or the subways had stopped running? Talk about chaos! Imagine what that does to the blood pressure, let alone the cardiopulmonary. You had to dream up all sorts of complicated transportation arrangements, like car pools, taxis, special buses, limos or bumboats.

"Bumboats?" Burt asked, "What're they?"

"They're old tugboats taken out of service, not much good for anything. They use them once in awhile to haul junk, or pig iron or garbage. The company, on occasion, would hire one to take us across the river. It was an exercise just to board these tubs and then jockey for a downwind position to avoid the stench. Had to walk across the bridge a couple of times."

"What bridge?"

"Brooklyn."

"Say that sounds interesting. Think you and I could do that sometime?" Burt said.

Phil looked at him as though he was kidding.

"No, seriously, I'd like that."

"OK. When?"

Burt could see Phil wasn't keen for this wild idea. But before he could back out Burt suggested, "How about Thursday?"

On Thursday morning they met at the station, bought a cup of coffee and a newspaper, and boarded the 5:45. Burt thought Phil was dressed a bit casual for a gentleman used to hobnobbing with all sorts of professionals in the business world. He had on jogging shoes, a short jacket with odd-colored sleeves, and a baseball cap. He *had* played ball in his younger days. They got to Atlantic Avenue, Brooklyn and Phil led the way out to the street and down a hole in the sidewalk to a subway platform, just as a train poured in. Burt had heard a lot about graffiti, but he hadn't ridden the subway in years and now, in reality, he wasn't sure it was a train. Instead, he was reminded of a camouflaged line of weapons carriers moving up to the front. He couldn't tell where the doors were until they slammed open and bodies came tumbling out and some tumbled in. He didn't think he boarded the train under his own power. It seemed more like he was carried in, and just in time, too, as the doors slammed shut. He felt he could have lost his hat, or worse, his arm.

"Gotta move fast," said his old friend, "or they'll trample you."

Burt could also see what they mean by sardines. There was no place to sit, so he learned about strap hanging. They swung and swayed to the next station, where everybody was thrown off balance like a line of dominoes as the motorman applied the brakes. None of the straphangers dared let go of the strap for fear of being deposited at the wrong station. Then the dominoes were straight again as the train lurched toward the next stop.

They pulled into the station near the bridge and climbed out of the hole up into a sunny day. They worked their way up the approach and onto the bridge and along a wooden walkway, well worn by both pedestrians and cyclists. The massive stone structures, with their arches, looked cathedral-like. The suspension cables cascading down from their high towers glistened in the sun like an enormous spider web after a shower. Burt had to have a picture of this spectacle and warned Phil he was going to lie down on his back to get a good angle shot.

"Go ahead, I'll make believe I don't know you."

A kindly old lady stopped and looked down at Burt with much concern. "Oh dear! Are you all right?" Very thoughtful of the old dear, Burt thought. She must be from out of town, a fellow New Yorker would simply step over me. After picking himself up and

Naked In A Coat of Armor

explaining his peculiar behavior, she just shook her head and flashed him a pretty smile.

They had a good view of the old schooners moored at the South Street Seaport and the Twin Towers of the World Trade Center as they approached the dominant skyline. They left the bridge and ambled past City Hall, down Broadway to St. Paul's, where they stepped inside to pay their respects. Then Burt led Phil out to the graveyard. He wanted to read the messages carved on stone tags by folks long ago, even though he supposed his friend thought, "What kind of a nut goes wandering around cemeteries, anyway?"

Burt got the feeling that Phil was getting more and more nervous as they continued towards Wall Street, then realized what it was that bothered him. He was afraid of running into someone who would recognize him, a colleague maybe, someone from the office. Burt wondered if it was because he thought it would make him homesick for the job.

Burt was getting hungry about now and suggested that they get some lunch at a nice tavern. He'd been looking forward to this, and surely Phil knew of several such spots in the financial district where they served a good businessman's lunch. But, again, Phil didn't seem too enthusiastic. This was all commonplace to him, Burt knew, but to him it was an adventure. Phil spied a frankfurter vendor across the street.

"How about a hotdog, Burt?"

"Look, I didn't come to the financial capital of the world to buy a hotdog, and from a vendor yet. I want a roast beef sandwich on real rye, Jewish rye, with crust and a large stein of beer. That's what I want."

"OK, OK." Phil saw there was no use arguing and turned into Exchange Place. There was what they were looking for, or what Burt was looking for–a super-fancy deli. It was called "Club 76." The place was a noisy bustle, overflowing with pinstripes, gold watches and fraternity rings. The décor was just right, with solid-wood paneling, overstuffed benches, ornamental chandeliers and the longest brass rail Burt had ever seen.

Servers were in spotless white, wearing tall starched hats, enticing customers to try delicacies from around the world, some Burt had never heard of. Phil, now in his environment, forgot his baseball cap and pushed through the happy crowd like a ferret in hot pursuit of some quarry. He spied a tiny table that might seat three in a squeeze. The third, a woman already seated, was sipping a Martini and reading a paperback. Burt guessed her to be an executive secretary.

"Mind if we join you?" Phil asked, surprising Burt with his casual approach.

"Help yourself," the secretary answered without lifting her eyes from her romantic novel. Burt wondered if she was aware of what she was sipping. They hung their coats on the backs of chairs to reserve their places and fetched roast beef sandwiches, piled high with rare meat, and pickles that tasted of dill, the best Burt had ever had. Or, he reflected, perhaps the environment had something to do with it. When they finished eating, Phil thought it a good idea to swing by the restroom on the way out, and Burt agreed. That tankard of beer was extra large. But swing by was all they did, since the place was crowded.

"Come on," said Phil, "we'll walk down to Battery Park and go there."

Well, the latrines there were locked. Suddenly, a perfectly normal function became an abnormal emergency. Burt felt sorry for Phil. There just was no choice but to go across the street to his office. They took the express elevator to the fourteenth floor. The rocket-like speed pressed Burt's stomach down onto his bladder, which could have proved very embarrassing. Fortunately, they arrived high and dry. Of course, they found those lavatories also locked, and for a moment Burt thought poor Phil was going to tear the knob off the door. But he composed himself and, after taking a deep breath, he marched into his Alma Mater as nonchalantly as possible. The sweet young receptionist greeted him with open arms and a big hug. Now, ordinarily Phil would have enjoyed this warm greeting, but her enthusiastic squeeze almost proved his Waterloo.

"Quick," he hissed, "Let me have the key to the restroom."

The girl must have thought him very rude the way he snatched it from her and went dancing down the hall, with Burt a close second.

Phil was still in a hurry when he returned the key, but this time his rush was to get out of there and head for home.

What's His Name

He came directly towards Burt with a cordial smile and his hand outstretched. "Burt, how are you? What's new?"

"Oh, I'm fine, thanks, ah ah..." Burt answered, struggling to remember this fellow's name. God, how embarrassing, he thought. I know him like my own brother, but do you think I could remember his name?

"Too bad about Freddie, huh?"

"What about Freddie?" Burt asked.

"Haven't you heard? He was in an accident."

It's no use, Burt thought. I have to ask him. "Freddie who?"

"Miller–Freddie Miller! He caught the blank look on Burt's face. "Don't you remember the guy that told all the funny stories at your retirement dinner?"

"Oh sure, I remember," Burt said just above a mumble.

"What about Charlie Wernor. Seen him lately?"

"Charlie who?"

"Wernor," he repeated with disgust. "Wernor." "Come on, Ecles–I mean Eichwald–we went fishing with him last year. He won the pool. Remember he caught the first fish?"

"Yeah, now I'm with you," Burt said. He couldn't help thinking this fellow sure knows how to make a guy squirm.

"Wonder how what's-his-name is doing?" he continued, it being his turn to fumble. "You know the clown who always bragged about how good he was on the bowling team? God, this is embarrassing. I know him like my own brother, but I just can't think of his name."

"Well," Burt said, now feeling very self-righteous. "Don't feel too bad, because I'll be damned if I can remember your name."

Beggar Man

"Look at this, Burt" his friend Joe announced from behind his morning paper, "the Transit Authority wants to make it illegal for beggars to panhandle on subway property." He said it with emphasis, to impress Burt that he was right on top of the current events.

"Yeah," Burt answered, indifferently, "the court threw it out. Unconstitutional, they said." Joe's jaw fell open, but he stayed behind his paper. "How come you're so goddamn smart?"

"I read the papers too."

"I think," Joe continued, "They kick that unconstitutional bit around too haphazardly. They twist it and stretch and warp it for each individual's liking. What does it look like with those derelicts spread out all over the place? How do you think respectable tourists feel when they confront a spectacle like that in our great city? They're going to take their money somewhere else. Those people slow down the flow of traffic, not to mention the flow of commerce and profit."

"Joe, you can't see beyond the money and profit part of it. If it doesn't have a monetary value, then it has no value for you at all. And to answer the other part of your question, tourists who have visited great cities all over the world have found beggars in every one of them. It's part of the tour. No, we don't need another law. What we need is to enforce the existing laws. If panhandling is wrong and offensive, then we need to address the cause. In the meantime, I would rather have a ragamuffin stake out his little corner in the subway station, break out his tin cup and sit quietly. It beats having some drug-crazed punk tap me on the head with a pipe and snatch my wallet in time to push me into the path of the Lexington Avenue express."

"Well, I think it's the beggars and the bag ladies and the homeless that cause all the trouble. They're just a lazy lot getting something for nothing. They should get off their duffs and get a job and earn a living," Joe said.

"I agree with you a hundred percent, but when you tell them to go to work you've got to have work for them to go to. They're not all bums, you know. Some of them are in trouble through no fault of their own. Some are genuinely in need of help. You can't just lump people all in the same bag like shake-and-bake."

Joe started to fold his paper. They finished their coffee and took the escalator down to the subway platform. A nun with a sweet smile greeted them at the bottom of the steps, begging, for a good cause.

"See what I mean?" Burt said. "There are all kinds.

Didn't you notice the Salvation Army at the head of the stairs? Come to think of it, even the government is a beggar. Every time they're looking for volunteers, they're looking for something for nothing. I hate to blame everything on human nature, but it does seem natural. When we're on our knees to pray, most of the time we're begging for forgiveness or something. Panhandlers have been with us since hundreds of years before Christ. And when he showed up, he told us to be good to the poor. Give until it hurts."

"Yeah, I know all about that too," Joe said. "But I don't buy it all. Carnegie had a different slant. He warned, 'Those who would administer wisely must, indeed, be wise, for one of the serious obstacles to the improvement of our race is indiscriminate charity.'"

When Joe was finished with that tidbit, Burt went into a singsong: "Hark! Hark! The dogs do bark / The beggars are coming to town / Some in rags, some in tags / And some in velvet gowns." "The poor," he said, "will always be with us." Then he said, "Not to change the subject, but see that woman?"

"Which one?"

"The one buckling under the weight of her sable. Watch."

She stepped in front of the panhandler, looked up and down the platform, then, satisfied that she had an audience, she opened her Gucci purse and dropped a coin into the beggar's cup. The loud rattle announcing her benevolence was not from the size of the coin but because of the height she dropped it from.

The beggar leaned over, peered into his cup, then looked up at the woman and said, "Chee tanks, lady."

"Burt, did you hear the one about the beggar that knocked on the priest's door and asked for some food?" He didn't wait for an answer. "The priest went back into the house and returned with a dry crust of bread and gave it to the fellow, saying, 'My good man, not for your sake nor for my sake do I give you this bread but for the Lord's sake.' The beggar turned the crust over in his hand a couple times and said, 'Well then, for Chrissake, Father, could you put a bit of butter on it?'" Burt laughed a bit, but then said, "It isn't funny. Something's got to be done about getting these people off the streets."

"Yeah," he agreed. "Let's duck into O'Brien's Pub and get a couple of pints and a bite to eat."

Morning

Burt felt a touch ever so gentle, and when he opened one eye, Lora said, "Come, I need a toaster man." He wondered how this woman could be so chipper on a cold, rainy, sleety morning such as this.

"We have to make our own sunshine this morning," she declared as though she heard his thoughts. Then she left to attend to her kitchen.

Burt rolled over to face the wall, thinking he really ought to stir. The other eye opened slowly. He wanted to be fair to Lora. He raised his leaden old frame and sat on the edge of the bed, waiting for his eyes to focus. He wondered if he should risk standing up. In the vertical position, he stretched his arms horizontally, rotated them just a little and pressed them back to the scapulars, in an effort to pull himself out of the set he'd taken during the night. He was very careful with all this for fear of breaking something. He remembered his Air Force calisthenics: "Suck up that gut and look proud." Boy, he thought, they ought to see this old dog now. He scratched his head and his loins and moved to relieve his bladder. "Well, we've got us another day," he told the stranger in the mirror. Then, after sluicing his face, he combed his hair. *Always come to the breakfast table with your hair combed*, he told himself, *she likes that*.

Naked In A Coat of Armor

The sheep in his slippers felt warm and, wrapping himself in his favorite old bathrobe, he dragged across the linoleum to the captain's chair in his corner. He knew he was alive because he could smell the coffee. It was Wednesday, a bacon and egg day, his favorite, though a hot poultice of porridge would do a body good on a morning like that.

He sat at the table beside the window by the toaster and listened to his thoughts. Don't need salt, the bacon has enough. A dash of pepper is just right. Shame to throw pepper into that clear ox eye. Miserable out there, nobody at the bird feeders. The toast has popped up and has to be buttered immediately and stacked on top of the toaster to keep it warm, so the butter can seep into it.

He watched his wife from across the table. She liked to eat the center of her toast first, the part that was nicely saturated. She saved little corners of crust to be eaten with dabs of gooseberry jam. He wondered if shared little idiosyncrasies aren't a part of drawing couples closer. "I love this woman," he thought for the billionth time.

He took a sip of coffee and his thoughts changed their tone. He thought how he liked his coffee in a mug with half-and-half and a dab of honey. Now she spiked it with milk so it wasn't really half-and-half any more. Who was she trying to kid? Her doctor must have told her something about cholesterol. He thought, irrelevantly, how the coffee should be poured with the pot held high so the force would give a proper blend.

The electronic dictator blared the latest news: an apartment house in the Bronx disappeared; there was a big bang and it shook the neighbors up. There would be an investigation. Bridge tolls to go up. A couple of cars sailing along the Thruway suddenly found themselves in the water with large chunks of bridge on top of them. There would be an investigation.

"Pass the jam, please."

America's brand new embassy in Moscow was full of bugs and must be torn down before it could be occupied. There would be an investigation.

"Did you hear that?" Burt muttered, "That's hard to believe."

Rapes in Central Park. AIDS had reached epidemic proportions. Willard Scott, the cheery weatherman said not to worry, it would clear. "Partially sunny today, partially cloudy tomorrow." He reminded the audience that people live to be a hundred in spite of it all, providing names.

The President and First Lady were on holiday.

"You know," Burt said, when I see him waving to all on his way to the helicopter, I worry that one of these days he's going to trip over his dog or something."

Lora laughed. "That would be the last straw."

Burt left the table, the caffeine prodding him to activity. He thought of writing a little something that morning while he was fresh. Trouble was, everything should be done in the morning, while he was fresh. The kitchen faucet was dripping faster now. He grumbled as he pulled his jacket on and snatched his hat off the hook and drove into the weather to the plumber's supply for a repair kit.

Why I go to that particular shop, I'm not sure, he thought. *They screw me as much there as anywhere*

Naked In A Coat of Armor

else. They were helpful though, and congenial too. One of them must have belonged to the Fire Department, because he always had the latest "Didja hear the one about–?" Crazy guys, always good for a laugh, and a laugh was good for Burt this morning. He left and drove past the cemetery on the way home. He hadn't been in there since they'd buried their John. Lora diligently tended to the graves, cutting, weeding, trimming and planting. He didn't get it. What's the use? was his thought. Those under ground wouldn't care, and what did it do for those above grade? He hated to have her puttering alone with her grief but supposed it comforted her. Around Christmas time, he usually trimmed the evergreens and Lora made blankets with the cuttings and decorated them with red bows and pinecones to place on the graves.

It stopped raining. He was brooding and felt a chill. *Dammit, you can't keep him warm any more,* he thought as he kicked the back door open.

He glanced at the faucet-repair instructions with contempt. First shut off the water supply to the faucet. (Wonder why?) Loosen the set screw and lift handle. (Come, come, get on with it.)

"It's time for our coffee break," Lora called.

At twelve she called him for lunch. *It's twelve? What happened to eleven?*

Lora usually served a cup of soup, one of her specialties. She layered an interesting sandwich and poured a cup of tea. Before sitting down to this good lunch, Burt switched the TV to their favorite game show. But that was too often precisely the moment when "We pause for the following important messages" would occur–not a pause, but a bloody unimportant intrusion. Very rude. A gracious woman spit out words in machine-gun rhythm, extolling the virtues of various feminine sanitary products. A gentle doctor in a long white gown, dripping with bedside manner, announced that we can now have our hemorrhoids removed with less discomfort by a laser procedure. A Hollywood actress, now a senior citizen, introduced us to a special diaper for the incontinent. A lovely young lady shared the particulars of her favorite douche, the one with the flexible nozzle. A new remedy for diarrhea was proclaimed as far better than the old one.

With his appetite ruined and his show gone sour, Bert was in an ugly mood. He sulked and retreated to his study, his hideout, closed the door and settled down to read. A copy of Thompson's *Generation of Swine* on his desk repelled him. The sun's rays streaming in through the window were sliced up by the venetian blinds. He dozed in its warmth. Five or ten minutes later, when he awoke, he felt refreshed, and the insults seamed to be mollified.

Chapter 24

It Hurts Only When I Laugh

Supper was good. Lora's suppers were always good. He left the table and folded his frame into the recliner, the one he liked to refer to as the "Command Module," and unfolded his paper. Soon his stomach began to rumble and churn with symptoms of indigestion. *The price we pay for gluttony*, Burt thought. After three days of discomfort, he thought he had better have it checked out.

It was embarrassing for a six-foot macho male to go crying with a bellyache to his sweet female doctor. "This might be nothing at all, Doc," Burt said, "probably rich eating. Yesterday I had a cheeseburger with fries. The day before I had roast rack of lamb."

"Gourmet, huh?" groaned the medic, who was probably a vegetarian. She looked at him with disgust. "Does this hurt?" she asked, pressing here and there on his belly. It did, and he thought of those delicate little rib chops wallowing in rich brown sauce…and he felt nauseous. She scribbled something on a pad, tore it off and handed it to him.

"I want you to go down to the lab for an abdominal sonogram. It looks like gallstones." Her diagnosis was close enough for her to make an appointment for him with a surgeon.

"A surgeon? What for?"

"I want him to confirm my diagnosis. Burt suspected she put it that way to calm his qualms.

He stepped into a crowded waiting room, where no one was smiling. The pulp in the magazine rack was current, about three weeks old. He selected a magazine and sat, trying to look nonchalant, but the churning inside reminded him to worry.

"I'm reserving a bed in the hospital for you," said the surgeon after examining him. On the way there, I want you to stop at the lab and have a CAT scan taken. I need a better look at what I'm looking for."

At the lab, Burt looked in awe at the elaborate equipment. They slid him into something resembling a barrel. The technician left him and closed the heavy door. He was very interested as things began to hum. Lights of assorted colors flashed; bells and beeps sounded off. He was fascinated and traced wires to and from switches. Then it suddenly occurred to him that he was alone in a lead-shielded radioactive room too dangerous for the technician to even talk to him. He felt deserted and scared.

Presently a recording, no less, instructed him to take a deeep breath...hooold it...breathe. Take a deeep breath...hooold it...breathe. Burt couldn't help thinking, *What if the recording machine malfunctions? I could still be holding my breath!*

All the while, a light was spinning around the circumference of the barrel, taking dozens of pictures of his innards. He imagined lying on a magician's table being cut in two by a radioactive saw.

"That's it!" said the technician, as he escorted Burt to the little booth where he'd hung his shirt and pants, "Have a good day." Burt wondered if he really cared what sort of day he had.

Naked In A Coat of Armor

As he drove up to the hospital, a somber pile of bricks he noticed did nothing to improve his frame of mind. Instead, it reminded him of the maximum-security prison in Manhattan known as "The Tombs."

Admissions called for an attendant, who appeared about twenty minutes later. She instructed him to get into a wheelchair (already he was seen as an invalid) and delivered him to the elevator. The altimeter flashed "5" and they disembarked.

He was wheeled into a room where a pleasant nurse greeted him with, "Hello, I'm Monica, your nurse on duty. What are you in for?" What am I in for? Burt thought, *Wish I knew. I'm sure I didn't commit a felony.*

"Surgery...gallbladder," he told her.

"You can get into bed and I'll be right back." With that, she was gone. Right back was about thirty minutes later.

"I'm going to check your vital signs," she said. After she was satisfied that his systems were AOK, she announced, "You mustn't take any food or water. You will be fed intravenously." She stabbed him with an I.V. needle. As she hung a plastic bag on a pole, he watched the slow drip...drip that was supposed to nourish him, and he sadly thought of steak and potatoes.

"I'll be right back."

She was gone for the day. He learned in the military that the quickest way to get through a long line is to read your way through and was glad he had brought lots of reading material to the hospital.

At 1:15 A.M. a voice boomed out of the darkness, "Hello, we have to check your vital signs." Burt, usually unconscious at that hour, wondered, *Do the signs change that quickly?* 5:00 A.M., and a different voice needed a blood sample. He was numb and indifferent. "Be right back," said the voice as it left the room. 7:10 A.M., a nurse he hadn't seen before inquired, "Did you sleep well?"

"I think so," he muttered, wishing she would go away.

"Have you had a BM?"

"A what?"

"A bowel movement."

"No."

"Do you have difficulty urinating?"

"No." He wanted to tell her, "Only when you piss me off." He wondered how these bodily functions could be difficult or even possible when he hadn't had as much as a teaspoon of food or water for the past twenty-four hours.

"I'll be right back."

Breakfast was served...for his roommate, that is. The smell of his coffee was excruciating. "Good appetite, buddy," he teased. Burt operated his bed for a sitting position and settled back to read. 8:20 A.M. A custodian came to mop the floor.

"Good morning," he cheerfully greeted as he sloshed his mop back and forth like swabbing a deck. When he was finished he asked, "Can I get you something?"

"No thanks."

"I'll be right back," he said, even though he wouldn't be back until 8:20 A.M. the next day. Was he practicing his English or just pulling people's leg?

Naked In A Coat of Armor

Burt began to suspect that the staff was on a slowdown prior to a strike.

Burt's family doctor came in to tell him he was scheduled for surgery the following morning and that he must have a chest x-ray before they could operate. Burt waited all day, but no one from the x-ray dept showed. 10:00 P.M. His nurse told him he must have an enema. "Be right back."

10:20 P.M. she returned with a cylinder cradled in her arm. *Good God*, he thought, *the thing looks more like a fire extinguisher than an instrument designed for delicate applications.*

He felt the warmth coursing throughout his plumbing system, all twenty-eight feet of it.

"Now you must hold that. Hold it for as long as you can," chirped the sweet nurse with a silly grin, as she made for the door. He made a frantic lunge for the lavatory, only to be pulled up short, forgetting he was tied to the damned IV hanging from the portable post. Steering his IV post carefully, he and it made it just in time. The evacuation was complete. At first it seemed it would never stop.

He was reluctant but compelled to check, for fear he might have passed something valuable, like a spleen or perhaps a kidney or something. He decided to strangle the first one to ask, "Did you have a bowel movement?"

A big, burly, good-natured man came in and drew the curtains around his bed. "Howya doin'?" he boomed. "I've come to give you a shave." Without waiting to hear how he was doing, he commenced arranging his tools and said. "Do you know why they have palm trees in Florida?" Just then, his roommate, who was a bit unsteady, lost his balance and came crashing through Burt's curtain, knocking Burt's IV pole over onto him, scaring the living daylights out of him and the tonsorial artist. Luckily no one was hurt. But Burt's attendant, still in shock, forgot the punch line to his joke, and Burt would never know why they have palm trees in Florida.

On the morning of the scheduled surgery, Burt's doctor came to inquire how he felt and was upset to learn that he still hadn't had the all-important chest x-ray. She left the room and, almost immediately, a technician appeared and whisked him off to the photo lab. He couldn't help feeling a bit apprehensive. He pictured the surgeon standing over him in his green regalia, scalpel poised, his aides assembled around him. "No x-ray? How could he tell what to remove?

One-thirty p.m. Burt was transferred to a gurney and wheeled to the OR...last on the production line. A nurse recited in a lightning-like monotone a long list of did-you-evers, are-you-allergic-tos and have-you-been-befores. She didn't need the list on the paper she held; she knew the spiel by heart and was bored.

"Look here, nurse, you'll have to speak more slowly. I'm a tired old man, and I can't keep up with you. I haven't the slightest idea of what you're saying." She giggled and apologized.

At last he was transferred from gurney to operating table. A gentleman from India introduced himself as the anesthesiologist and offered words of comfort. His assistant on the other side was a pleasant female from the Orient. They stretched Burt's arms out and stabbed him with something. He began to visualize what the crucifixion must have been like, and braced himself for the sponge of vinegar.

"Hold this over your face and take deep breaths," the doctor instructed as he handed Burt a plastic mask. Burt remembered the mask he wore on bombing missions. Periodically it was necessary to knead it in his hand to crush the ice crystals of frozen breath. He looked up at the great bank of special lighting and wished he hadn't read so many Robin Cook stories about gruesome surgical procedures. He was going to stay awake as long as possible.

The big clock read 2:00 P.M. Somehow he was back on the gurney being wheeled out of the operating room. Burt panicked and demanded, "Wait, why have you changed your mind?"

"It's done. We're all finished," the doctor said, smiling. The clock showed 4:00 P.M. So much for trying to stay awake.

Burt was now in a dimly-lit recovery room with some bodies covered with sheets and lined up along the tile wall. He strained to hear whether anyone was breathing. Could this be the morgue? Was Rigor Mortis hovering in the wings? Back in his own room and reassured, he was quite content to take a nap. But of course he was rudely interrupted. "We must check your...

"Yeah, I know, I know, my vital signs."

A woman marched up and down the hall periodically all day long every day. The staccato rhythm of her stiletto heels sounded as though she was tap-dancing. After listening to this for a couple of days, Burt decided he must see who the dancer was. The next time reheard her start on her mission, he made a quick move to sit up and peek but found that his new tattoo was quite sore and collapsed back into his pillows. *The hell with it*, he decided.

His feelings were mixed about this surgery. Even though he had no choice, he was now a member of the cutup club. After all, up until then he'd hung onto all his parts, even his tonsils, and for eighty years. It was not easy to accept that, now, his torso had been violated by some stranger who had been mucking around inside of him.

His loving daughter, the artist, brought a book to cheer her dad. It was called *1401 Things That Piss Me Off*. Burt decided to add two more, the latter being, "It hurts when I laugh." It's frightening to think he could pop the staples that hold him together.

After a good breakfast, he decided to take a walk. "You must walk a little every day," he was told. After trying to put his bathrobe on while tethered to the IV pole, he wondered if he could have hanged himself. He took his dancing partner and shuffled off down the hall, past the nurses' station to the foreign end.

A nurse who had been very nice to him smiled and said, "I'm glad to see you're taking your morning stroll, Mr. 'E'."

"I'm looking for the exit."

"Oh no you don't...not yet."

He heard the cadence before he saw the tap dancer. She was a big woman, well groomed, smart in a tailored suit, wearing too much perfume, a sheath of papers in her hand and a pencil clamped behind her ear. Her glasses slid down on her nose so that she could glare over them. She seemed to have no sense of humor, all business–probably the financial secretary.

Naked In A Coat of Armor

Burt and "Ivy" waltzed back to their room. His dancing partner stood guard while he napped before lunch. He woke just in time to see his tray being whisked away. "You haven't touched your lunch," said the dietician over her shoulder, gliding out of the room. Burt thought wistfully, They let you sleep through mealtime but never through vital-signs time.

At last he was discharged. How wonderful it was to be back home! Orange juice, poached eggs, rye toast and real coffee.

After a few days he reported to the doctor's office to have the hardware removed. "I know you," smiled the doctor when he came in, offering his hand for a shake. "Let's see now...say, that looks good—everything went well. How do you feel? Talk to me."

"It hurts only when I laugh."

Burt saw he really did want to chat; he wanted to distract him. He had a four-letter word for each of the eighteen staples he plucked, but he kept them to himself.

A Wee Dram

The phone vibrated in its cradle as though announcing an urgent message. Fogarty picked it up and said, "Hello? Mrs. Murphy? Are ye arl roight? Ye are? could oi do a favor for an old lady? Of course oi can. Would oi pop in at Flanigan's and fetch you a bottle whiskey? Did ye say Flanigan's? Whiskey? Well, of course—oi'll be back in two shakes." The message didn't register until he hung up.

"Broidie," he called to his wife, pulling his cap on. "How old be Mrs. Murphy?"

"She'll be nointy-two if she lives till Tuesday, bless the old dear."

Fogarty was back in the two shakes he promised and banging on Mrs. Murphy's apartment door. He could hear the old girl shuffling along the hall, and it seemed a long time before she was fiddling at the lock to let him in. She led the way back and said, "Will ye sit, Mr. Fogarty, and share a little nip with an old lady?"

"'Twould be moi pleasure, Mrs. Murphy, but only a wee dram, moind you."

The old lady put two foggy glasses on the table and poured a goodly dollop into each. Two anise cookies were on a pretty china saucer. Anise? Yes, she learned that from her neighbor, Mrs. Rotollo. "Anissa cookie, atsa nice widda the wine," she had said.

Fogarty noticed that though her hand wasn't very steady, but the tired old woman didn't spill a drop of the amber. "How be ye feelin' these days, Mrs. Murphy?"

"I'm foine, thank ye, as long oi don't forget me medicine."

His eyes drifted from the knurled hand clutching the bottle, and he was sure he caught her flashing a wink at him. He looked into the ancient face and saw traces of the beautiful colleen that had been there long, long ago. He wondered how often she had tripped over life's lumps and picked herself up to come all this way. "To your health Mrs. Murphy," he said, raising his glass.

The drink felt warm all the way down to his toes. "Oi must be off now. Carl me again when ye be needing your medicine."

Naked In A Coat of Armor

Mrs. Schultz was leaning out of her front room window, her arms folded on the sill to support her great bulk. The traffic wouldn't let Fogarty cross the street, so he had to stop and greet the woman. "'Tis a broight marnin', Mrs. Schultz."

"I maybe shouldn't tell you, Mr. Fogarty," said she in her preacher's tone, "but you should not shop for Mrs. Murphy. I mean, in der liquid schtore. Do you know vot?" she continued with her solemn sermon, "eine alcoholic see ist yet."

"Sweet Mary, Mother of God, an alcoholic at nointy-two? My dear Mrs., Schultz, even if your gossip be true, oil shop for Mrs. Murphy for as long as oi can, bless her hart. Good day, Madam." He tipped his hat and crossed the street.

"That nosey parker should live so long," he muttered to himself.

Hitch Hike

The canoe was lashed on the roof of the car. He had packed his gear the night before, wanting to get an early start. It would take eight hours from Tupper Lake to Long Island. Stopped in town to grab a cup of coffee. When he got back to the car, there stood an old man, haphazardly jerking his thumb for a ride. He was clean-shaven and neat in appearance. He wore a baseball cap, like the ones that advertise Merrill Lynch, the Mets, or I love NY. His was bright blue with the Maltese cross of the Veterans of Foreign Wars on it.

"Where you going Dad?" Burt saw that the "dad" bit jarred him.

"Veterans Hospital, down the road a bit." Burt watched him out of the corner of his eye, scrutinizing the stubble on his face. "Didn't stand very close to your razor this morning did you, Sonny?"

"If I had I wouldn't have been on time to pick you up. And what's that "Sonny" bit? They called me Pappy in the service. I suppose you're all of two years older than I."

"Smart ass." He pulled out a flask of something and took a slug, then passed it to Burt.

"No thanks."

"Suit yourself."

"How far is this hospital?"

"Just keep goin'. I'll tell you when." Burt began to wonder what he let himself in for. But then he reassured him, as though he heard Burt's thoughts. "Got to get down there to get my check-up and see the guys once in a while."

"I see you belong to the VFW," Burt said.

"Yeah."

"Me too."

"Wouldn't have guessed it by that chapeau your wearing," the passenger said.

"Yeah, I know. Yours is the in-thing right now, but it's like being branded so every one knows what herd you belong to."

"You got a point. Like them bumper stickers. They tell a lot about people."

"Yes." Burt said. "Did you ever wonder what kind of person drives the board the baby is on?"

"Right, or what kind of a guy would stuff his mother-in-law in the trunk and wheel her around. And who cares if you love your dog? Or even that you have one."

"What outfit where you in?"

"First Armored Division...Bastogne." He looked at Burt, waiting to see if he could top that. "Eighth Air Force," Burt said.

"We were some glad to see you flyboys finally show up a couple of times when we were being squeezed pretty bad."

"The flying weather was pretty lousy," Burt reminded him, hoping he would understand why the "flyboys" only showed a couple of times. "It was the worst winter in Europe in twenty years.

We couldn't see the plane ahead of us when we were terracing down the runway on take-off. In fact, two big-ass birds piled up before they got off the ground. Killed fourteen people. We barely pulled up over them with the load we were carrying."

"We foot soldiers didn't hear much about things like that," the elder man said.

"We were scheduled to bomb the German supply lines at Daun and worried about getting too close to you guys. We flew in so low we even took some small-arms fire. I remember, I flew the day before Christmas and the day after."

"You can drop me off at next traffic light."

Burt pulled over and let him out.

"So long, buddy, thanks a lot."

"Watch out for the traffic," Burt called after him as he pulled back into the mainstream. It was then he heard it, that gut-wrenching scream of brakes. He could see a pile in his rear-view mirror. The bright blue hat lay in the street nearby. A few minutes later, an ambulance passed by, going the other way. Burt hoped it would be in time. It was eight hours to Long Island.

Terminal

If at eighty you find your tired old body is stretched out on a gurney in a house of medicine, you're over the hill, probably at the foot of it and will soon be under it. Green goblins hover over you, wearing masks and old-fashioned dust caps so you can't recognize who's who. They've inserted a spiteful looking instrument up your brudel and forced a tube down your gullet. Very rude. A couple of electrodes are taped to your chest and two more to your ankles. Red wires go here and under, blue go there and over, something like knitting a sweater. Tubes enter your body and tubes leave your body. A bag hangs on the side to catch the detours. You're looking like an anemic meatball on a bed of spaghetti.

The clergy is waiting in the wings, ready to administer the last of the rights you may have coming to you. The only visitors are high-tech machines standing around. You think they have nothing to say. All they do is go, "tut tut" and wink at each other while they hum and click, flash lights, ring bells and gong-gongs. But then you find out they have been telling secrets in some foreign language. And you hope the staff can translate them. The only thing on television is a squiggly line across the screen with alternating high peaks and low dips, which leaves you feeling just like that…oscillating. A bottle swings overhead, and you know it's not bourbon. Besides, it's out of reach.

Naked In A Coat of Armor

You are now just a live cadaver, a blob for the medics to meddle with and maul, while they exercise their trials and errors. The cash register rings with every painful breath you draw. The payoff is that all this costs you or yours a fortune, when in actual fact they should be paying you for the privilege to meddle and maul while learning.

Somehow Burt got the silly notion that, over the hill, the ride on the down side would be smooth and untroubled. Instead, there were boulders in the pathway, low-hanging branches and potholes.

When I get to the point where I can no longer see what I'm looking at, smell what I'm sniffing, feel what I'm touching, he thought, *and when my taste buds can't recognize a delicious morsel in my mouth... please! Let me go. Let me go, I say; don't mess around. Cut those lines, set me adrift. If you like, I'll donate what's left of me to the kids in med school. But, mind you, I'm not ready for the compost yet.*

Magnus (Tribute)

Ninety three...can you believe? Just think how remarkable it is to have come all this way. Dad, if the bit about three-score and ten is true, you've beat the odds; you're on overtime. You have seen the beginning of this old century and are looking forward to seeing the beginning of the new. All the way from horse and buggy to high-tech. Someone before him put just that in a better light than he can, Burt decided. The author wrote, "You are what is commonly known as a senior citizen: one who was here before the pill and population explosion." Yes, Burt thought, he was here before television, penicillin, polio shots, antibiotics, and Frisbees. Before frozen foods, nylon, radar, florescent lights, credit cards and ballpoint pens. For him, time-sharing meant togetherness, not computers; a chip meant off the block, hardware was hardware, software wasn't even a word. Coeds never wore slacks.

He was here before panty hose and drip-dry clothes, before icemakers and dishwashers, clothes dryers, freezers and electric blankets. Before men wore long hair and earrings and women wore tuxedos. Before yogurt, Ann Landers, plastic, the forty-hour week, and minimum wages. He got married first, then lived together. When you were gay, you were merry. How quaint can you be?

Closets were for clothes, not for coming out of. Bunnies were small rabbits, and rabbits were not Volkswagens. He was here before Frank Sinatra and cup-size bras.

Girls wore Peter Pan collars and thought cleavage was what the butchers did. He was ahead of Batman, Rudolph the Red-Nosed Reindeer and Snoopy; before DDT, vitamin pills, Jeeps, disposable diapers and pizza.

Cheerios, instant anything and McDonald's were all unheard of. He thought fast food was what you ate during Lent. He was before Madonna; before radios, tape recorders, electric typewriters, word processors, electronic music, disco dancing (something not all bad).

In his day cigar and cigarette smoking was fashionable, grass was for mowing, coke was a refreshing drink, and pot was something to cook in.

Naked In A Coat of Armor

If he'd been asked to explain CIA, MS, NATO, ERA, or HUD, he'd have said it was alphabet soup.

He was one of today's senior citizens, one of a hardy bunch, when you thought of how the world had changed and the adjustments he'd had to make.

Magnus Adrian Louie (that's an alias) Lindborg came from a little Hamlet called Balsjo, on the east coast of Sweden, a couple of hundred miles south of the Arctic circle, where his parents had a farm. The homestead had been in the family for over two hundred years. He was the oldest of eight children. When he was around twenty years old, he decided that farming wasn't that great, so he packed his bag and signed onto a freighter as ship's carpenter, plying between Europe and Louisiana. He also learned to cut hair, and when the wood butchering got slow, he'd cut hair. After a few trips, he jumped ship and settled down in New Orleans and opened up a barbershop on Canal Street and Magazine Avenue. Burt heard tell that he got to making a little hooch in the cellar to sort of supplement the barber shop, and he prospered–so much so that it was a question of whether the still was supplementing the shop or the other way around. The law was prohibition and, when the cops got wise to him, it was then the Emigration people put him on a slow boat to Holland.

In 1927, after he straightened out his papers and became legal, he lost no time in signing onto another boat, this time bound for New York. He had heard about another Swede out on the Island in a place called Islip. His buddy got him a job working for the State, building the Pilgrim State Hospital.

Now, Magnus Adrian, AKA Louie, was a very independent individual (some would say square-headed) and he soon got to arguing with the union. When the shop steward started dropping bricks down on him accidentally, he figured he had better get out of there.

Things were tough back then, in the WPA days. Louie owned an old ambulance, a big gray box of a thing. It had a generator almost as big as the engine itself, and often it wouldn't gen and the battery wouldn't bat and the carburetor wouldn't carb. Seemed like the ship's carpenter was always "tinkering wid dem damn tings." Well, he'd rattle all the way out east with it, buy up produce in season and peddle it from door to door. Potatoes and cabbage in the fall and corn and lettuce in the spring. "Is it fresh?" the ladies would ask. "Yaw, yaw, the first crap of the spring," he would answer. "Oi, yoi, yoi."

The plumber down the road, also a Swede, introduced him to a pretty widow and they fell in love. He and Burt's mom got married.

He got a job with Good Roads making asphalt. From there, he became a construction foreman. He built bridges, roads and factories. Burt was out of work for some time and his mom twisted Louie's arm to give him a job. He took one look at Burt's skinny frame and just shook his head. But finally he took Burt on a road-repair project. The first assignment they gave Burt was to haul cement in an enormous wheelbarrow from the mixer down a narrow board ramp into the roadbed. The mixer operator loaded the man-size wheelbarrow to the brim. Burt could not distinguish whether he managed to steer the barrow to the bottom of the plank or if it wheeled him to that point. When he tipped it up to dump it, the sticky load pulled him up with it and he went sailing between the handlebars, right over the top, ass over tea cups into the wet, slushy mud. To some people, that was very funny. Looking back at it, Burt felt sure the old man planned that deliberately, hoping to get rid of him. It worked.

Dorothea and Magnus opened their home and welcomed several foster children. Some of them kept in touch for years afterwards. The place was always full of kids. Many a time, Dorothea had to chase the louts out, zapping them with a wet dishtowel. So you see, Magnus had a busy life, so busy that for fifty years he had no contact with the folks back home. Not until his sister Hilma contacted the Salvation Army to locate their long-lost brother did they find out where the guy was. Soon after, he met a man who, coincidentally, had a summer home across the street from the Lindborg homestead. And it was Lennard who insisted on taking Magnus home for a visit. Dorothea and Burt got him down to the airport OK, but when he tried to yet through the security gate, the gongs and bells and flashing lights took off, causing a lot of raised eyebrows. They made him empty his pockets and ushered him through. Again and again, he triggered the alarms. Security carefully swept him with their electronic wand, and it lit up every time. Dorothea and Burt began to think he would have to walk to Sweden. Finally, they took him into the back room, and there they discovered he had a steel pin in his hip, a souvenir from a past auto accident. They were all relieved to see him board his flight at last. The little hometown went all out to greet their native son, with reporters, red carpet, brass band, the whole bit. All his brothers made for a wonderful reunion.

Magnus was not a saint. He had a couple of flaws. For instance, he liked cigars (Copenhagen), girls, "yin" and blackberry brandy. He eventually quit the cigars. He was pretty foxy, too. When friends and family would invite him over for Thanksgiving or Christmas dinner, he'd be wary until he checked to see who was offering the best menu. One time Burt and Lora had him over for Christmas goose. Lora had ordered a beautiful, fat Wisconsin goose, and the old man was sure to be there. But, alas, that damn bird must have walked all the way from Wisconsin, for it was the toughest thing ever to appear on a plate. Needless to say, they didn't see Burt's dad for Christmas dinner ever again.

Ninety-three years! That's a big block of time. Burt wrote in the birthday card, "Dad, God bless you and let's look forward to another party for the ninety fourth." He planned and organized a party to celebrate Magnus's ninety-fourth birthday. A great time was had by some twenty-five guests. Magnus Adrian (AKA Louie) Lindborg passed away in his ninety-fifth year.

Surprise

"I'd like to have a pig roast," Calvin announced over a cup of coffee one morning. Burt's cousin liked to play around with his Bar-B-Q; in fact, he was quite the cook. "Yes. I've wanted to try one for years," Calvin said. My neighbor and I used to talk about it

Naked In A Coat of Armor

year in and year out but never did anything about it. After awhile he moved to Florida, and I grew too old. Trouble is I can't swing anything like that, living in a condominium."

"Hardly."

"Do you think I could have it here on your place?" he asked after mulling it over in his head a couple of minutes.

"Sure, help yourself. But leave me out of it," Burt said.

"Well, I'd like you to stick around and carve the carcass for us."

"Listen, just because I was in the butcher business as a kid doesn't mean that I know how to carve. The butcher cuts the meat for the chef. The chef carves it for the guests," Burt explained, trying to worm his way out of it.

"Aw, come on; you can do it. You know some of my friends; besides, Susanne wants to get in on it, too."

Nothing more was said about it till a week or so later.

"Well, it's on," announced Cal. Got the pig on order, and the rotisserie. The whole bit." He was all smiles, raring to go. "Will August the nineteenth be ok with you?"

"Sure, whatever you say; just leave me out of it."

"You will cut it up for us, won't you?" Cal said, revealing some anxiety.

"Yeah, I guess so."

Come the big day, and the people started to parade to the back yard. Burt kept a low profile and stayed in the living room reading his paper.

"Daddy aren't you going to come out and meet the folks?" his daughter, Susanne, asked.

"Nah, leave me alone, you go ahead and enjoy; it's your party." He could see she was getting nervous. So after a while Burt ambled out to be sociable. The first one he saw by the garage was his old buddy Big Bob the Swede. That caught him off guard.

"What the hell are you doing here? he sputtered.

"I don't know. Someone said there's a party going on here."

Then Burt spotted Gerry. God almighty, all the way from Wisconsin. He couldn't believe it! And Dorothy with him, too. They gave each other a thirty-year hug and then burst into tears. Burt roamed around in shock. Everybody seemed to know something he didn't. He greeted all his local friends, and then he saw Terry and Mona from England, and Don from South Carolina. He began to think something was screwy. There was young Stan...and Len...a couple of Boy Scouts of his–oh, such a long time ago!–and now with their wives and children.

Susanne led him over to a fellow and asked him, "Dad, do you know this gentleman?" Burt couldn't place him right away. But then—.no! He couldn't believe it! It couldn't be! Whitey, the waist gunner on the B-24 fifty years before in England, now a sheep rancher from South Dakota. Burt was overwhelmed, trying to crowd all their resume's into such a short time on such short notice. What a happy occasion! Lora and Dorothy had a wonderful time reminiscing. All four of them had lived in Savanna, Georgia for a few weeks when Gerry and Burt were in training prior to going overseas in 1944.

Naked In A Coat of Armor

The pig, complete with an apple in its mouth, looked a bit anemic and forlorn to the amateur cooks. But as it slowly turned on the spit and changed to a golden color, it looked quite edible. The proof was that, while licking greasy fingers, all agreed it was a great success. Cal and his helper, Bernie, were pretty proud of their project. Bernie offered a blessing and, while surveying this wonderful menu, Burt couldn't help feeling how appropriate it was.

During the quiet that happens when feasting is done, Susanne introduced everyone to a This-Is-Your-Life book she'd assembled for Burt. While his daughter commenced to read excerpts from it, Burt finally came to the realization that they were celebrating his eightieth birthday, even though the anniversary would not be until September. That was another way to throw him off the scent. Imagine! A complete surprise...on his own property. How his Susanne did all that work and kept it a secret from her old dad, he could not figure out. His Lora sauntered over and gave him a big kiss and whispered, "Happy birthday, Sweetheart."

Sandy took pictures and later presented him with a beautiful album. She had caught all the guests, in all the moods. This day he would never forget.

Last Exit

Three days after the festive occasion, they were in the garden having a bite of lunch when Terry and Mona stopped in to say their good-byes before returning to England.

"Thanks for a lovely time. Wasn't it a great party?" Mona said. But Lora didn't answer. She couldn't. She had lost her speech momentarily and was frustrated and annoyed at not being able to get the words out.

All of them, of course, were frightened. Burt put his arm around Lora's shoulders and asked if she would like to go inside and lie down for awhile, but she refused. She regained her speech in a moment and, although embarrassed, seemed to feel better. The next day, they went to see the cardiologist, who, after a preliminary examination, admitted Lora to the hospital. It seemed she had suffered a minor stroke due to a blockage in the carotid artery.

After necessary surgery, she rallied and longed to get back home. They spent two happy days together. The weather was clement, and they walked in the garden. Lora watched the fish in the pond and fed them.

At lunch, she leaned to one side in her chair as though looking for something on the floor. "What are you looking for, Honey?" Burt asked, but she could not answer.

Emergency responded in a hurry and took her back to the hospital, where tests proved she had suffered a major stroke.

Day in and day out, Burt sat beside her bed, holding her and telling her how much he loved her, knowing that she knew he did. Her condition deteriorated a little each day, until she settled into a peaceful coma. Burt called Susanne, convinced that this was the end, afraid to be alone. His wife, his Lora,

Naked In A Coat of Armor

his love of fifty-one years died the next day, September 20, 1995.

After Susanne left to go back to work in New Hampshire, Burt thumbed through the photos taken at his party just a month before. The last picture in the album haunted him. Lora's pretty face was somehow distorted. She stared and her eyes sparkled in an unnatural way. Her teeth were clenched in determination. Her fingers seemed to be clawing the checkered cloth on the picnic table as though she was clinging to her last breath, her last carotid surge, the last heartbeat. It seemed symbolic, as if she was bracing herself in the turn of the ramp on the last exit. Was she harboring something that she couldn't share with him? Did she know something the others didn't?

Though tears warped his focus, Burt saw that Rigor Mortis was still over there in the corner. "Rigor," Burt said, "you've been so quiet, listening to me all this time. I'm flattered."

The specter tightened his black cape around his bony frame and, without any expression—or feeling—simply spoke the command.

"Let's go, Burt."

The End

Eugene A. Aichroth

About the Author

Eugene A. Aichroth is a veteran of World War II, serving in the Army Air Corps (later the Air Force).

Born in England, he spent some of his earliest childhood exiled with his family in Germany, near his oddly-cruel paternal grandparents. When his parents managed passage to America, he and his brothers spent several years at an orphanage in his mother's native England until money could be earned for their passage too.

His war bride from St. Louis, Lillian, became the center of his life.